A WINDLESS PLACE

Also by Toni Fuhrman

One Who Loves
The Second Mrs. Price

A WINDLESS PLACE

A novel by

TONI FUHRMAN

Adelaide Books
New York / Lisbon
2019

A WINDLESS PLACE

A novel

By Toni Fuhrman

Author photo by Jennifer Skelly & Auston James

Published by Adelaide Books, New York / Lisbon
adelaidebooks.org

Editor-in-Chief
Stevan V. Nikolic

For any information, please address Adelaide Books
at info@adelaidebooks.org

or write to:

Adelaide Books
244 Fifth Ave. Suite D27
New York, NY, 10001

ISBN-10: 1-950437-84-1

ISBN-13: 978-1-950437-84-9

Printed in the United States of America

For Helen and George—together in

"the immense edifice of memory."

Margaret, are you grieving
Over Goldengrove unleaving?
Leaves, like the things of man, you
With your fresh thoughts care for, can you?
Ah! as the heart grows older
It will come to such sights colder
By and by, nor spare a sigh
Though worlds of wanwood leafmeal lie;
And yet you will weep and know why.

Now no matter, child, the name:
Sorrow's springs are the same.
Nor mouth had, no nor mind, expressed
What heart heard of, ghost guessed:
It is the blight man was born for,
It is Margaret you mourn for.

Gerard Manley Hopkins
"Spring and Fall: To a Young Child"

Mais elle, sa vie etait froide comme un grenier dont la lucarne est au nord, et l'ennui, arraignee silencieuse, filait sa toile dans l'ombre a tous les coins de son coeur.

Gustave Flaubert
Madame Bovary

But her life was as cold as an attic facing north; and boredom, like a silent spider, was weaving its web in the shadows, in every corner of her heart.

Francis Steegmuller translation

CHAPTER 1

I think we never recover from our first bout with hero worship. How and why a particular person triggers it is perhaps unknowable, although I think for me it was that Gina was my absolute antithesis—everything I admired and could not hope to be.

I was fourteen when Regina Gregorka moved into our neighborhood, together with Phil, her husband; Ellie, their three-year-old daughter; Rags, their dog; and their things. Even at her young age—she was in her twenties—Gina had an impressive collection of "things."

"Having my things around me makes me feel more comfortable," she would say.

Her eyes would seek out a rosewood end table or a spindly side chair; her nervous fingers would trace the pattern of a cameo brooch or caress a gauzy silk scarf wound around her neck.

Ellie was Gina's prize possession—her pride, the hand-held mirror in which she saw herself growing up again, in saucy sweet perfection. Her indulgence toward Ellie was selfish, blind—and captivating. I envied the child almost as much as I admired her mother. I suppose I wanted to be both Gina and her daughter, both mother and child. But that was later. At first, there was just Gina. Supremely herself. Resolutely and joyfully what she was.

Gina moved into the neighborhood on a sunny summer day in the heart of the 1950s. Dwight D. Eisenhower was President, with Richard Nixon taking a back seat as VP. The Second World War and the Korean War were well behind us; Joseph McCarthy and his Communist Red Scare tactics had been defused. Women had resumed their traditional roles. On the radio, "Rock Around the Clock" was a top single; a television set was still a luxury. In our small town, there was no racial tension because racial barriers were strictly, if invisibly, upheld. Diversity was miles away, in the steel towns on nearby Lake Erie; in Cleveland, Detroit, Chicago. Nonconformity was distant thunder. In Upton, Ohio, all was placid—at least until Gina moved in.

That day, there was a light breeze fanning the oak and maple trees that lined Parish Avenue. As it was a Saturday morning, many of our neighbors were outdoors, puttering in their front yards, watching their children, exchanging sporadic remarks while they eyed this important event.

Across the street, Mrs. Boetcher was sweeping her sidewalk, as she did almost every day, while she chatted with Mrs. Mowby, who was sprucing up her curbside dahlia plants. One house up from us, Mr. Granger sat on his porch steps, sipping coffee and calling out neighborly insults to Mr. Simon, across the street from him, who was revving up his lawnmower and who, Mr. Granger insisted, mowed his lawn far too early in the day, while it was still wet with dew. He and Mr. Simon competed for the street's greenest and trimmest grass.

Gina moved into the house next door to us—a comfortable, two-story white frame house with a big front porch. On the porch was a green-painted swing hanging from chains. The narrow, neglected back yard was graced with a big willow tree and enclosed by a picket fence badly in need of paint.

She rushed in and out of the house all day, directing two sweaty, gigantic moving men. Her man-tailored shirt was yellow, open at the neck, tied in a knot above her waist; her pants were black, skin tight, stopping above her ankles. Her calves and ankles, I noticed, were slightly pudgy. On her bare feet were scuffed brown penny loafers. Her hair was short, curly, a glossy brown shot through with reddish highlights when sunlight touched it.

I thought she was dazzling. I watched her at every opportunity, riding my bike leisurely past her house, sitting on my front steps with a book propped up so that I could peer over the unread pages.

I was sitting on the front steps when the two men broke for lunch, opening their creased brown paper bags as they sat on the grassy curb near the van, the beer cans they held in their hands dripping with frost from the ice chest nearby. Gina walked toward me, waving cheerfully, as though we were old friends.

"Can I join you?" she asked.

I nodded, then ducked my head, not knowing what to say.

"Whew! What a day," she said, plunking herself down beside me. She reached into her shirt pocket and withdrew a pack of cigarettes. A small book of matches was tucked inside the cellophane wrap. "I'm dying for a smoke. Want one?"

She held the pack out to me. It was white with horizontal gold stripes, a gold crest over the word "Kent," a blue band at the top.

I shook my head, but I was immensely flattered.

She tapped the pack, extracted a long, filter-tipped cigarette, lit up. Her expression was one I would come to know well—amused, a little smug—as though she knew something about me that I hadn't yet discovered. Close up, her skin was pale, somewhat freckled; her eyebrows carefully plucked; her brown, almond-shaped eyes lightly framed with mascara.

"I feel like I've just come in from outer space and landed in Our Town, America," she said, blowing out smoke from reddened lips and small, slightly upturned, nose. Her cigarette tip was smudged with lipstick. "Are the natives friendly?"

I tittered self-consciously, then looked around at the neighboring houses, the curious residents: Mrs. Boetcher, sweeping her spotless sidewalk; Mrs. Mowby, staking her top-heavy dinnerplate dahlia; Mr. Simon, adjusting his ancient lawnmower. They had paused in their activities to follow Gina's movements while she crossed the lawn to our front steps and sat down with me. They looked away self-consciously as she picked them out one by one with sharp, farsighted eyes, squinting slightly, as though she were targeting them with a rifle, or an arrow.

"Neighbors," she said, in a low voice. "The bane of my life."

I started to ask what she meant by "bane," but stopped, not wanting to show my ignorance. I was already harboring a secret pride in my language skills. I nodded knowingly instead, scanning the neighborhood with hostile eyes. I was sure "bane" must be something suitably bad.

Gina leaned back, resting against the porch rail. She looked at me with narrowed eyes as she smoked.

"You're very pretty," she said. "What's your name?"

I blushed, looked down, unable to meet that cool, assessing gaze. I agonized over my appearance, not sure if I was attractive or hopelessly ordinary, wanting to be vivid, striking, but seeing reflected in the mirror a fairness which made me seem all of one hue. I envied my friend Sharon her creamy skin and short dark curls.

"Maggie," I said, glancing up at her briefly.

"You're quite extraordinary," Gina continued, as though I were an object of scientific study. I came to accept and admire this ability in Gina to direct all of her attention toward one person or one object with stunning concentration. "Your hair and your eyes are almost the same color—a tawny brown, I'd say—and your skin is so fair—no freckles."

She looked away, allowing me to recover from her microscopic examination.

"So, Maggie," she said, after a few moments, as though she were continuing a thought. "You're going to be my nearest neighbor. I hope we'll be good friends."

I realized as she said this that I wanted it, too; that I had already taken her part against the neighbors, who continued to watch her movements as she sat with me, smoking a cigarette; that I was ready to defend her against any and all criticism, even from my family. All of this instant loyalty was based on her friendly smile, her white teeth, her proffered cigarette, her resentment toward oppressive neighbors.

"I'm Gina, by the way. My husband, Phil, is on the road. Ellie, my little girl, is staying with my mother in Hillsville while I move us in."

She pushed her stub of a cigarette against the concrete step and stood up, leisurely raising her arms. She stretched, revealing a broad expanse of skin between her knotted shirt and her pants; then she yawned, crinkling her eyes, tilting her head to one side as she smiled—another characteristic expression I would come to know.

"Got to get back to the business at hand," she said. "Nice talking to you, Maggie."

"Can I help?" I asked, hearing the eagerness in my voice.

"I may take you up on that offer," she said, as she walked toward the moving van.

I realized she was refusing my offer, but her wave as she looked back at me was so friendly that I was glad I had spoken up.

Along with most of my neighbors, I watched Gina on and off for the rest of the afternoon. She seemed to like being watched; perhaps we sensed this. Her gestures were big, dramatic. Her voice, her lusty, contagious laughter, carried across the lawns, across the street. When she disappeared into the house, there was a curious lull, as though a curtain had fallen on a performance. Then she would appear again, ordering the moving men, coaxing them, teasing them. They grunted, sweated, performed. We watched, withholding nothing but our applause.

At last, the women went inside to prepare dinner. The children huddled in restless groups waiting to be called to wash up. The moving men slid the metal ramp into the back of the van, slammed the doors shut, and drove away.

Gina waved back as one hairy arm emerged from the open window of the van and saluted her. Then she stood looking at her house, hands on hips. She picked up a piece of wrapping paper that littered the small front yard as she walked toward the front steps. I couldn't see her from my porch, but I could hear the groan of the porch swing as she sat down, the slow rasp of the chains as she swung back and forth. I listened for a while before I went inside.

CHAPTER 2

After our first meeting on the porch, the day Gina moved in next door, I saw her almost every day. She was always generous in her compliments to me, a fledgling adult, awkward and uneasy with the mysterious changes in my body that had me sprouting breasts and the occasional pimple. She bolstered my confidence whenever she could, admiring my hair and eyes, my figure, my skin. I, however, dismissed most of what she said, confining my admiration to a female ideal of vivid color and contrast, like Gina herself.

Gina must have recognized and accepted my speechless admiration from the moment we met. But she was gracious with her admirers, rewarding them with her attention and her approval.

Perhaps it was her attention that awed me, initially. Attention in my family was offhand, often backhanded. To be female was to be relegated to background status. I had an older brother and a younger brother. Win, my older brother, was a high school senior that year—good-looking, popular. My mother, Kate, could not see or hear anyone else when he was in the room. Frank, my father, expanded visibly whenever he contemplated his firstborn.

Timothy, my younger brother, had been born perfect, fully developed, and dead. He had captured my mother's imagination ever since.

I was, I thought unfortunately, much like my mother—fair, mild, pleasing in a negative, because not imposing, sense. I daydreamed constantly about making a dramatic statement, either with my appearance or with something I said or did. Instead, relatives and friends of the family referred to me as "sweet," "pretty," "the image of her mother." Whenever I opened my mouth in company, the words that came out were scarcely above a whisper; whatever I said was indistinct, forgettable.

I was much more open and chatty with Gina. That was probably one of the reasons I admired her. She brought out the best in me, or what I considered to be the best. I felt safe with her, in that I knew she would never embarrass me or put me in an untenable position. My mother, unknowingly—my father and brother, all knowingly—could make me wince with the pain of self-consciousness, and often did. But Gina just let me be.

She had her own family, of course. A husband, a daughter, a dog. But she seemed to genuinely enjoy my frequent visits, to encourage them. I was so smitten I didn't need much encouragement.

"Well, what do you think?" she said to me one day, some weeks after she and her family had moved in. "I think I've finally made my mark on the place. What do you think? Do you like it?"

I was flattered, as always, that she solicited my opinion. I walked through the living room with her, admiring her somewhat ornate furniture, the velvet drapes, the Turkish carpet, the pictures on the wall (mostly landscapes), the occasional porcelain figurine or knick-knack, the mirrors.

There was a gilt-framed mirror in the living room that I particularly admired. It hung over the fireplace, replicating the shape of the fireplace and mantelpiece. The frame was magnificent in its intricacy, imposing in its size. My eyes always went to it whenever I walked into the room.

"Look at us," Gina said to me, as we wound up our tour and stood before the mirror. "We're gorgeous, the two of us, don't you think?" Then she laughed—her booming, hearty, reverberating laugh.

I sometimes, in my own thoughts, viewed Gina's family as a sort of entourage, surrounding and attending on her, reflecting her vividness rather than shining their own light. Phil, her husband, was, a "nice-guy" type, who had been attractive enough, entertaining enough, to win her. A premed-school dropout who sold hospital equipment, he was on the road a lot. He and Gina had moved several times since they had married, to towns near Toledo and Cleveland. They were now returning to their hometown area, buying their first house. Phil was ten or twelve years older than Gina. He had been married before.

"But no children," Gina had said. "I wouldn't have taken him if there were any burrs attached."

I liked Phil, but I never got to know him well. He teased me, paid me the minor attention that I needed in order to feel welcome and important in their family. His frequent absences became more obvious as I came to know them better.

Ellie, their daughter, was a self-assured, rotund, three-year-old explosive device—often in my charge, often to my dismay. But she was, like her mother, so warm, so appealing, so loving, so outgoing, that I could, and did, forgive her childish mischief and misbehavior.

Ellie had a speech defect that Gina was convinced was only temporary and would disappear overnight—as soon as she reached a certain level of development, as yet undetermined. For the present, she was allowed her own mode of expression. Following Gina's lead, everyone was expected to understand and respond to her peculiar form of gibberish.

"Rish a mergir," Ellie would say to me, when I would greet her after her nap. I had quickly made myself available for babysitting whenever Gina had an errand or craved an evening away from home.

"She's out shopping," I would say, having developed an expert ear. "She'll be back soon, with a present for you. Something very special, she said."

Ellie would then lead me through a series of rituals and activities, most of which were developed by her or by her mother. The rituals included brushing her long, fine, light brown hair, followed by an afternoon snack of the Jell-O of the day, or a sandwich spread thinly with egg salad, or cookies and milk to make her mustache, or "rushash"—a source of mirth that never lost its appeal. Then, we would inspect her "little family" of dolls and stuffed animals, and play with Rags, the large, indulgent, nondescript dog that I was always tripping over—perhaps because he seemed to be a cross between an Old English Sheepdog and a brown pile carpet. We would finish up with a game, a book, or a walk around the neighborhood.

No one except her mother could completely understand Ellie, but everyone liked her. The neighborhood children soon learned to put their own translations into service, often disputing among themselves as to whom belonged the closest interpretation, the clearest understanding.

Ellie, in her good-natured way, accepted most of the plausible interpretations—only occasionally resorting to screams of rage and frustration.

Gina was an affectionate, indulgent wife and mother, but she struggled with her stay-at-home role, complaining often, loudly, of her lost opportunities, her unused gifts, even though she said she had freely chosen her role.

"I should have been a singer," she said to me one afternoon, as she did some light housekeeping in her living room. She was puffing on a cigarette, her voice already somewhat gravelly from her smoking. "I had a talent. Everyone said so. I even sang in a nightclub once."

"Tell me," I said. "When? What did you sing? What did you wear?"

"Oh, well, it was only for one night. 'Amateur Night,' they called it. But I was good. You should have heard the applause. I wore this black tulle dress—remind me to show it to you, I still have it. I sang 'My Funny Valentine.' You could see I had their full attention. And the applause—even the band clapped for me."

She fell silent, lost in thought, reliving those five minutes of fame.

"Are you sorry?" I said.

"Sorry I sang?" Gina said, teasing me.

"Sorry you aren't singing now, still."

"I am singing now, still," she said. "I sing all the time, every day."

"You know what I mean," I insisted, wanting to hear her regrets, her longing. But she refused to humor me. She was feeling exuberant; she was more often cheerful than melancholy in those early days.

"Don't I sing in the church choir?" she said, dancing around the living room with a feather duster in her hand, sweeping it across a table here, a windowsill there. "Am I not the star of the church choir?"

She began to sing the *Kyrie Eleison* from a High Mass she was rehearsing, jazzing up the Latin until it sounded like a torch song. I laughed helplessly, feeling guilty, but unable to stop. Gina went on to burlesque the *Agnus Dei*, pausing only when Ellie rushed in from the back yard, shouting "Whagis? Whagis?"

Gina's response was to toss the feather duster aside and gather up Ellie in her arms, dancing her around the room, singing to her daughter in Ellie's own barely intelligible language.

CHAPTER 3

My mother disapproved of Gina from the start. My friendship with and admiration for our new neighbor were a constant source of tension between us. I don't know where the disapproval came from, originally, although events would prove her more than right. She was aloof with Gina from the beginning of their acquaintance, declining invitations to her house, seeing her in company only when social or church functions made it inevitable.

Gina sensed her disapproval, even remarking on it to me, but she seemed to laugh it off, as she did almost everything in those early days. My fierce loyalty to Gina increased with each derogatory remark, every unspoken criticism. I wondered at my mother's callous attitude. Kate was soft-spoken, reserved, seldom hazarding an opinion about her relatives and friends, even within the family. Her immediate dislike of Gina, her ongoing disapproval, were, for me, unaccountable.

"You should be with your friends," she said on one occasion, when I told her I was going "next door" for a while.

"I am with my friend," I responded.

"I mean with friends your age. Your school friends. You know very well what I mean."

"Why can't I have a friend Gina's age?" I said, challenge in every syllable. "What's wrong with that?"

"I didn't say there was anything 'wrong' with it," she said, backing down, as she always did, when directly confronted. "I don't mind it when you babysit for her, or even stop by occasionally, but you're spending so much time there. She's married. She's experienced. I don't know why she would want you around so much . . ."

Her voice trailed off. I looked at her with the contempt that teenagers can so easily summon for a parent who is blind to the obvious.

"Maybe, just maybe, she wants me around because she likes me, she likes my company."

I turned away from her, stomping out of the house, slamming the front door behind me.

Of course, the truth was that Gina liked having me around because I was her best audience. I, however, was aware only of her warm, offhand welcome whenever I knocked on her door or joined her on the front porch swing. I never questioned her preference for my company. I was simply grateful for it.

That summer, we had our usual number of picnics, informal backyard barbecues, and neighborhood get-togethers. For the past year or so, I had considered it beneath me to attend these functions. But that summer I tagged along with my parents quite willingly, hoping to meet with Gina, quite content to sit close by and observe her when I did.

Gina shone in company, while Phil was at his best and most amusing when he was with her on those occasions. At first, our friends and neighbors welcomed their appearance, clamored for their attention. They made a good-looking couple. Phil was slim and athletic. He wore his casual clothes with style. Gina always wore something eye-catching.

The first neighborhood function they attended, shortly after they moved into the house next door, was in our back yard. My mother had invited them with the encouragement of my father, but she was probably just as curious about them as was my father and the rest of the neighborhood.

It had been a hot June day. The prickly warmth was just beginning to recede as the neighbors drifted in, with their macaroni salads, scalloped potatoes, plates of fresh celery, carrots, and cucumbers, cookies and cake. My father brought the backyard barbecue fire to the pitch of perfection as he prepared to sear the hamburgers and hot dogs. There were beer and soft drinks chilling in an ice-filled keg. Noisy neighborhood children scrambled for soda pop or lemonade, running across adjoining back yards in mock haste, trying to outshout each other. I sat in dignified silence at the picnic table, nibbling on carrot sticks, responding politely to the good-natured teasing of family friends. Most of them had wiped my nose or plied me with hot dogs and potato chips as I scurried among them only a few summers before.

My brother Win, as usual, set himself up as instigator, delighted to make me squirm with embarrassment. Christened Francis Mercer Lowin Junior and called Win ever since—he was seldom at these get-togethers, having recently gotten his ticket to freedom in the form of a very used Pontiac. But, on this evening, he was at home, and hungry. He was put to work helping Frank serve the main course.

"Hey, Mags, catch," he said, holding a plate of sizzling hot dogs as if about to toss it across the few feet that separated us. I put my hands up in protest, protecting the dazzling white of my new sleeveless blouse.

"You jerk," I said, as he backed off, sliding the platter across the picnic table toward me.

"Gotcha," he said, seemingly content.

My friends said that having an older brother was a boon, since it brought boys into the house and older boys into my company, but I had yet to reap the harvest of this blessing. I considered him mostly as a punishment for my being second in line.

"Behave yourself, Buddy," said Frank, glancing at him with a half-amused frown. "And get over here."

"Yes sir, Pop sir," said Win, standing at attention as my father heaped another platter with hamburgers.

I ate in silence for a while, listening to Rosemary Clooney sing "Come on-a My House" on the radio positioned in the kitchen window, responding politely when a neighbor solicited my attention, nursing my self-consciousness—wondering if I would ever outgrow the blushing stage.

There was a momentary hush and a little stir. I looked up to see Phil and Gina walk across the back yard, Ellie in tow, greeting their new neighbors, accepting welcomes and introductions.

Gina always made an entrance when she joined a group, but it was a long time before I realized that her entrances were deliberate, studied. She was vivid, in her coloring, in the clothes she chose to wear. Her voice was pitched a little above those around her. Her laugh was loud, infectious. No one could resist her laughter. That evening, no one even tried.

She was wearing a light sundress that clung to her slim upper body, with sandals on her bare feet. The dress, sleeveless, scoop-necked, was etched with small red flowers. The full skirt seemed to float when she moved. Her fingernails and toenails were painted a matching red. Gina was slightly over medium height, slightly rotund, but she carried herself so well, dressed herself so knowingly, that I seldom heard anyone criticize her figure. Her legs and ankles were somewhat thick and unshapely, her hips a little too wide—but walking across the lawn toward us on that June evening, she was strikingly attractive, her head held high, her movements smooth and sure, her bare neck and shoulders shining, sculpted, in the late afternoon light.

"Hi, sweet thing," she said to me, sitting down beside me after greetings were over. She held a hand in front of her mouth and stage whispered, "The natives are friendly tonight, thank God."

I looked around at the neighbors gazing at Gina in the afterglow of her appearance. The company seemed to have come alive. The noise level approached a din. She nudged me and smiled, signaling her success. In those early days, Gina could make me feel like a privileged participant simply by singling me out in company. I nodded, then nudged her in turn, silently congratulating her.

As I looked around, I noticed Win staring at Gina. He hadn't yet met our new neighbors, being busy with his own engrossing affairs. He was standing a few feet away from us in temporary immobility, a platter of meat in his hands, his mouth slightly open, a look of surprise, or perhaps disbelief, on his face. Gina ignored him for a few moments, allowing him to stare at her, then turned toward him.

"Say, young Adonis," she said, lifting her chin, calmly assessing him, "Are those hot dogs for show or can we have some?"

Win shuddered, as though he were being jerked awake. He put the platter in front of us with a mumbled response. It was such a triumph for me to catch my confident, smooth-talking older brother in an awkward moment that I giggled. I swallowed with a gulp as Win turned a furious face toward me.

"So, you're Win," Gina said, tucking a hot dog inside a bun, coating it with mustard and relish. "I've heard a lot about you. From your parents," she added, as Win continued to glare at me. "I'm Gina. Your new neighbor. I hope we'll be friends."

Gina talked on, Win listened, and I observed, marveling at her ability to draw anyone into conversation—even my normally inattentive older brother. He seemed mesmerized by her voice, her movements, her youth. Men, regardless of age, seemed to be irresistibly drawn to her.

I was jealous of Win that evening, without even knowing it. I felt I had a prior claim on Gina. I resented her interest in my older brother, his obvious admiration. It was, however, a jealousy tinged with the humility of youth and inexperience. When Win moved on with his platter of hot dogs and hamburgers, and Gina again focused on me, I was grateful.

"Your brother's an attractive young man," Gina remarked. Then, perhaps seeing my feelings registered on my face, she quickly added, "And quite full of himself, isn't he?"

She asked, as if it were an afterthought, "How old is he?"

"Seventeen. Almost eighteen."

"A dangerous age," Gina said. "Too many possibilities."

On that warm June evening, Gina came among us a relative stranger—and left having been eagerly accepted into our neighborhood. The neighbors embraced both her and Phil, jostled for their attention, made a fuss over Ellie, who wore a starched blue party dress and tiny patent leather shoes with white socks.

Except for Win, Gina was careful to focus on the women in attendance—Mrs. Granger, Mrs. Morgan, Wilifred Muncie (a distant cousin), Frances Baird, Helen Mowby. They welcomed her, fussed over her, buzzed around Phil, making more noise than the radio blaring in the background (my dad had switched stations to a big band sound).

When the last hamburger had been grilled, my father joined the group, adding his booming voice. He stood with his plate of food, asking Gina about her choir singing, telling tales about the neighbors that brought shrieks of protest and encouraging laughter.

"Now, Freddie, here, he couldn't carry a tune if Eisenhower himself was in the room, and his sidekick Nixon was playing piano accompaniment."

My father nudged Wilifred Muncie's stout, carrot-haired husband.

"Remember when he led the congregation at High Mass last Easter, and everybody was singing off key because of him? Why, he even drowned us out last Christmas at the

Grangers' party. We had to lock him up with a keg of beer to shut him up."

Gina turned to Fred, who was loudly protesting his musical abilities, and gestured toward my father. "I suppose Caruso here can carry a tune?"

"About as easily as I can carry my wife," said Fred promptly, nodding toward large, deep-bosomed Wilifred, who laughed along with the rest of us. Wilifred and Fred were known in the neighborhood as Tweedledee and Tweedledum.

Gina talked to everyone in turn, her almond eyes merry and teasing, as though she had known them all for years—but once or twice I noticed an expression on her face, a wandering look in her eyes, that indicated her attention was tinged with what might have been boredom, or impatience.

Just before the party broke up, several of Win's friends showed up in a battered but still defiantly red Buick convertible, minus a muffler, and whisked him away. Gina watched them thoughtfully as they shouted for Win, the convertible burping and idling in the driveway, the car radio screaming out "Shake, Rattle, and Roll" at full volume. As Win joined them, he waved in the general direction of the party, then leapt into the back seat, amid greetings and protests.

"See ya, folks," he shouted, as the convertible backed out of the driveway. There were a few desultory waves and parting comments, then we all turned back to Gina, who was just a beat behind us. There was a look of longing on her face as she watched the convertible drive away down the street.

"Those were the days, hey, babe?" said Phil, putting an arm around Gina's shoulders.

Gina shrugged, dislodging Phil's arm from her shoulder. She laughed her loud, infectious laugh.

"We'd all have to be crazy to want that again, wouldn't we?"

She looked around at her solid, middle-aged neighbors.

"The angst, the misery, the pimples."

Everyone launched into tales of teenage woe, their own or their children's. I listened, a little apart from them, wishing my underage friends could pick me up and whisk me away in a convertible.

The sun set gracefully behind us. Pink clouds brushed with purple drifted across the sky. We ate, drank, fed the noisy, grubby children, sending them off to play tag and catch "lightning bugs." I watched them, remembering, with a chill, the savage games of childhood—how we would sometimes pluck the luminous essence of the harmless little firefly before crushing its wriggling, mutilated body between stones.

When Gina and Phil left to put their small, cranky, incoherent daughter to bed, we watched them go with a hush of regret—Ellie clinging to Phil as he carried her across the lawn to their back yard, her pretty blue dress crushed and soiled, her shoes scuffed, her cries fading as she succumbed to sleep. Then, our neighbors gathered up their empty plates and platters, their whining children, calling out "Good evening!" and "Thank you!" as they leisurely made their way back to their houses.

I sat at the picnic table, nibbling the last of Wilifred's famed oatmeal raisin cookies, while my parents cleared away the debris—until my father threatened dire consequences for anyone not helping with the cleanup. I swept away the last of the crumpled napkins and crushed beer cans just as the mosquitoes began to test our still pale and tender flesh.

CHAPTER 4

"I hate this goddamned house," Gina said to me on one of my visits that summer, as we sat idly in the living room. "It's old. It's rotting. It's full of worms and vermin. Look at that ceiling! Do you see that crack? If we stomp our feet, we'll probably bring down a rain of plaster on our heads. It's pitiful. Do you know how many layers of wallpaper were on the living room walls? At least twelve. At least. I lost count. Picking it off with my fingernails. I thought I'd never make it to the bare wall, so I could paint it!"

I tried to remember what the room had looked like when Mrs. Ennis lived there, but I had only been in the house a few times, when I was much younger. Mrs. Ennis was a widow, and elderly. I remembered it only as old-fashioned, fusty. I never liked the smell of it.

Gina lit a cigarette, offered me one, then shook her head, teasingly, when I refused it.

"I love to paint. Paint is clean and smells good. It makes everything new, fresh. But wallpaper! Stiff, smelly, reeking of glue."

Without a pause, she turned her attention to the carpet underneath our feet.

"How do you like this rug? It's Turkish. Does that mean anything to you, Maggie? Woven, thread by thread, by thin, overworked, underprivileged laborers—probably female—with a genius for design. Phil hit the roof when I showed him the bill, but, hell, he can afford it. I feel energized every time I put my foot on it, every time I walk across it. The oak flooring really sets it off. Did you ever see such a gorgeous floor? Our last apartment had this hideous linoleum under the carpeting. I was so ashamed of it. I told Phil we had to get wall-to-wall carpeting, even though we knew we wouldn't be there long. We ended up getting a remnant that more or less fit the room. I couldn't wait to get out of that place."

I waited, breathless, for her next remark, feeling as if I were on a roller coaster ride, sitting behind Gina, who was controlling every twist and turn.

"There's something elegant about these old houses," Gina continued. "They're so—finished. Do you see that molding around the ceiling? Do you see how intricate it is? I painted that molding with loving care, let me tell you. Phil offered to do it, but I wouldn't let him near it. I'm going to wallpaper the bathroom next. Look here, pet. Let me show you the pattern I picked out. No, let's go upstairs with it. You need to see it in its proper setting. It's like a rich wine-colored brocade. Burgundy wine. Come upstairs."

I opened my mouth to point out to her that she hated wallpaper—*You just said so!*—but I kept silent as she led me down the hall to the stairway, fanning her hand with a forward gesture to hurry me along.

"I polished every railing of this staircase. See how it shines? I love the feel of polished wood. You could slide down this banister and never feel it underneath you. In fact, I did. After I polished it. Good God, this stair carpeting has to go. It's incredibly worn and threadbare. Can you imagine anyone actually selecting this ugly green wool, then looking at it, year after year? It's like vomit. Jesus Christ, I'll be a grandmother before I get this drafty old barn in shape. Just like the grandmother we bought it from. Old and full of shit. Literally. We could hardly get her off the subject of her chronic constipation long enough to talk about the house. She was a sweet old thing, though, Mrs. Ennis. I understand she's living with her daughter and her family in Pittsburgh. She cried when she signed the closing papers. Wept real tears over her signature. Well, who can blame her? This house is a treasure. We could sell it tomorrow for twice what we paid for it."

I think Gina was lonely that summer. Phil worked long hours; he was often traveling. Gina was left to fix up her new home, and look after their daughter. Despite her initial popularity with the neighbors, they did not seek her out as they had at first. Most of them were older than she was, busy with their own children, their own lives.

My mother in particular kept a careful distance. I found this puzzling, a little irritating, but not that surprising. Kate didn't like sitting in a clutch of women, sipping coffee and gossiping. She didn't play cards. She didn't shop just for the pleasure of shopping. She kept herself to herself. If she had free time during the day, she sat down to read. When my father was at home, she was with him. Aside from his hunting, fishing, and boating, she shared in his activities, taking pleasure in his pleasures—whether it was the unfailing delight of an open fire, nature in all its beauty and variety, long rides in the country, or sociable gatherings with family and friends—usually culminating around a piano, with whatever musical instruments and vocal talents were at hand. My mother took care of our needs, but she was a companion to my father, not to us. We were apart from her. We accepted this. We didn't know anything else.

That summer, my visits with Gina, though often unannounced, were always welcome—although I never knew what to expect when I knocked on the screen door, calling out, "Gina? Are you there?"

Sometimes I joined her in the back yard, as she puttered in her small flower garden, or painted the neglected picket fence. I brought my friends Prue and Sharon with me several times. We would entertain Ellie, or look after her while Gina worked around the house. After the initial awkwardness, Prue and Sharon tried to talk to Gina as though she were one of us. But they weren't as comfortable with her as I was, so it was usually just me who knocked on her door, then waited for her cheerful, "Maggie! Come in, pet."

We would chat in a casual way, moving around more slowly as the days got hotter. I would help her with whatever she was doing, or simply watch her, content in my idleness, sipping lemonade or iced tea, refusing her jokingly proffered cigarettes, listening to her complaints, her lamentations, rejoicing with her when she was in high spirits. Unlike my mother, Gina didn't hide her feelings from me, or from anyone.

My bedroom was on the second floor, above the porch, facing the front of the house. One morning, very early, I opened my eyes to the sound of birds chirping hesitantly in the maple tree close to the east-facing window, and a tapping on the window facing north, over the porch. I raised my head, rubbing my eyes in wonder when I saw Gina looking in at me, beckoning me to open the window.

"Good morning, sleepyhead," she said, when I raised the window. "Get dressed, quickly. We're going for a walk."

"But how—?"

"I climbed up the trellis," she said, promptly. "Now, hurry! Before the sun comes up."

I dressed in seconds, grabbed a sweater, and climbed out the window, shutting it softly behind me. Then Gina climbed down the trellis that edged the porch. I followed. The trellis creaked in protest, but it held fast. I put my feet on the ground, exhaling, just then realizing I had been holding my breath.

"Come. Quietly," said Gina.

We walked along the driveway to the back of the house, staying on the grassy edge to avoid disturbing the loose gravel, breaking into a run as we skirted the back yard. We were breathless and laughing by the time we reached the little-used road behind the house.

"Oh, Maggie, isn't it glorious?" Gina said, stretching her bare arms up over her head, turning around and around, doing a little dance in the street. "Isn't it wonderful just to be alive? Let's walk, very fast. I want to be outside of town when the sun comes up."

Gina walked, as she said she would, very fast. I walked with her, sometimes skipping to keep up with her long strides. In a few minutes, we were on the outskirts of our small town. We saw no one, heard only the increasing chatter of the birds, a train whistle that seemed to herald the dawn. We crossed over the tracks, walked past Baird's Lumberyard, then entered a cornfield by way of a tractor path just beyond the lumberyard.

It was still chilly. I pulled my sweater around me.

"Aren't you cold?" I said, looking at Gina's bare arms. She was wearing loose slacks, a light shirt, tennis shoes—her outfit of choice that summer.

"Cold? Cold?" She looked at me in mock astonishment. "I am as warm as toast. Warm as a day in August. Warm as a cat in front of a fire. How could I be cold? How can you be cold?"

"I don't know. I guess maybe I'm imagining it," I said.

Gina did indeed look warm and content that morning—her skin flushed with exercise, her freckles standing out across her small nose, her short brown hair carelessly curling around her face. She could barely contain her intense high spirits, a sort of driving force that propelled her along the streets, then through the field of fresh young corn stalks. We weaved our way in and out of the endless rows, laughing at nothing, anything. I began to feel warm as well, until at last I pulled off my sweater, triumphantly sailing it over my head.

We had been moving toward a small clump of oak trees in the center of the vast field. We sat down, leaning against the largest of the trees as the sun rose over the greenish-gold corn. Beyond the field, a white farmhouse with a red barn behind it gleamed like a not-yet-dry oil painting.

We were panting, laughing, but we quickly grew still as the day brightened around us.

I looked at Gina and saw that her eyes were closed.

"All I want from life this morning is to be here, to be alive, to listen to the birds, to feel the sun on my face."

She sighed, turning her face slightly toward me without opening her eyes. "Feel it," she said. "Just feel it. It's a gift. A blessing."

Gina scoffed at most religions, even her own, but she often expressed her happiness, her surging spirits, in religious terms—as if what she was feeling could not be otherwise contained. That early morning, with her eyes closed, her face held up toward the sun, she was like a young novitiate expressing her devotion.

After a few minutes, during which I didn't talk, didn't move, scarcely breathed, for fear of shattering the hum of contentment I felt, Gina stirred, opened her eyes, and said, matter-of-factly, "Phil's probably still asleep, and Ellie will wake up soon. Let's go home, Maggie."

We retraced our steps and were home in twenty minutes or so, just as the neighborhood was beginning to come awake. We heard murmurs through the open windows, the sound of a screen door slamming, children's voices raised in fluty, sleepy half sobs. We parted in my back yard, Gina unlatching the little back gate that opened onto her garden.

"Have a good day, chicken," she said, softly, as we crossed our separate yards. "Thanks for keeping me company."

After that first morning, we took a number of early walks, sometimes taking a new route, sometimes returning to the cornfield or another favorite spot. The streets outside of Upton were easy to access. They led to hilly country roads, tractor paths, wooded cloisters, and a cemetery with smooth, green, moist grass, stones for sitting, sunning ourselves, while we mused about lives buried just beneath us.

"I don't want to live to be old," Gina said to me one morning, when we had walked to the cemetery. "I want to die before my body starts to rot."

"That sounds so hideous," I said, shivering, looking around at the tombstones. "Maybe they were happy, some of them, even if they were old."

"Maybe," said Gina, skeptically. "Maybe. But I doubt it. People are only happy when they're young, like you, and full of hope."

"But I'm not *especially* happy," I said, mentally tabulating my self-doubts, my family grievances.

"Oh, but you are, Maggie, you are."

Gina put her arm around my shoulder, squeezing my arm briefly before she let go.

"You're just not aware of it. As soon as you become aware of it, it begins to go away."

"But that's *crazy*," I wailed, feeling cross, cheated. "How can I enjoy it if I don't even know about it?"

"Don't whine, my dear. I didn't say it was fair, did I?"

"But aren't you happy?" I said, stubbornly insistent. "Don't you like being married, having a house, a husband, a little girl? Not being told what to do all the time?"

"I'm not *especially* happy," said Gina, mocking my adolescent whine.

I sat down on a nearby tombstone, kicking my shoe irritably against the worn engraving.

"I can't wait to grow up. I can't wait to be on my own, to do what I want to do."

"What do you want to do that you can't do now?"

"Just—everything," I said, despising my own incoherence. "Everything I can't do because I'm too young and too—stupid."

"Like what?"

Gina's voice was soft, encouraging.

"Like—drive a car. Live on my own. Do something important, something that matters. Say what I mean without sounding like such a jerk."

I raised my eyes to gauge Gina's reaction. She stood with her arms across her chest, grasping her elbows. She had a pensive expression on her face—as though she had forgotten me and was thinking of something else altogether.

"The happiest time of my life was when I was about your age, when I was in high school," Gina said, dreamily, sitting down near me, resting her head on a carved angel.

"That's because you were so pretty and popular," I said.

Gina often talked of her high school days, her popularity, the boys who admired her.

"As are you," Gina said, as if responding to a cue. "If you could only see it."

We sat in silence for a while—the rising sun warming the stones, sipping the moisture from the grass. Gradually, my frustrations fell away from me.

Those early morning walks had a magical quality, a brief period of freedom from restraint and the almost overwhelming responsibility of growing up, keeping up, in company with my peers. I longed for escape. Gina gave me that, by knocking on my bedroom window that first morning, inviting me to join her for a walk. I sensed, even then, that Regina Gregorka did not tailor her life with a plain stitch. She embroidered it with brilliant threads of color and exotic, bewildering patterns—like her Turkish carpet. That, for me, was the enchantment.

CHAPTER 5

The last walk Gina and I took that summer was in September, two or three miles outside of town, on Old Creek Road, in an area of unpaved roads and a hill flanked by trees. The road led down to a bridge built over a quiet creek. On the other side of the creek was a heavily wooded property owned by Fred Muncie, with a gate barring an overgrown tractor path that led to an old shack, seldom used anymore.

It was unusually chilly that morning, with a paper-thin crust of frost. We were both wearing warm jackets, thick socks and shoes, recalling our earlier warm summer walks.

"Look at that tree, Maggie," she said, pointing to a small maple at the side of the road. "See how yellow the leaves are already."

"So pretty," I said.

"But our summer is gone."

I warmed to her description of the past months as "our summer." I was a high school student now. My friends, studies, school activities were filling up my days. Gina seemed to distance herself from me as fall approached and the temperature dropped. I had wondered about this, a little, but I was young and involved with my own life's drama, so I didn't give it much thought.

We walked briskly down the hill, taking the middle of the road, as we always did, for we were alone at that early hour. Our breath hovered in front of us as we made our way toward the bottom of the hill, and the bridge that was our goal. Gina grabbed my hand, pulling me into a run the last few hundred feet. We arrived at the little bridge laughing, gasping for breath.

We stood on the bridge, elbows resting on the rail, and watched the creek while our breath returned to normal. The creek was shallow. The clear water leaped and scurried over the rocks, gurgling and sighing as it ran under us, chasing itself endlessly toward town along the winding creek bed. We listened to the creek, the twitter of birds, the hushed rustle of trees.

After a long time, Gina said, very softly but emphatically, "I hate this time of year."

I was startled out of my reverie.

"Hate it?" I said, looking around at the first changing colors, feeling a breeze rush against my face and lift my hair. "But it's so—so—" I struggled for words, wanting to defend the beauty of autumn, the almost blissful melancholy it aroused in me.

"Everything is dying," Gina continued, as though she hadn't heard me. "Can't you see it? Can't you smell it? It's death, moving in on us."

She shivered, looked away. I stared at her, almost frightened, and then looked down in confusion. I had seen Gina depressed before. I had learned to avoid her when she was moody. But on our walks she had seemed immune to despondence.

"Do you know, I've never been out of the Midwest," Gina continued, after a time. "I haven't even been to Canada, or Washington, D.C., let alone London or Paris or Bangkok."

"Are you sorry you got married and settled down?" I said, thinking of myself more than of Gina, of my plans to see the world, to be the heroine of my own adventure story. I couldn't imagine "settling down" without having lived out my fantasies.

"I thought being married would be fun. Phil was so much fun. I thought we'd just go on having—fun."

She wasn't talking to me anymore. She did this sometimes when she was in one of her "moods." It didn't matter whether I was there or not, and at that moment I wished I hadn't been there.

"Marriage is dreary, my dear, so dreary. It's a life sentence that you live out one day at a time, waiting for visiting day, waiting for parole, waiting for the courage to break out." She paused, then said, "Waiting for a miracle."

"I like Phil," I said, timidly.

"Everybody likes Phil," said Gina. "Even I like Phil. Phil is one of the good guys. Good for a laugh. Good for a joke. Good looking …"

We stood in silence, leaning on the rail, looking down at the water dancing beneath us.

Gina laughed suddenly, not her joyful morning laugh but bitterly.

"Every girl should be issued a warning about uniforms. 'Men in uniforms are dangerous. Keep off. Keep away.' Phil was made to wear a uniform. God must have looked at him in his lieutenant's stripes and said, 'We're not going to let anything too bad happen to him because we don't want to mess up his uniform.' When I met him—he was just back from Korea, on disability—he was all shiny and new; all his bumps and bruises had been nursed away. He made me laugh. Beware, Maggie, my pet, of a man who can make you laugh. They are armed with the ultimate weapon. They're irresistible. If he's older, 'been around,' as they say, with that tempting crust of sophistication older men get ... And if he looks at you like ..."

She stopped, sighed. "Ah, we had such good times back then. We just—played. Around here, around the area. We 'spent' every weekend as though it were currency. We didn't have much money, either of us, but we played as though we had all the money in the world. There wasn't a nightspot or a live band in a fifty-square-mile area that we missed. As far east as Cleveland. As far west as Cedar Point. You should have seen us dance! God, we were good. We never got tired in those days. Never. We drank too much. We drove too fast. We slept most of the day away, then we started all over again. One night, Phil said, 'Hey, babe, why don't we get married? We're so good together.' And I said—"

Gina stopped. I glanced at her, uncomfortable with her mood but eager for her to continue her story.

"You said—?" I prompted her.

"And so they were married," Gina continued, as though I were not there, "standing, not quite sober, in front of a Justice of the Peace. And the handsome young officer stepped out of his dazzling uniform, started selling medical supplies. While the fair maiden—now something called a 'wife'—got down on her knees to scrub the floors of their three-room apartment. The music stopped. The dancing stopped. There wasn't much time to play. There was never enough money—Phil's first wife took care of that. Before long, the new 'wife' was looking for ways to make her escape. But, of course, she couldn't escape. She was pregnant."

"Oh," I said, feeling very young and inadequate. I thought about Ellie, their bright, appealing little girl, who darted in and out of every house in the neighborhood, speaking in riddles, often leading a small pack of children who seemed to understand her sometimes incomprehensible commands.

"I wasn't a very good mother—at first," Gina said, after another long silence. "I resented her. I resented her—claim on me. But then—"

She looked up, her eyes sweeping across the woods and the creek, the brightening sky, still streaked with reds and pinks, then resting on me for just a moment. She smiled, with a half-sigh, half-grunt of wonder.

"Well," she said, backing away from the railing. "You know how she grows on you. Let's go, young and innocent one. I've bent your ear enough for one day. What do I need Father Flint for? I've got you for a confessor."

She started up the hill at a slow jog. I followed, walking at first, still deep in reflection, then running to catch up to her.

"C'mon, slowpoke," she called over her shoulder. "I have mouths to feed, beds to make, critical shopping lists to compile. Let us return with all speed to home base."

We walked back quickly, in silence, following the creek until it edged away from the road and made a sharp turn to the west, where it skirted the town, then meandered for a mile or two before it joined Pin River.

I was as anxious as she was to get home so that I could be with friends of my own age, with my own inexperience. My legs and feet felt weighted down. I looked for familiar houses, the unpaved road that led to our adjoining back yards. Gina took long strides, looking straight ahead, swinging her arms, deep in her own rhythm. We parted with barely a nod between us.

I ran into the house, banging the door behind me, calling out, "Hey, Mom, what's for breakfast? I'm starved!"

CHAPTER 6

I continued to sit with Ellie, willingly, whenever I was asked, for I was always in need of money for clothes, small purchases, after-school sodas and sundaes at Zimmer's—the local hangout. Gina welcomed me whenever I joined her on her creaky porch swing, or knocked on the back door while she was preparing dinner. But the closeness I had felt with her during that first summer seemed to have dissipated, with little regret on my side.

I could almost hear my mother's sigh of relief when school resumed and my high school life commenced. I turned to my friends for the shared solace of taking on adolescence. There was a certain prickly dread, an excitement that hung over us, as we confronted each new experience, each new feeling. I couldn't entrust that period of my life to any adult, even one I admired as much as I did Gina.

My mother's approach to managing issues was by indirection. When problems arose, Kate dealt with them in her own way, but never head-on. I knew that she disapproved of the time I spent with Gina, but she never confronted me with it.

Kate's beauty was subdued, receding. At that period of my life, I could only admire beauty that was vivid, striking. By any objective comparison, she was far more attractive than Gina, even though she was more than a dozen years older. But when I looked at my mother, I saw a reflection of my own light hair and eyes. I could not yet approve of either.

Her eyes were not as pale as mine; the hazel was tinged with green. She wore very little makeup, so it was only up close that a casual observer saw the green surrounding the iris, the long, slightly curving eyelashes. She was slim, with slender, shapely legs and ankles, which Gina openly envied. She seldom raised her voice, either in joy or in anger, but she managed to convey her opinion and judgment to everyone in the family.

We were all familiar with her stubborn evasiveness, but Win could sweet-talk her to get his way, while my father shouted, stomping around the house. I often ran away to the comfort and solitude of my messy room when she refused the argument I longed to engage her in, pounding my rumpled bed in frustration. Lying on my back, I would stare at the cracks in the ceiling, wiping away tears of anger and self-pity.

"Why don't you like Gina?" I had demanded one day, while my mother was preparing dinner. "What did she do or say that's so bad?"

"Nothing at all," she said. "As far as I know, she hasn't done anything wrong since she's been here."

"Then, what's the problem?" I said, my voice rising with my irritation. "Why don't you want me to spend time with her?"

"I never said that," she replied.

"You don't *have* to say it," I said, with dramatic emphasis. "You're barely friendly with her. When I try to talk about her, you—you—"

I stopped, frustrated, as usual, by lack of evidence. My mother listened patiently when I talked about Gina, or anything else for that matter. But she could appear to be listening and not listening at the same time. I don't remember that we ever sat down face to face when we were talking. She was always doing something else, which increased my irritation. I seemed unable to command her undivided attention.

I took a deep breath, tried again. "Look, Mom, just tell me. I'll listen. I'll try to understand."

Sometimes, as I did then, watching my mother begin dinner preparations, I felt our roles were reversed, that I was the tolerant parent, trying to communicate with an obstinate child.

Kate broke lettuce into a salad bowl as she considered her next words. I sat at the kitchen table in a caricature of patience, hands overlapping each other at the table's edge, top fingers strumming against the hand beneath it. There was a prolonged silence.

"Why don't you just say what you're thinking?" I said, trying to sound poignant, appealing. "Gina never stops to think about what she's going to say."

"You like that about her, don't you?" Kate said.

"Of course I do. We can talk to each other. Not like—this."

I waved my arm in her general direction, then slapped the table sharply.

"But don't you see, Maggie ..."

"See—what?"

I caught at her response, urging her on.

"That's not always ... good."

I waited a couple of beats, but she didn't elaborate.

"Why, Mom, why isn't it always—*good*," I said, sarcastically.

"Gina is not—she's not—she isn't what she appears to be."

At last, I thought, she has thrown me a small meaty bone of contention.

"But that's one of the things I like best about her," I said. "She's so natural, so—up front. She's *exactly* what she appears to be."

Kate raised her head, looking out the window at the long narrow back yard, her hands poised gracefully over the salad bowl, a leaf of lettuce quivering between them. I waited. Even in my anger, I could sense her struggle to find the words to describe her feelings.

"Gina reminds me of—someone," she said, still staring out the window. Her hair was pulled back in a careless French twist. The late afternoon light outlined her clean-cut, regular profile. She looked young, vulnerable. "An old—girlfriend of mine. Her name was Mary Louise."

"Yes? And?"

"She was so bright, so lively. Everybody liked her. She was popular, even with the girls. We were friends in high school. And then ..."

"And then—what?"

"And then I found out—things—about her. I found out she never told the truth, not quite. She lied a little bit, about everything. She also lied a lot about—a few things."

"Like—what?"

"She told lies about—about me. Hurtful things. We had a disagreement. There was this boy she liked, who liked me … She was jealous and … She lied about me, and then she laughed about it."

After a moment, she added, "She wanted to hurt me, I think—because I was so easy to hurt."

"What did she say about you?"

She shrugged, dismissing the question, or not wanting to remember.

"But what does this have to do with—"

"Gina?"

"Yes. Gina."

"Just that—I don't believe—don't quite believe—anything she says."

I waited, then responded, my voice rising, "And that's *all*?"

"I've said this before. Gina is—much older than you, much more experienced."

As usual, my mother's calm, reasonable response aroused my anger. I sputtered out my response.

"So you—you don't *quite* believe what she says—but you don't know *why*? And she's more *experienced* than I am—maybe because she's *older* than me?"

"Well … yes."

Kate began tearing at lettuce leaves again, her fingers busy, her eyes on her work. Once again, she had withdrawn from the confrontation.

"Well, *Mom*," I said, "since you don't want to talk about it anymore, I guess I'll go on visiting Gina—being friends with her—and babysitting Ellie, and being—being—" I groped for suitable words, for dignity "—a good neighbor—" then stopped to take a breath before adding, "because you haven't given me one good reason *not* to. Not *one*."

I waited to hear my mother's response, to defend my position. But there was no response. My mother continued to prepare the salad in silence, chopping celery, slicing a tomato, blending the fragile vegetables carefully with her hands.

After a time, I got up from the table and left the kitchen, having gotten in the last blow, but knowing I was retreating in defeat from an unmoving opponent.

CHAPTER 7

In the fall of that year, when my parents entertained their friends with beer and music, I sometimes listened at the floor register in the upstairs hallway.

The black metal register, its louvers open to admit heat and air upstairs, was built into the living room ceiling, allowing heat from the coal-burning furnace in the basement to travel upstairs. When I was unable to sleep, or feeling curious, I curled up close to the vent, listening to the sounds coming from below.

My mother usually played the piano. My father sang, plucked on a guitar or mandolin, breathed into his harmonica, or hauled out his accordion. On those occasions when Gina was there with Phil, she, of course, sang. Phil rarely joined in, preferring to jokingly comment on the amateur nature of the musicians. Wilifred and Fred Muncie were usually there—Freddie bravely defending his right to sing, even if out of tune—as was Sam Baird, who owned Baird's Lumberyard, a small, voluble Scotsman as well as a good tenor. His wife, Frances, towered over him, monitoring Sam as though he were a naughty child.

The music was almost guaranteed to make me sleepy, as it was the "old" songs, songs nobody sang anymore—tunes from the songbooks my mother kept inside the piano bench, often sung in harmony. "Let Me Call You Sweetheart" or "You Must Have Been a Beautiful Baby" or "Deep Purple" or "Shine on, Harvest Moon."

I listened at the vent only on those evenings when Win was out. If he were to catch me in the act, he would delight in exposing me to the company. But Win was usually off with his friends, or with a current girlfriend, so I listened until my eyes grew heavy. Then I'd tiptoe back to my warm bed, lulled to sleep by the muffled music and laughter below me.

When I had friends overnight, to spend the evening in gossip and giggling, my parents spent most of the evening upstairs. Early in the evening, I would herd the girls into the relative privacy of the kitchen or the "side room," formerly a porch, which had been enclosed and now served as a place to relax, listen to the radio, or watch television.

My friends and I would await the unannounced but expected arrival of a group of boys from our class—who would come in, hover awkwardly for a while, then leave—after which we would dissect their incomprehensible behavior.

Later, while we were arranging blankets and bedding in the living room, I would run upstairs to check on my parents and say goodnight, but they were always in their bedroom. I never once caught them near the vent.

Occasionally, Win and his friends would bound in late at night, turn on all the lights, rouse us out of our blanketed nests in the living room—so that they could see us protest loudly in our shorty nightgowns or ruffled PJs. They would raid the refrigerator and then run out the back door to their car, roaring off in the night with shouts of laughter. This, I knew, gave my parties an aura of success. As a result, I was often honored with the task of hosting an overnight.

That first year in high school was a relatively innocent time for my friends and me. We were limited in what we could do, or avoid doing, because we had little means of escape. We had not yet graduated to driver's licenses and the liberty of cars. We had each other's houses, we had Zimmer's after school, we had adult-supervised dances and activities, and we had a few darkly exciting trysting sites in our small downtown area.

There was one other option: to date an older boy, a boy with a driver's license, a car, the freedom we craved. Win was a logical target for my friends, but only one of my select group, Sharon, stood a chance. She, however, spurned him, preferring Andrew, one of his classmates, whom she deemed "cuter" and "more mature." Win, who was popular in his own right, shrugged this off, calling her a "too-young chick."

I set my sights on Charlie Fox, who was tall, well built, on the football team, with dark, slicked-back hair, and a blue and white Chevy hardtop. He was a junior, in the class below Win's, and considered a catch. He was in my first-year French class, and often at the dances I attended with my girlfriends. I had never spoken to him but I watched him surreptitiously, coveting him but unable to get his attention. At last, I brought my problem to Gina, who offered her solution with a casual, offhand authority.

"You must learn how to flirt," she said.

"Is that something you need to learn?"

"Of course," she replied. "You learn it just like anything else—like tying your shoes or riding a bike or—" She smiled, finding the right simile, "like learning a foreign language."

"Ah. *Oui*," I said, knowingly.

"Now. Where do you sit in French class, and where does he sit?"

"I'm in the front. He's in the back."

"That won't do. You need to be a couple of rows across from him, a little in front of him."

"But I can't see the board as well if I move back."

"Bother the blackboard. We've got more important things to think about."

I laughed at Gina's impudence, and listened intently to what she had to say.

The next day, I changed my seat in class, telling Miss Bridges—frumpy, middle-aged, but accommodating—that the light from the window was hurting my eyes. I took a seat where I could see Charlie, as I took down notes, by turning my head to the right and looking across at him, two aisles away and one seat back.

When he looked up from his notes, casually looking around, I was ready for him. Following Gina's instructions, I caught his eye and returned his somewhat surprised glance. I didn't smile. I didn't blink. I tried very hard not to blush. After a moment or two, I turned my head to face front, focusing my attention on Miss Bridges. I didn't look at him again.

During the next two or three classes, I did exactly as I had done that first day. At the end of that time, Charlie was looking at me whenever I chose to look across at him.

"Right," said Gina, when I reported my success to her. "On to the next step."

When Charlie walked into French class the next day, he was looking for me. This time, when I glanced across at him, and saw him staring back at me, I smiled, managing, without difficulty, to let him see me blush before I turned away. When we left class, Charlie was right behind me, with a slight comment about Miss Bridges—"What a peahen!"—that made me laugh. He seemed gratified by my response.

On Friday night, I went to a dance at the school gym with Prue and Sharon, after a brief stop at Gina's, who was ready with her makeup tools.

"Just a touch," she said, darkening my eyebrows, then applying a dab of mascara to my lashes. "So he can't resist you. Forget the lipstick. Let him concentrate on your eyes."

"But how do you know he'll be there?" I said, examining myself in Gina's triple-sided mirror.

"He will be."

He was there. He sought me out with his eyes as he had in class, then awkwardly approached me.

"Dance?" he said, ignoring my giggling girlfriends.

I nodded. He took my hand, then led me onto the crowded gym floor. I glanced back at my friends, who gazed at us in awe.

I hadn't been to many dances before, hadn't danced with many boys, but I was carefully nonchalant. It was a slow dance. We didn't speak a word, or look at each other. I knew, even with my limited experience, that he and I would never have much to say to each other. It was enough that he was following exactly the script that Gina had prepared for us.

As we moved through the slow, swaying steps of the Moonglows' "Sincerely," my head tucked up against his, I felt something hard and pointed push against my skirt. I pulled back, but Charlie drew me in close, pushing himself against me. My thoughts switched suddenly from a sort of preening triumph to dismay, as I calculated the length of the song and my options for its duration. I pulled away again, attempting to say something light, casual, but Charlie wasn't interested. He drew me in, closed his eyes, moved me around the dimly lit gym—while I danced as well as I could with my rear end jutting out. At the end of the song, he returned me to my friends, smiled at me, and walked away.

We danced again, two or three times, wordlessly disputing the amount of space between his pelvis and mine. Then he left with his friends Jerry and Sid, both juniors. Shortly after, I left with Prue and Sharon.

The three of us were standing outside the school entrance, hunching our shoulders against the chill evening air, preparing to walk back to our homes, when Charlie drove up beside us in his Chevy hardtop, with Jerry and Sid in the back seat.

"Wanna ride?" he said to me.

I looked at my friends. They nodded, I nodded, and we got in the car, Prue and Sharon crowding into the back seat with Jerry and Sid.

"Do you know where we live?" I asked Charlie, as we drove away from the school.

"Sure," he said. "You in a hurry to get home?"

I glanced back at Prue and Sharon, who were mimicking a struggle for space amidst squeals and giggles. Both the boys seemed determined to seat them on their laps.

"I guess not," I replied, wondering what Gina would advise in this situation, but quite sure she would approve.

Charlie took Overlook Road, which led out of town, toward the lake. Soon we were on open road. He put his arm around my shoulder, pulling me close to him. I thought smugly of the success of my first flirtation. It had grown quiet in the back seat, but the radio was loud, "Sh-Boom" overriding the silence, the purr of the motor reassuring, as the Chevy sped down the dark road. At the end of the road, a few miles ahead, was the entrance to Lake Park, a popular rendezvous for young couples. I had opened the starting gate, and baited the hound. I had to run the course.

At Lake Park, the parking spaces that faced the lake were all but filled. It was a clear night, moonless but starlit. We passed car after car with forms huddled together or, more ominous for me, revealing no forms at all. Far down the row, almost to the exit, Charlie pulled into an empty space. He turned off the engine but switched the battery on, so that the heat, and the noise of the radio, continued to surround us.

I wanted to peek at the two pairs in the back seat, but I couldn't bring myself to turn around. I could hear things, though—a sigh, a small pop as two mouths disengaged, brief skirmishes, lengthy silences.

Charlie turned to me and began to kiss me.

I had never "necked" before. At first, I found it not unpleasant. Then, as he pressed his lips against mine for longer and longer periods, I grew impatient, feeling nothing but the abrasiveness of his skin, mouth, and teeth against mine. After a while, I felt his tongue pushing against my lips, working its way into my mouth. It felt hard and pointed, like his penis pushing against me on the dance floor. I resisted, just as I had resisted earlier in the evening, but this didn't seem to bother Charlie, who retreated somewhat, just as he had on the dance floor, then began again.

At last, weary of the struggle, I pulled away, saying, "We'd better get home now."

Surprisingly, Charlie did not argue. He started the engine. The two couples in the back seat shifted, laughed, adjusted themselves noisily. Charlie backed out of the parking space and sped back to Upton, everyone seemingly satisfied with the events of the night.

After that, Charlie and I dated—not enough to go steady, but enough to be recognized as a couple at school functions and Friday night dances. I gave Gina an edited account of my first evening with Charlie. I wanted to share my success with her, but not my reluctance to participate in the intimacy necessary to maintain a steady boyfriend. I was sure that she would find my attitude silly and immature.

I liked Charlie but I knew that I would never know him any better than I already did; that he was not interested in getting to know me any better than he already had. He took me out in his car, danced with me, kissed me, said very little but probably more than I did, and seemed content to go on just as we were.

I, however, was not content. Inexperienced though I was, I knew what it was I wanted in a "steady," and it wasn't Charlie Fox.

Eventually, having exchanged far more kisses than words, Charlie and I went our separate ways, without drama, almost without discussion. Our names were no longer linked—nor, to my relief, were we.

CHAPTER 8

During that season of teenage experimentation, I saw very little of Win. He was eighteen, a senior, full of himself and his affairs. He had no time for a younger sister just launching herself into high school. My parents discussed his comings and goings as though he were a potentate—my mother preparing feasts for his evenings at home, my father heralding his triumphs on the basketball court, his chances for a scholarship.

"He'll be the first in our family to go to college," Frank said, proudly. "The first on either side of the family."

"Better wait till I get in," said Win.

"Oh, you'll get in, my boy. You'll get in."

"What if he doesn't?" I said, blandly.

Kate had prepared a special dinner for Win, even though it was a Tuesday evening. I was enjoying the fresh apple pie, after the stew of beef chuck and tender vegetables, but willing enough to dampen my father's enthusiasm.

"Nonsense," he responded, promptly. "Win has kept up his grades all through school, and he's the best player this town has ever seen."

"Well, at least since your day," Win said, winking at me.

"I wasn't bad, up until I broke my arm, but you're better. State will want you, I'm dead sure."

"I hope you're right, Pop. Well, gotta go."

He planted a loud kiss on Kate's cheek. "That was great, Mom. Too bad they don't give out scholarships for baking pies."

"Big Tuesday night on the town?" I said, scraping the last flaky bits of crust off my plate.

"That's cute," he said, cuffing me lightly as he headed for the back door, grabbing his leather jacket from off a hook near the door. "I'll remember you to Benson."

"Don't you *dare*," I shouted, alarmed, starting up from my chair. But Win was already out the door.

Ben Henderson Junior—everybody called him Benson—was a close friend of Win's. I worshipped him from afar. Win had only to threaten me with exposure to harass me.

Benson was good looking in a laid-back, unaffected James Dean sort of way, with wavy brown hair, brown eyes, a lazy smile. He was slender, well built, not as tall as Win. He always had a greeting for me. "How ya doin', Sis? You're lookin' good today." Something like that. I couldn't remember when I had not had a crush on him.

I sat down again, but it was a while before I calmed down enough to hear my father and mother talking quietly about Win.

"I'd still like to know where he's going all these evenings," said my mother, as she cleared away the dishes. "I could smell your Old Spice on him."

"He told you. He's out with his friends."

Frank was leaning back comfortably, working a toothpick into a back tooth.

"It's not like him," said Kate. "He's in training. His friends have called more than once when he was supposed to be out with them—"

"So he's out with a girl. Is that so bad?"

"What girl? He hasn't mentioned a girl in months."

"You're not saying—"

My father stopped. Kate looked over at him, shook her head. I maintained my deeply reflective state just long enough to reassure them I hadn't seen or heard this last exchange. Then I got up from the table.

I left the kitchen, mumbling that I had homework to finish. I walked slowly upstairs to my bedroom, where I sprawled across my bed, pondering what they had said—and what they had not said.

I had heard a rumor about Win and an "older woman" at school, overheard some earlier talk between my parents—some reference to Gina and Win—but I hadn't thought about it seriously. To me, it seemed preposterous. After all, I was Gina's friend. I was Win's sister. I would know if …

Then I realized I did know—something—a movement seen only in the act of turning away from it, words heard only after the sound of them had ceased.

It had been on a Friday afternoon, late in the day, just before Halloween. I'd knocked on Gina's door, wanting her advice on clothes and makeup for a school dance. A jaunty pumpkin face grinned at me from the front window as I waited. There was no answer. I rapped on the door again, then peered inside through the glass panel that framed the upper half of the door, narrowing my sight by pressing my hands against the sides of my face.

At the top of the stairs, which directly faced the door, I saw a movement, as of someone backing away. Then I saw Gina, heard her say something. She was wrapping a loose robe around herself, a savagely patterned kimono I particularly admired—turquoise, splashed with peacocks and huge exotic flowers. She glided down the stairs on bare feet, opened the door.

"I was napping, Maggie," she said.

She yawned, leisurely, so that I could see the pink roof of her mouth.

"Gina, there's a dance tonight—" I began, eagerly.

"Not now, sweet," she said. Her voice was tolerant but impatient.

"But Gina, it's—"

"I know. It's urgent. But I can't help you now. You see, I'm—" She paused, bit her bottom lip. "I'm indisposed."

"What?"

"I'm not feeling well. I'm sickly. You remember, we talked about this before. I get this way almost every month."

Her voice dropped to a lower register, became more impatient.

"Wear that pink sweater that suits you so well. Make up your eyes a little, like I showed you. No lipstick. You'll look wonderful."

"But—"

"Tell me all about it tomorrow. I'll feel better then."

She closed the door, softly but firmly. Disappointed, I turned away, walking slowly down the porch stairs, cutting across the lawn to my front door, thinking about the pumpkin in Gina's front window, the movement at the top of the stairs as I peered inside through the glass door panel, Gina's voice—muffled, indistinct—saying something to someone I could not see …

Then—distracted by my own concerns—it was forgotten.

As I closed the front door behind me, my mother came out of the kitchen, wiping her hands on a towel, calling out, "Maggie? Will you run next door and get Win? He's in the basement. Gina's washer overflowed, and Phil's off somewhere with Ellie. Hurry, please. Win has your dad's car. He's supposed to pick up your dad in a few minutes."

"He's not there, Mom," I said. "Gina's sick."

"But he said—"

"I was just there. Gina's all by herself."

Kate shrugged and returned to the kitchen.

I sat down on the couch, mentally fingering each item in my wardrobe, concentrating on my pink sweater, and how it might look with my gray plaid skirt.

A few minutes later, I heard Win calling a careless greeting to Kate as he came in through the back door.

"You'd better hurry," Kate said to him. "Your dad's waiting for you."

CHAPTER 9

It was that autumn, I think, when I first began to see my mother as a person apart from the family she tended. Soft as she was, I had always thought of her as too fragile to thrive outside the environment of our home. But her resistance to Gina had changed my perception. It made me reckon with the quiet force of her.

She was a woman who never imposed herself upon anyone or anything. She hovered quietly on the surface, going through the motions but holding back, holding in—the genuine kernel of her being hidden beneath layers of reserve.

My father loved her passionately, but even he could not break down her guard. He was always more affectionate than she was, more demonstrative, more argumentative, more complacent. He embraced her, petted her, cajoled her, admired her, shouted at her, threatened her, walked away from her in disgust—but she kept her defenses intact, her fortress secure.

I had been an unheeding witness to this ongoing domestic drama, but that autumn I was alert, protective of my friendship with Gina, eager to prove my wisdom, my maturity, admiring candor above all, offended by any hint of reticence.

My critical observation of my mother spilled over, quite naturally, into self-criticism. I felt I was like her in too many ways. Gina was my ideal, but Kate was, perhaps, my fate. My resistance was strong, unyielding. I could not change the fact that I resembled her, but I felt I could sculpt my own character. I waged a silent, vigilant war against those tendencies that seemed to mimic her inwardness, her constraint, embracing and championing all that was outgoing, straightforward, unreflective.

"Why do I have to look like this?" I said to Gina at one of our sessions before her ornate, three-way dressing-table mirror. "Why can't I look like you, or like Sharon?"

"You little fool," Gina said, stroking my hair back with her flat-bottomed brush while I sat on the cushioned stool in front of the vanity table. "I told you the first time we talked you were lovely, and I tell you now you're getting more so all the time."

"You say that because you've never wanted to be any different than what you are," I replied peevishly, but I was searching my reflection for confirmation of all she said.

"Of course not. Why should I? Why should you? If we all looked the same, who would be pretty? Who would stand out? If there were only one kind of flower in the world, with a single fragrance, who would bother to look at it, or put the scent of it in a bottle?"

She laughed good-naturedly as she picked up a vial of cologne and sprayed my hair with it. It smelled like lavender.

I looked at her reflection in the mirror as she stood behind me.

"Do you think I look like my mother?"

She looked critically at my reflection in the mirror, seeming to give this question she had heard before her serious consideration.

"Yes. You do," she said.

Before my disappointment registered on my face, she went on. "You look like your mother, but also like your father, a little, and a bit like—what was her name?—the blonde in the movie that was playing last week. And you look like a great aunt of mine who could have been a movie star. And you look like a chum of mine back in high school."

She paused, while I tried to visualize this array of images. "But, really, you don't look like any of them."

I frowned, trying to decide if I was pleased or disappointed. Gina studied me in the mirror. She was about to say something when Ellie ran into the room from her bedroom, where she had been playing with and cooing to her dolls and stuffed animals.

"Rajishbash," she said, coming to a full stop before her mother, tugging at Gina's sleeve.

"Rags is bad?" said Gina with some surprise. "What did he do?"

"Meshumup engrumpetum," Ellie replied, like a small captain reporting reluctantly on her troops.

"He messed up your little family?"

"Meshumup en*grump*etum," Ellie said, emphatically, stomping her foot.

"Oh, he did, did he? He *growled* at Porky and Judy and Bozo and the others?"

Relishing the hint of menace she heard in Gina's voice, Ellie crossed her arms in front of her chest, nodding her head up and down.

At this point, Rags himself lumbered slowly into the bedroom. He had followed Ellie out of her room, but he moved in majestic slow motion, never showing the least inclination to hurry. Rags was a large furry dog of indeterminate origin, whose sole function in life, as far as I could tell, was to follow in Gina's footsteps. His unruly brown coat wrapped around his body like an ill-fitting garment. His sad, resigned expression was fixed on a long face hung with even longer floppy ears.

"Well, Ragamuffin, what do you have to say for yourself?" said Gina, facing Rags with her hands on her hips, her neck craned.

Ellie watched her mother in evident delight. Rags, once he was securely within the room and close to Gina, flopped down with a groan, resting a tired chin on the floor.

"Didn't I tell you to look after Ellie? Didn't I?"

Gina tapped her foot, waiting impatiently for Rags' defense, but he could only manage a half-yawn and a guilty, averted glance.

"We've talked about this before, you know. This is a repeat offense. You are not to threaten Ellie's little family, nor are you to touch your wet nose to them, nor are you to growl at them, no matter what they do to you. Is that understood?"

Rags' bushy eyebrows shifted alternately as he listened. He lifted his head, turned it slowly toward an outstretched paw, repositioning himself so that his head was turned away from Gina.

"It's just so hard to get good help these days," continued Gina, turning to me for confirmation. "You put your trust in someone and look what happens." She shook her head in disgust.

Ellie, giggling, threw herself against Gina, hugging her, her small face turned up in rapturous delight.

"Whashwedodaraj?" she demanded, glaring at the dog.

"Hmmm," said Gina thoughtfully. "You're quite right. Rags must pay for his foul deed. What shall we do with him?"

Ellie attached herself more firmly to her mother's side, a grim smile on her eager little face.

"Ragamuffin," said Gina, solemnly, "you are hereby denied your afternoon game of fetch and placed on one week's parole."

"Whashat?" Ellie's voice was hopeful.

"That means I'm going to be watching him like a hawk," said Gina.

She placed Ellie on the stool I had just vacated, scrutinizing her in the mirror.

"Now, *Madame*, what can I do for you today? A new hairdo, perhaps, or a manicure?" She lifted a small, grubby hand with chipped pink polish close to her face. "Ah, yes, I think a manicure, and our latest upswept hairdo. *Madame* will look very smart for her afternoon tea party."

Rags sighed and closed his eyes, resigned to his fate as perpetual underdog. I felt a momentary affinity with him as I flopped down on the bed. I propped my chin on my hands, watching the mother and daughter *tableau*. In that moment, I wanted to *be* Ellie, my pride and self-confidence in the keeping of this playful, affectionate woman I so much admired.

"Ah, yes, I see your cheeks have turned quite pale from your ordeal. A little pink—there—and there—yes, very good—and the slightest hint on the lips. Much better. Now for the *coiffure*."

She worked the French for effect as she swept back Ellie's long, light brown hair with a brush. Ellie giggled and squirmed.

"Upswept. The very thing for *Madame*. You see. Just so. Perfection."

She pinned Ellie's hair on top of her head, stepped back to gauge the effect, then knelt beside her and grasped a small hand. "The finishing touch, *Madame*. 'Ruby Red.' Our latest color." She dabbed a bit of garish color on each nail, reached for the other hand. "There. And there. You see? *Voila*!"

Gina stood up. Holding her securely around the waist, she posed Ellie in a standing position on the stool.

"Pretty as a picture! Maggie? Look at *Madame*."

"Pretty as a picture," I repeated.

"Go and show your little family, *Madame*. And *Madame* will come back, I hope, very soon."

Gina lifted her down to the floor. Smoothing her crushed and soiled red velveteen dress, Ellie marched out of the room, stepping haughtily over Rags, who had stretched out on his side with his eyes closed, his head close to Gina's feet.

CHAPTER 10

"What happened to Timothy when he was born?" I asked my mother one afternoon, apropos of nothing—except a passing thought that my younger brother would have been only a few years older than Ellie, had he lived. "Was he sick or—" I hesitated. "Was there something wrong with him?"

"He was perfect—a perfect child," my mother answered quickly.

Her face, before she turned away from me, had the look of a defenseless animal startled out of its sleep by a rude kick.

We were housecleaning, moving from room to room with a vacuum, dust rags, and a bottle of Johnson's furniture wax—my mother efficient and thorough, me dragging my feet, waiting to be dismissed so that I could join my friends. It was a Saturday afternoon. Sharon and Prue and I planned to prowl around the downtown area, looking for clothes, trying on shoes, perhaps taking in a matinee at our one small theater.

My mother and I seldom faced each other in conversation. We circled, avoiding eye contact and any sudden, threatening closing in of the space between us. There was no challenge in my question. It was the simple utterance of a thought. But I saw at once that she was quivering from its effect.

My teenage sensitivity did not yet extend beyond my own skin, so I felt a small swell of triumph before she switched on the vacuum, turning her back to me. I waited for her to finish, relishing the emotion I had created in her. She vacuumed around the couch, side tables, piano, armchairs; then moved from the living room to the dining room—used occasionally as a dining room but more often as a family room—where she continued to vacuum around the drop-leaf table, the side chairs pushed against the wall, the lounge chairs, floor lamps, bookshelves. I followed her, waxing and polishing, zealous in my pursuit, undaunted by her attempt to avoid the topic. When, at last, she switched off the vacuum and exhaled softly, the breath left her body with a gasp, like the air inside the vacuum bag.

"So, what happened to him, Mom?" I said, as though there had been no interval while the vacuum roared. I suppose I was pushed to cruelty by boredom, and perhaps a lingering resentment of her too cool, too distant authority.

"We—don't know—exactly," she said.

"But he died," I said. "There must have been a reason."

"It was—we think it was—because the doctor didn't come soon enough."

"Weren't you in the hospital?"

"Yes. The nurses—"

I looked up from the table I was waxing. She still had her hand on the vacuum cleaner handle, but she seemed to have forgotten it was there.

"Mom?" I said, with a prick of conscience, followed immediately by exasperation.

Why couldn't she just say what she was thinking?

"The nurses— We think the nurses kept him inside me too long. They—wanted to wait for the doctor to come. He — We think he was—smothered."

I stared at her, ashamed of myself at last.

"I'm sorry," I said, awkwardly, not sure if I was sorry for what I had done, or sorry for Timothy, a perfect child born minutes after his time, or perhaps sorry for being born alive and healthy, flourishing into my second decade.

"Let's finish," she said.

She switched on the vacuum, shutting me out. Shutting me out again!

My regret surged into anger, like the vacuum cleaner as it sputtered, hissed, and swallowed up the silence. After all, I had lost a brother. Didn't I have the right to know about him? Didn't she want to know how I felt?

But she had turned away, both from me and from any further conversation. All I heard was the whine of the machine as it was pushed forward and pulled back, propelled ahead and then forced to retreat, again and again.

CHAPTER 11

No one, as far as I knew, could touch that carefully protected center where my mother lived, not even my father, though perhaps he came closest. I often saw my own frustration reflected in his angry shouts that hung in the air like shards of glass, then fell harmlessly to the ground, where Kate ignored them, or swept them aside with a few curt words.

I had always felt that there was a deep, abiding love between my parents, all exposed on my father's side, except in his moments of anger—on my mother's side mostly silent, secretive. Sometimes, jealous of their affection for each other, I wondered if they loved their children as much as they loved each other, but I was never able to resolve this question in my mind. Nor was I able to determine if the love of husband and wife should supersede their love for me, their child. Win seemed oblivious to anything so subtle, so I never included him in my musings.

I was convinced that I was, to some extent, an outsider in my own family, feeling both more and less than I thought I should, more a witness to, than a participant in, the volatile relationship between my parents—the tension that bounced among us like an electrically charged wire. When I took sides, as I sometime felt obliged to do, I threw off caution and consistency, defending one or the other, an unwelcome referee.

"There's no point in talking to you," my father said to her one night, slamming his fist on the kitchen table, pushing it away from him as he stood up. The legs of the table emitted a high-pitched shriek as they scraped the floor. "You're bullheaded and stubborn. You refuse to see what's right in front of your face."

The topic was money, my mother's incapacity for understanding its importance, and my father's inability to earn enough of it to satisfy her capacity for spending it.

"I'm working ten, twelve hours a day, selling insurance to people who don't know what they want, toadying up to bellyaching men, to women who can't make up their minds—"

"That's not fair, Dad," I interjected. "Lots of women can make up their minds."

"I come home tired, worn out, and I have to deal with these bills—"

"I pay all the bills," Kate said, quietly.

"You pay them with the money I earn, working sixty hours a week—"

"I work sixteen hours a day," she said, still not raising her voice.

"Like hell you do," Frank said, illogically. When he was in a good mood, he was adamant that she "take it easy," urging her not to work so hard.

"Well, she does," I said, not satisfied with her defense. "You're not around, you just said so. You don't see—"

"I'm trying to make things easier for you, to give you a better life," said my father, ignoring me.

"But you just said—"

"Maggie," my mother said. "Keep out of this." As I opened my mouth to protest, she added, "Please."

I stomped out of the kitchen, my father's booming lamentation, my mother's murmured response, following me upstairs to my bedroom, where I fell on my bed with a thud and a squeal of springs.

Why was I defending my mother, when she could move me to the same angry outbursts as she did my father, with her silence, her lack of response? Yet—she needed defending against a mind as prickly, as irrational, as my father's.

Why on earth were they married to each other? What could have drawn such polar opposites together in marriage and caged them up, to growl and lash out at each other, for life? Why did I feel compelled to interfere—not as the voice of reason, but in defense of my mother, who provoked me beyond reason with her stoical acceptance, her self-containment, so that I often attacked her with the same relish as my father was doing at that very moment?

Unable to answer any of these questions, I closed my eyes and fell into a light sleep, from which I woke a half hour later, refreshed.

When I went downstairs and walked into the kitchen, my mother was sitting at the table, reading the evening paper. As she turned the crisp, crackly pages of the newspaper, my father, who was standing behind her, leaned over and kissed the back of her neck, where her hair was swept up into a careless twist.

CHAPTER 12

I was as aware of Win as I needed to be, considering that he was an older brother, the object of my envy and admiration, the only surviving son of my unquiet father and my impassive mother.

I trembled whenever my father began to scowl and sputter, readying myself to draw off the verbal assault from my mother, to challenge her lack of force, or to escape, seething and baffled by both opponents. Win, on the other hand, never took sides, never took offense. He somehow trusted that the spark between our parents would always reignite, no matter how low the temperature dropped, or how ashen the hearth.

Win came and went as he pleased, cheerful and resilient, riding out his last year in high school with a minimum of effort, seemingly confident that he would be comfortably installed at the state university in the coming year—not willing to forfeit any of this year's pleasures for next year's plans.

"I wish I were as tall as Win," I said to my mother disconsolately, standing on a step stool in the living room while she pinned up a dress she was hemming for me. It was early evening. We had just finished dinner and the dishes.

"Why on earth would you want to be six feet tall?" my mother said. Kate was of medium height, as was I.

"You'd never have to hem a dress for me, for one thing."

"No, I doubt if we could even find a dress that would cover your knees."

I sighed dramatically, fingering the soft green wool fabric, squirming under the unaccustomed stillness of my position.

"Stop fussing, Maggie."

"Yeah, Mags, stop fussing," Win echoed, coming in the door just behind me.

I craned my neck to scowl at him. Used to his direct, in-my-face teasing, I was surprised to see his expression of dreamy absentmindedness.

"So you're home, finally, Win," Kate said, her voice low.

She looked up at him, looked again, quickly, then resumed her pinning.

"Did I miss something?" said Win, stretching his arms up, eyes closed, then assuming his usual expression and tone of voice as his arms came down, his eyes snapped open.

"Yes. Dinner," I said.

"We were wondering where you were," Kate said, her voice mild, her eyes on the hem of my skirt.

"Didn't I tell you? Major change of plans. Senior Christmas party stuff. Had to go to Hillsville for a look at the hall."

"You sure took a good long look," I said.

"Shut up, Freshman."

"Peggy called," Kate said.

"Oh, yeah? She couldn't go with us. Some test or assignment, I don't know. We went to Dingo's afterwards, for a burger. Sorry about dinner. Any dessert?"

"Yes. A pudding. Have some, if you're still hungry."

Kate wove the last pin into the hem of my dress and stood up. She looked at Win for a moment, slightly squinting her eyes, as if she were trying to find something. Win brushed past her as he strode in the direction of the kitchen, calling back, "Thanks, Mom."

"What's with him?" I said, stepping off the stool carefully, so as not to jab my legs with the pins. I hurried to the full-length mirror that hung inside the living room closet door and scanned my image. Yes. Much better. Nice to have good legs. I had my mother to thank for that.

I looked over my shoulder, smiling at her, expecting her to be looking back at me. But she wasn't. She was looking at Win as he disappeared into the kitchen, listening as the door of the refrigerator opened and closed, frowning as Win's loud, off-tune whistle started up, peaked, and abruptly stopped as he began eating the pudding.

Later that same evening, Win went out again, "To see Peggy," he said to Mom and Dad. I went to bed, *The Hound of the Baskervilles* in hand, but the murmur of voices below me kept drawing my attention, until I closed the book and tiptoed out into the hall, kneeling near the register vent in the floor, my cotton nightgown wadded up under my knees. As I looked down onto the living room beneath me, I could see my parents talking quietly on the couch.

At first I couldn't unravel the low-keyed conversation or make sense of what they said. Only the tone of their voices filtered up to me—my mother's insistent, my father's staccato—like listening to the melody of a song without the lyrics. Gradually, I began to catch at words and phrases.

"Don't tell me that, Frank."

Then, my mother's voice, again, saying, "It *is* serious."

I heard a muffled dissent from my father. There was a pause, then my mother's voice, indistinct.

"She wouldn't do that," my father said, his voice emphatic. "She's not a ..."

The vital word was obscured by a discreet whisper. I shifted my position, so that my ear was closer to the register.

My mother said, emphatically, "Win doesn't know ..."

Again, the end of the sentence dissolved into a murmur.

I raised my head, alert, sniffing the air, as if for clues. What about Win? And who was "she"? I pressed my ear against the register, eager for more information, but my parents were shifting. I heard them get up, my father yawning, my mother laughing—a very little laugh. I realized he had grabbed at her, playfully. They were wrestling like a pair of kids.

I heard, "Stop it, Frank, be serious," and my father saying, "I want to lick your neck." Then their voices became murmurs again as they went into the kitchen.

I got up and tiptoed back to bed, intrigued by what I'd heard.

Was Win in trouble? With a girl? It didn't seem to be Peggy. We all knew Peggy. Peggy wasn't a "she," to be discussed in hushed tones. They must have been talking about Gina. But what did they know? *How* did they know?

We never talked about anything important, anything *real*, in our family. Everybody went around doing whatever they were doing, thinking their own thoughts, never saying out loud what they were thinking. What was the point of having a family if no one knew what anyone else was thinking?

I sighed and snuggled under the covers, feeling left out, as usual. It seemed as though the only way I was to know about anything was to *force* my family to talk—as I had when my mother and I talked about baby Timothy. Or I had to figure it out for myself—as I had just before Halloween, when I thought I saw someone—*was* it Win?—at the top of the stairs at Gina's house.

But I felt smug as well. I had my suspicions, just as they did. I knew as much as they knew—perhaps more.

I'll get to the bottom of this, I thought. *See if I don't.*

A delicious warm sleepiness stole over me. It was a mystery, but I would solve it—just like Sherlock Holmes!

CHAPTER 13

I hadn't seen Gina for a while and was beginning to feel the lack of her company, when she hailed me one day as Prue and I were returning from school. She was sitting on her porch swing. She called out a cheerful greeting, waving a hand with a cigarette in it, creating a little eddy of gray smoke close to her head.

I waved goodbye to Prue, then ran up the steps of the porch.

"How nice you look," said Gina, who always noticed what I wore and how I looked. "How smart!"

She nodded her approval, scanning my plaid skirt, high-necked sweater, and light wool jacket, all in shades of autumn, a soft melding of brown, yellow, orange, and red.

"I like your shoes," she added.

I sat beside her on the swing and stretched my legs out so that she could admire my shoes, brown leather, with flat heels and a tassel. My outfit was new, a tribute to my persistence, as I'd let my mother have no peace until she agreed I needed more clothes, then persuaded my father to agree with her.

"Smoke?" Gina said, arching an eyebrow.

Occasionally, as on that first day when Gina moved in, she offered me a cigarette. I always refused, she always laughed at my refusal, and that was that. I knew she was teasing me, not pressing me to smoke. That day, however, feeling cocky, unusually confident in my new clothes, her compliments fresh in my mind, I nodded, holding out two fingers in a "V."

Gina's eyebrows went up in surprise and amusement, but she pulled a pack out of her slacks pocket, tapping the package to disengage a cigarette. She extracted a book of matches from the cellophane, watching me as I held the cigarette to my lips. I tried not to stare cross-eyed at the small flame she touched to its tip.

I pulled in a minute quantity of smoke, then immediately blew it out, concentrating on the sensation in my lungs. The important thing was not to cough. Coughing and choking were for beginners. I was determined to begin in the middle.

"When did you start?" said Gina, leaning back. She lifted her feet, so that the swing was in motion again.

"Oh, I don't know. A while ago, I guess."

I had never held a cigarette in my mouth before, but I applauded myself for my cool response. The motion of the swing, however, was putting that lie to a vigorous test.

"Glorious day, isn't it? So sunny and warm. And almost winter."

"Yes," I murmured, overwhelmed by smoke and motion sickness.

I looked at the cigarette in my hand, watching the pinky-gray ash grow and nibble at the white paper. How many more puffs would it take for it to dissolve and go away?

Abruptly, Gina stopped the swing. She turned toward me, tucking one leg under her as she dragged at her cigarette.

"Now," she said, inhaling deeply, blowing out between lips pursed as if to whistle, "Tell me. What have you been up to? Besides smoking, of course."

She lifted her chin to exhale, eyes half-closed, lashes spiky with mascara.

"Nothing much," I said, tongue-tied, as usual, in the face of such a direct question.

I puffed at the cigarette, despising my muteness. Just then a cough bubbled to the surface. I quickly swallowed it, together with a lot of smoke.

"You know, you must never wear anything too bright," Gina was saying, when I had recovered enough from the painfully stifled cough to hear her. "Your coloring is all of one hue. You don't want your clothes to be overwhelming."

I nodded, grateful for her voice, wondering if my own was in working order.

"My waist is too big," I muttered, with only a slight crack.

"Nonsense," Gina replied smoothly. "Your measurements are almost perfect. Didn't we mark them down last month?"

I nodded. "My waist—"

"What? 24? 24 ½?"

"25," I said, bleakly.

"You have a lovely figure," Gina said. "We'll put you on some exercises for your waist. Just watch those colors. Nothing glaring. What you're wearing is just right."

I relaxed, conscious I was able to breathe normally again. The urge to cough had receded. Suddenly, I laughed. Then Gina laughed. The swing creaked on its rusty chains as she set it in motion again.

"Are you okay?" she said.

"Yes. I'm fine."

"You are, you know," she replied. "Tell me about school. Any new boyfriends? Do you need an advanced course in the art and techniques of flirting?"

I had often wondered what it was about Gina that made her easy to talk to, that made me feel open and confident—so different than I felt with my mother and even, to some extent, with my friends who, like me, were paddling through the reefs and swells of adolescence—barely able to steer. Gina seemed to delight in what I thought, said, and did, to enjoy guiding me with her wisdom and experience.

I began to talk, no longer self-conscious. I unburdened myself with the same feeling of relief I had felt only moments before, after stifling the urge to cough, when the breath gushed back into my body. I told her about Earl, the boy I was dating—only a freshman, but not bad looking, and better than nothing—and my latest quarrel with Prue, who started talking the moment I picked up the phone, not even waiting to make sure it was me and not my mom—and Sharon's popularity—was she really that pretty, or was it her clothes, her confidence?—and how I hated algebra.

When I stopped, the only sound was the creak of the swing, along with the muted afternoon sounds of the neighborhood. A small child, a few houses down, was weeping plaintively.

In the front room, screened windows opening onto the porch, Ellie was talking to her "little family" of dolls and stuffed animals. I thought I heard, "*Engine engine could could could*" —then realized I was putting my own interpretation to her mumbo jumbo.

Gina lit another cigarette. She was smoking thoughtfully, one leg tucked under her, the other dangling so that she could keep the swing in gentle motion, pushing off with her toe, rolling back onto the heel of her penny loafers. In the late afternoon light, her short brown hair—cut "Italian style"—had a reddish tinge. A few freckles stood out across her unpowdered nose. She was dressed with characteristic flair, in loose, brown tweed slacks and a golden brown sweater with a furled collar. Tucked underneath the collar was a gold chain, on which was suspended an intricately wrought medallion. It gave the outfit a certain importance, as though she were expecting company.

"I haven't seen much of you and your family lately," she said, at last.

"Mom's been busy," I said, then wondered why I had said it, as though to defend her.

Gina said, "I'm sure." Then, "I don't think your mother likes me."

I was silent. What could I say?

"Or, perhaps she doesn't care much for women friends."

I felt compelled to respond to the question in her voice, so I said, "I'm sure that's true."

After a moment, I repeated, with more conviction, "Yes. That's true."

Gina continued to smoke in silence, guiding the swing with heel and toe, while I thought about what she had said.

Who were my mother's friends? When did she sit in the kitchen with a pot of coffee between her and a woman friend, and talk away the morning? Who did she go shopping with? Was she ever on the phone for more than five minutes, with anyone?

My mind clicked through these questions as though they had never occurred to me before. I realized they had not.

It wasn't that my mother had no friends. It was that she and my father had the same friends, while my father had friends apart from her. Win and I, of course, had friends apart from them. Why had she no special friends of her own? I puzzled over this, not yet used to analyzing family members. I wondered if she were lonely.

"Penny for them," said Gina.

I shook my head. "Just thinking."

"Funny, aren't we?"

"What?" I said, with some surprise.

"Funny. Comic. Not laugh-out-loud funny but—strange and amusing."

"Do you think so?"

There was an edge to my voice, as I was still thinking of my mother, but Gina went on, as though she hadn't heard me.

"The way we fool each other. The masks we put on. Almost no one knows who we are underneath. Maybe no one at all. What are you thinking right this minute? Would you tell me? Could you tell me, even if you tried? We're all bottled up inside, full of fizz and ready to explode if we're uncorked. We never say what we mean. Not exactly. And we certainly never mean to say exactly what we're thinking. Anything rather than expose our inmost thoughts. Slimy things, our inmost thoughts. Slugs creeping about inside us, hideous to look at. Who would want to see? Not I. I keep my inmost thoughts hidden, even from me."

She laughed, suddenly, whether at herself or at the expression on my face, I didn't know.

Wasn't this exactly what I'd been thinking about my family? Hadn't she just put into words the very emptiness I felt at home, knowing that our feelings were all locked inside us, that there seemed to be no way to let them out, that some of those thoughts and feelings were so bad we were afraid to let anyone know what they were?

"Not a pretty picture, I know," she said. "Let's talk about something pleasant. Sugar and spice, not snakes and snails. Speaking of which—"

Gina leaned forward and called through the window screen, "How are you, little spice of my life?"

"*Mershishnum*," came the prompt response.

"That's fine, my love. Carry on."

Gina turned back to me.

"Don't you wish we could all communicate so well?"

"No slugs inside her," I said.

"No slugs," she agreed.

CHAPTER 14

Winter came. There was, finally, no holding it back. The holidays passed quietly, and I, as usual, did not get my wish. My parents had one or two non-family gatherings, to which Gina and Phil were not invited, or did not choose to come. I didn't ask, nor did I listen at the register.

At home, a sort of watchfulness lingered over us. I watched Kate. Kate watched Win. Frank reined in his temper, lavishing goodwill on us all, contemplating his wife and son—even me, at times—with satisfaction.

Win alone remained oblivious. "Seventeen is a dangerous age," Gina had said to me, last year, when she first met him. "Too many possibilities." Were there more possibilities, now that Win was eighteen?

Our parents imposed no rules, so Win came and went as he pleased, carefully avoiding the outrageous. This, we both knew, was the only forbidden behavior in my parents' unspoken canon.

"Tell Mom I'm going out with Mick and Sonowski," Win said to me on a bleak February afternoon.

"Tell her yourself."

I was on the phone with Prue, idly flipping the pages of my French workbook while conjugating boys and girls of our acquaintance.

"She's not in the nest. Must be out snaring something for dinner. Tell her not to wait for me."

"Where are you going?"

"To look at girls. By the way, Sonowski says you might be worth looking at in a year or so."

He slammed the door behind him. Prue's sigh seeped through the wire.

"He doesn't even know I'm alive," she said.

"He probably said that just to make you jealous."

"But he didn't know you were talking to me!" There followed a pause and a hopeful, "Did he?"

"Maybe," I said, feeling generous. "After all, we've been talking long enough."

I accepted my role as Win's younger sister with what I presumed was grace and dignity. I had to deal with girlfriends who angled to be near him, following me home, breathlessly accepting my invitations to "come in for a minute." Then, antenna extended for any Win vibrations, they looked around, speaking politely to Kate and absentmindedly to me as they memorized the setting. After a while, they left, disappointed, for Win was seldom there, and never on display. Prue, at least, was a childhood friend whose allegiance to me, I assumed, would outlast her admiration for my brother.

My mother came in with a bag of groceries. The day, which had never been bright, grew dim, then dark. There was something cozy and restful about those brief winter days that expired like a worn flashlight battery, followed by a long evening of electric light, heat rising from the floor registers, the rustling sounds of Kate moving around the kitchen, the first enticing aroma of dinner.

I sat in the dark living room, looking through the dining room to the kitchen, where Kate was moving under bright light, her movements measured, deliberate—the perpetual dance of meal preparation.

She looked tranquil and centered, the language of her body graceful, all of a piece. The setting belonged to her. She was totally unselfconscious. I realized, with a pang, that if she knew I was watching her, the dance would become stilted, constrained. Unlike Gina, who glittered when she was watched, my mother was most herself when she was alone. I wondered—*Am I like that?* Something in me denied all that was Kate in me—pale, hidden, receding, unknowable. I uncurled myself from the couch and went into the kitchen.

"Win won't be home for dinner," I said.

"Oh? Why?"

"Out with friends."

"Oh." She looked away from me, considering this. "Your father is working late. There's just us for dinner."

"I need to read *The Scarlet Letter.*"

"Go ahead. We'll read at the table."

We sat in silence and ate. Kate quietly turned the pages of a magazine, while I began Nathaniel Hawthorne's story of Hester Prynne. I stopped frequently to savor the taste of the cucumber salad, the skillet casserole of ground beef and peas—and to glance at Kate, who looked up at me once or twice.

"This is good, Mom," I said.

"I'm glad you like it," she said.

That was all we said to each other.

When we were finished, we cleared the dishes together, then I left her to do the washing up. Book in hand, I prowled the house, contracted in the winter because there was no screen door opening easily onto the front porch. I was looking for a place to land, where I might sit comfortably and open my book again.

I tried the living room couch, but the urge to nod off was overwhelming. I got up, determined to stay awake. I sat at the upright piano, picking out a tune with one finger as I read a paragraph or two, then wandered into the dining room. Not often used for dining—except for Thanksgiving and other special occasions—the room was more of a family room, with the drop-leaf dining table pushed against the wall, a few comfortable chairs, a cushioned window seat, some bookshelves.

I sat on the window seat and opened my book, but I couldn't concentrate. I got up and pushed open the door to the small paneled side room, unheated, but used occasionally for privacy, or to watch television. A worn couch and the console that housed the TV, radio, and record player dominated the room. I banged the door shut against the gust of cold air.

"Is that you, Win?" Kate called from the kitchen.

"Just me, Mom," I called back. "Why don't we heat the side room?"

Kate stood in the doorway to the kitchen, drying her hands with a dishtowel, the light behind her shining down on her hair. She looked wistful and quite lovely, a furrow between her brows, her chin tucked in, her head turned aside, as if listening.

"I told you, he's out with friends," I said, feeling inexplicably defensive. "Mick and Sonowski, he said."

"I feel so helpless," she said, quietly.

"Why?"

She looked across the room at me, surprised.

"Why what?"

"Why do you feel helpless?"

"Oh. Nothing."

She went back into the kitchen. I followed her, angry and determined.

"Why don't you just say what you're feeling? Just say it!"

Kate folded the towel; she hung it on a rack to dry.

"You're so—so *secretive*," I said. "You never come right out and say exactly what's on your mind. What are you worried about? What's going on with Win?"

"Why, nothing, I'm sure. Nothing."

She stood there, not looking at me, looking at the towel, then out the window, where she could see—nothing.

The front door slammed. Kate turned quickly, glancing past the anger on my face. It was my father. He tossed his worn briefcase on a chair, pulled off his overcoat, sat down on the couch with a thump.

"Dinner's still warm," said Kate, moving swiftly toward the living room, with me close behind her. "Are you hungry?"

"Hungry, and dead tired. I think I'd rather be shoveling coal for a living. Hi, Maggie."

"You did that already. Remember?"

Kate's frown had disappeared, her face clearing as she approached him.

Frank reached down to untie his shoes. "I remember. Did you know I shoveled coal for a living, Maggie? And I don't think I felt this done in at the end of the day."

"You were younger," said Kate, stooping down, pulling off his shoes.

"Well, you weren't any prettier than you are right this minute," said Frank.

He pulled her down beside him and kissed her. They sat close together, his arm around her, her head on his shoulder.

I smiled at them, because it was impossible not to, even though I felt the usual tug of jealousy. I could not make Kate feel less uneasy, or Frank feel less exhausted. They needed each other to renew themselves. Though not unwelcome, I was not necessary.

I went up to my bedroom and read more about Hester Prynne, who is forced to wear her shame on the outside of her body, for all the world to see. I wondered, as I read, what that would feel like. The murmur of my parents' voices in the kitchen floated up to me like the soothing sounds of background music. I fell asleep, fully clothed.

I woke up, late in the night, when the front door slammed again. I listened as Win took the stairs three at a time, not quietly, passing my room to his own. Then I got up, changed into a nightgown, sleepily brushed my teeth, and went back to bed—this time beneath the blankets and between freshly laundered rough white cotton sheets.

CHAPTER 15

There were rumors about Win and Gina among my friends and acquaintances at school, but I refused to believe them. Win was just the same—just as careless, just as brash and confident. Gina was years older; she was married; she was—Gina! It couldn't be. I shook my head, refuting the insistent hiss of gossip.

At school, I caught glimpses of Win now and then, usually with a group of fellow seniors, sometimes with Peggy. Peggy was pretty in a quiet way, with long, bouncy brown hair, and brown eyes that were almost always focused on Win. Her parents were well-to-do, so her clothes were the envy of every girl in school. She and Win had dated all through high school. Win, to give him due credit, seemed to prefer her to other, flashier girls who vied for his attention. He and Peggy did not, however, "go steady." Win was sometimes seen with other girls at dances and school functions. He seemed just the same to me, striding down the hall at school, or loud, occasionally raucous, when he was showing off with his buddies—ignoring me or tossing out an offhand, "Hey, Sis!" Nothing was different. Nothing had changed.

One day, I knocked on Gina's front door, not having seen her for several weeks.

"Hi, stranger!" she said, as she waved me inside.

Ellie ran up to me, clutching me at the waist with a muffled "Majee."

Even Rags sniffed me in a rather friendly way.

Gina preceded us down the dark little hall to the bright living room, where the afternoon sun glanced off the surfaces of the furniture and the hardwood floor, and lit up the reddish highlights in her glossy brown hair. There was a thin crust of snow on the ground outside. Gina had turned the heat up high, so that the radiators clacked and hummed, reassuringly noisy.

"Washa*dee*buddy," said Ellie, leading me to the center of the room, where a small table, low to the floor, had been set with miniature cups and plates. The table was surrounded by stuffed animals and dolls waiting at attention, pudgy arms resting on the edge of the table. The wool carpet beneath it, opulent with purple flowers, gave a garden party look to the setting. I clapped my hands together in genuine delight.

"Oh, how nice!" I said.

"We're having a tea party with Ellie's 'little family,'" said Gina. "Will you join us?"

I nodded, kneeling on the carpet behind a perfect pink-faced, pink-costumed doll with porcelain head and arms, seated next to a teddy bear missing eyes, an ear, as well as much of its stuffing.

"How nice!" I said, again, misty-eyed.

How could anything sinister happen in this house, with this joyful child, the sun shining through white gauze curtains, Gina looking so content?

Ellie chattered, mostly to her "little family," correcting their manners, lightly slapping a pudgy hand or paw if there was a misdemeanor. Gina poured real tea by teaspoonsful into the tiny cups. We sipped, then chewed on morsels of cookie, bumpy with chocolate chips.

After a while, Phil came in, slamming the door behind him, calling out a cheerful, "Where's my girls?"

He pulled off his overcoat, threw it on the sofa, pulled off his shoes, loosened his tie, unfastened the top button of his shirt, and dove into the center of our party—tickling Ellie, settling her on his crossed legs, chucking Gina under the chin, then acknowledging me with, "Well, I see I've got a trio of girls today. Hi, Blondie!"

I ducked my head, feeling myself blush. Gina had told me he admired my pale coloring. When I looked up, Phil had Ellie giggling uncontrollably as he wordlessly slapsticked his way through our tea party, sipping from a micro-cup, pinkie lifted delicately, chewing, then gagging, on bits of cookie. Gina soon chimed in with her own pantomime—the well-meaning but clumsy guest.

This was what I most admired in Gina and Phil's relationship—their mutual sense of fun and good humor. Not even Ellie could outplay them when they were feeling playful. I watched as they acted out their roles, vying with each other for laughs, topping each other with feats of mimed silliness. Ellie and I were weak with laughter. Ellie tumbled off her father's crossed legs, clutching her stomach. I covered my mouth to muffle my childlike giggles and guffaws.

When at last Phil unfolded his legs and got calmly to his feet, pursing his lips while he flicked invisible crumbs off his suit coat, tossing a "Thank you, ever so," back to us as he swaggered out of the room and upstairs, we collapsed against each other, exhausted.

The light had grown mellow. We sat, looking at each other, still aching a little from laughter. We listened to Phil whistling, moving around, upstairs.

I said, "I'd better get home."

"Mowasha*dee*buddy," Ellie whined.

"Not now, my pet," said Gina.

I got up, said goodbye.

"Come again soon," said Gina, recreating for a moment the formality of the tea party.

Ellie echoed, "Comegin*shoon*."

A frigid gust of air swept across my warm face as I shut the front door behind me. I shivered and ran home.

Although I barely noticed it at the time, the image that comes most to mind when I remember that boisterous winter tea party is that of Rags, in his usual flat-on-the-floor position, wearing his usual woebegone expression. Lying on the living room carpet a little apart from us, muzzle planted between his paws, his sad liquid brown eyes edged with white, he glanced from one of us to the other, bushy eyebrows arched inquiringly.

CHAPTER 16

The rumors about Win and Gina persisted—often embroidered, as rumors are when they persist. Someone told Prue, who told me, that Win had been seen in Hillsville with an attractive older woman—his next-door neighbor, as a matter of fact. Win and several of his friends had been seen with this woman, in a fast-moving car, driving out of town late one afternoon. This woman had been seen recently on a lonely stretch of beach, huddled in blankets with someone who might have been Win.

I dismissed the rumors with the sarcasm I thought, at the time, they deserved.

So what? Gina's a friend of the family. Maybe she was with someone else. Maybe even her husband! Does anybody know for sure?

I knew of Gina's penchant for walks—in the country, on the beach. But the rumors didn't go away. They still got back to me, in a roundabout way.

Perhaps the rumors persisted because of Win, so sure of himself, so immune to criticism. He didn't care what was said about him. He laughed off the smirk or the sidelong glance, muttering, "To hell with those goddamned gossips!" Having said what he felt, he shrugged off the whole business.

I knew my brother. He was eighteen. He was popular. He was graduating in less than two months. It was not in his nature to brood.

St. Jude's Catholic Church was less than two blocks from our home, but we always rushed to get to Sunday Mass on time, often not quite making it. This made my father furious.

"*Jesus Christ*," he said, on one of those Sunday mornings, drawing out the name like an intonation, "we're practically across the street. I can hear the goddamned choir from here. All we have to do is walk a few yards. What are you people doing?"

"We're getting ready," my mother said, calmly.

My father was at the foot of the stairs, grasping the banister as if to hold himself in check. Kate was at the top of the stairs, making a few last-minute adjustments to her outfit—a gray skirt and boxy jacket she had recently made. Win was whistling in the kitchen as he routed out a forbidden snack. I stood in the living room, preening in front of the full-length mirror that hung inside the closet door, arranging a lace chapel veil over my hair. I liked wearing the cream-colored mantilla. It made me feel like a romantic heroine.

"Why bother to go?" Frank shouted, rhetorically. "We're late as it is. We won't get there till the goddamned Offertory."

"Nonsense," said Kate, coming down the stairs. "The bells haven't even rung yet."

At that moment, the bells bonged against each other. Frank threw up his arms in despair.

"Do you see? That's it. The Frank Lowin family is once again the last to arrive. Let's just stay home, why don't we, and move right on to Sunday dinner."

"Great idea, Pop," said Win, striding out of the kitchen with the remains of a sweet roll in his mouth. "I'm starved."

"Win," said Kate. "You broke your fast. I thought you were going to Communion."

She frowned at him as she stood behind me, checking her appearance in the mirror.

"Good going, Win," I said, closing the closet door. "Now you've got your excuse."

There was a momentary hush, as though we had all caught our breath simultaneously, then silence all around as we realized the church bells had stopped.

"*Goddamn it!*" said Frank, banging his fist on the banister. "We're late for Mass *again*."

"We're ready. Let's go."

Kate's voice was quiet, steady, as she took Frank's arm. They went out the front door and started down the street.

Win elbowed me aside, hissing, "*You holier-than-thou little troublemaker!*"

He caught up with them in a few long-legged strides.

I followed in their wake, listening to the choir as it grew more distinct. They were singing the "*Kyrie Eleison*." I thought of the day Gina had given the ancient Latin hymn the lure of a torch song. Sunday Mass was an ordeal we all had to endure, but listening to the choir, trying to lift Gina's voice out of the clustered sound, waiting for her occasional solo hymn, made the hour move along more tolerably for me.

We entered the small anteroom of the church, where the bell ropes hung down, still swaying. A small stained glass window over the entrance cast a dim light. Frank gave us one last disapproving look, then opened the inner door.

Fred Muncie, stout and grimly suited, his carrot-colored hair slicked down, nodded to Frank, then ushered us down the left side aisle to a half-empty bench near the front of the church, close to the altar.

We positioned ourselves on the long padded kneeler, made the sign of the cross in unison, after which each of us, supposedly, offered up a silent prayer before we sat down.

The choir sang the last notes of the *Kyrie*, the organ held the endnote, then stopped. The voice of Father Flint rose in the silence like a persistent fly, buzzing in a Latin that was as familiar as the faces around us, though only vaguely understood. We stood up, then sat down; then stood up again to listen to the gospel; then sat down again to listen to the sermon.

Father Flint, who performed most of the ritual of the Mass with his back to us, in a language foreign to us, seemed self-conscious as he stepped down from the altar to stand at the podium and face us directly. He cleared his throat. There was a certain authenticity in the sound; we all knew he enjoyed his cigars.

I leaned to one side, so that I could see between the two heads in front of me, one rising out of a stiff collar, the other out of a fringe of lace. Father Flint was rubbing his hands together, glancing out over the congregation, picking out faces. I straightened my head, concentrating on the man in front of me—his neck, bristly with dark hair, rising out of the white collar, his bald spot like a pink oasis atop his skull.

Father Flint began, slow and deliberate.

"There are those among us who, in the words of today's gospel, 'have a devil' within themselves. There are others, like the crowds in the gospel, who are anxious to take up stones and cast them at the so-called guilty party."

He paused. There was a hush in the church, broken only by the whimpering high note of a child, swiftly silenced. I felt a thrill of anticipation. Father Flint seldom ventured outside the realm of generalities.

"Let me tell you," he continued, his voice low but audible, "you are wrong, all of you. Mistaken. Misdirected. There is a devil among us, but he doesn't sit hunched inside a guilty few of us. He is everywhere, quick and clever, slippery as an eel, elusive as a chimera, within us and outside of us in the blink of an eye. Unrelenting in his search for that which is weak in us, and frail, and vulnerable. Our eyes …"

He paused. I had leaned to the side to take another look at him, but I immediately straightened up to avoid his penetrating gaze. His eyes narrowed as he peered around at us. I was nearer to him than I cared to be.

"Our ears …"

He stopped again. The congregation held a collective breath.

"Our lips."

His voice wrapped around the words with relish, as though he were sipping soup from a spoon.

My mother, who was sitting to the left of me, made a little gasping sound, which caused me to look at her. Her head was lifted up from her neck proudly. Her hair was swept up into a French twist beneath her soft, gray felt hat, her profile cameo clean, except for a slight tremor in her chin. I thought I detected an expression of distaste, or disgust, but I wasn't sure. With Kate, it was difficult to tell.

My father, who was sitting next to her, shifted on the hard bench, pressing against her. I couldn't see Win, who sat closest to the aisle. He was apparently leaning back in his seat, as was I, to avoid the uncomfortable proximity of the priest.

"The devil," Father Flint continued, "cannot be cast out. He is firmly entrenched in our midst. He leads us into sins of the flesh. He revels in our downfall. He tempts us with sins of thought, and reassures us of our innocence. Most insidious of all, he delights in inciting us to sin in word, to 'gossip,' as it were. To spread the disease of our sinful thoughts. To broadcast what is conjecture as though it were fact. To audaciously sit in judgment."

He stopped, looked down at the podium, then out at us, his spectacles reflecting the light from the nearby stained glass windows. I was unable to resist taking sidelong glimpses of him, as though I were hypnotized by that glinting light.

There was a self-conscious shuffling, a cough or two, the high whine of a child. My mother, sitting next to me, was still. I could not tell what she was thinking or feeling. For Kate, her religion was as close, as private, as her innermost thoughts and feelings.

For a few minutes, I lost interest in the sermon, as Father Flint seemed to be reverting to his usual generalities. Then he said, "I do not condone the guilty parties, if guilty they are. Their conduct is inexcusable. They have sinned grievously. They must confess, do penance, vow to sin no more. The Church commands it. God demands it. *If*—"

Here he looked around at the congregation again.

"*If*—they are guilty."

I heard a distinct, "*Puh,*" of disgust. I leaned forward and turned toward Win to see him shake his head and turn away, planting his feet in the aisle as if to get up, to leave. Then Kate reached across Frank, putting her hand on Win's arm. Win nodded, almost imperceptibly, as Kate released her hold.

Again, Father Flint looked around at the congregation. Then, looking down at the missal, he read, quietly, without intonation, "*They therefore took up stones to cast at Him, but Jesus hid Himself, and went out from the temple.*

"Let us not cast stones," he said, looking up, "lest we injure the innocent, and display our own ignorance of the truth. Now, let us stand up and recite the *Creed.*"

Returning to the center of the altar, his back to us, the purple and gold of his vestment shimmering, he began. "*I believe in one God, the Father almighty, Maker of heaven and earth, and of all things visible and invisible.*"

The congregation stood up, abashed, chastised, forgiven—none of us daring to question our guilt, not even with a passing thought—and echoed the words of the *Nicene Creed*, our collective voice a fraction in arrears. I turned toward my mother to register my surprise at the unusual sermon, both in its topic and its brevity, but she was looking away from me, toward Frank, and Win.

"*And in one Lord Jesus Christ, the Only-begotten Son of God. Born of the Father before all ages. God of God; Light of Light; true God of true God.*"

The voice of the congregation began to swell as we recited the familiar words. We gathered momentum, reasserting ourselves as we continued. "*And I believe in the Holy Spirit, Lord and Giver of life, Who proceeds from the Father and the Son.*"

We intoned the concluding words with a great swell of confidence. "*And I believe in One, Holy, Catholic and Apostolic Church. I confess one Baptism for the remission of sins. And I look for the resurrection of the dead. And the life of the world to come. Amen.*"

Convinced once again of our privilege, our rightness, our salvation, the congregation sat down noisily—sighing, shuffling, coughing, blowing into a handkerchief here and there. The organ droned as Fred Muncie, together with three other dark-suited men, strode up the front and side aisles to the altar carrying long-handled wicker baskets. They genuflected, turned toward the congregation, then slid the basket down each aisle of benches, nodding as the parishioners dropped envelopes, bills, and loose change into the shallow interior.

I thought I could discern Gina's voice, clear and fluty, among the choir. I remembered Fred Muncie talking about her recently, as he sat with my parents.

"Son of a gun, she has a voice," he had said. "I listen to her singing up there behind us in the choir and think, *Damn!* She sings like a goddamned bird. Good looking, too. Pleasing to the eyes. Pleasing to the ears. Just as well we can't see her up there in the choir. Distracting, that kind of woman."

When each of us had been given an opportunity to contribute to the church, as well as to the procurement of Father Flint's cigars, Canadian whiskey, and modest household needs, the four men returned to the altar. They presented the collection to the priest, who acknowledged it with a nod. He then returned to the altar and began the Offertory prayers.

With a wave-like movement, we bent forward and positioned ourselves on the kneelers, hands clasped, heads bowed, ears attuned to the Latin prayers issuing from the priest and the muted responses of the choir. Father Flint held up a small white wafer, swallowed it, then drank from the chalice of wine and water mixed by the young altar boys attending him.

The choir began the poignant verses of the "*Agnus Dei.*"

Agnus Dei, qui tolis peccata mundi, miserere nobis.

I thought about the sermon. Who was Father Flint alluding to? Who were the guilty parties? Could it be Gina, up there in the crowded little balcony with its imposing organ, her voice rising above the others, as though she couldn't contain her joy in the song? What about Win? I leaned forward for a glimpse of him. He was looking down, moving his fingers as if playing at an invisible piano, then turning his hands over to examine the nails, first one hand, then the other. Before I looked away, he lifted his chin to expel a great yawn.

When it was time to walk up to Communion, Win stepped into the aisle, so that we could pass him and walk up to the Communion rail. The familiar feeling of self-satisfaction and dismay assaulted me as Father Flint mumbled the Latin intonation that began "*Corpus Dómini nostri Jesu Christi,*" then placed the wafer on my tongue. Satisfaction that, unlike Win, who had broken his fast—perhaps deliberately—I could take Communion; dismay that the wafer had once again lodged itself on the roof of my mouth. I felt sure that everyone could see my attempts to dislodge and swallow the holy bread as I returned to my seat.

I knelt, pressing my forehead against my folded hands, resisting the urge to smile as I silently recited the prayer that seemed to me so appropriate: *"Oh, Lord, I am not worthy that You should come under my roof, but only say the word and my soul will be healed."*

Sensing the impatience of his congregation, Father Flint hurried through the final prayers, offered us his last blessing, then preceded the altar boys into the sacristy.

Scarcely waiting for his purple vestment to disappear, we crowded into the aisles, nodding at each other, smiling, exchanging light comments—blessed, relieved, and absolved for another week.

After the chill of the church, the sun felt warm and welcoming. None of my close friends were gathered outside, so I stayed with my parents. Win had disappeared.

"Probably home already," my father said, as my mother looked around for him.

Gina didn't come out, or else I didn't see her.

We walked home, the three of us, my father restored to good humor, my mother preoccupied. I liked the walking home part of going to church on Sunday, especially when the sun was shining. I felt fresh and absolutely clean, having fully participated in the ritual. It was, after all, good to go to church with my family.

"Did you take the rib roast out of the refrigerator?" said Frank, his arm intertwined with Kate's, his walk jaunty, his chest thrust out.

"Yes," said Kate, absently.

"Good. I'll take care of it, hon. You just do the salad and potatoes and peas."

"All right," said Kate.

"A great day. A glorious afternoon," said Frank.

He winked at me as I walked beside him.

"Yes," said Kate.

"Beautiful wife. Beautiful daughter. I'm a lucky man."

I smiled up at him. My mother was staring straight ahead, just as she had in church, in the midst of the sermon. I wondered if she were feeling the dart of Father Flint's remarks, and why those remarks, which bounced harmlessly off my father, seemed to have rendered her silent, pensive.

"Kate?" he said.

"Yes?"

"Do we have garlic?"

"Yes."

"And plenty of black pepper?"

"Yes."

"By God, I'm a lucky man," said Frank. "A lucky man."

CHAPTER 17

As the days grew warmer, my mother began preparations for Win's graduation party. It was to be outdoors, with a canvas tent, open at the sides, to protect the food, as well as the guests, from the sun, or the possibility of rain. Kate notified relatives and family friends informally. She also made lists. Guest lists. Food lists. Cleaning lists. She tore recipes out of magazines for chicken casseroles, bean salads, deviled eggs, angel food cake. She leafed through cookbooks, looking at her notes from previous parties. We even went shopping at Spangleman's for new clothes—for her and for me—something she rarely did. She chose a black and white floral print dress with a swing skirt. I chose a turquoise sheath. Frank fumed about the expense, but went along with her plans. After all, it was for Win.

I wanted to ask her if Gina and Phil were on the guest list, but I couldn't bring myself to put the question. Something kept me from coming to the point—some warning signal emanating from Kate, brisk and preoccupied, determined to celebrate her only son's achievement, his release from the confines of our small town, his promising future. I finally asked Gina herself.

"But of course we're coming. You're our dear friends, our neighbors. We wouldn't miss the celebration for the world. I'm making Ellie a special dress for the occasion. Pink, with lace edging. Very smart. She squeals with excitement whenever we have a fitting."

At school, the rumors about Gina were on the wane; Win's name was no longer mentioned in conjunction with hers. She was still a lively topic for gossip in the neighborhood, but the stories were somewhat forced. There was the police officer who was seen (not by me) sitting on her porch steps after he had stopped her for speeding. There was another senior, Lloyd something-or-other, who delivered groceries, who was often seen (even by me) in her kitchen. There was someone in the choir, a dentist, or maybe an orthodontist, who was seen with her at a tavern, in Hillsville. The stories seemed vague, even a little ridiculous. They were eventually swallowed up by rumors about other people in our small, nosy community. Many of them involved unwanted pregnancies and hasty marriage plans. These rumors—bursting into bloom like spring flowers—were more immediate, more sensational.

I continued to see Gina whenever I could, at home avoiding mention of her or of my visits. Gina—even little Ellie—were like units of energy that could recharge me with a touch. There was a gaiety about them that made me feel good, a carelessness in their offhand approach to each small activity, a refreshing lack of self-consciousness in their relationship. Sometimes they seemed almost of an age with each other—Gina as childlike as Ellie; Ellie—mother to her "little family" of dolls and stuffed animals—pretending to be older and wiser than her four years.

I seldom saw Phil, perhaps because I wasn't babysitting for them as much as I had been, perhaps because he wasn't around much. Gina didn't tell me where he was. I didn't ask. When I was with Gina and Ellie, they seemed complete; there was nothing lacking. Phil was entertaining, good company, but—almost *like* company. There again. Gone again. I wondered—but never asked—how Gina felt about him.

She told me one night. The night of the ride. I never knew why Gina chose to confide in me. Perhaps because she had no close women friends. Perhaps because I was young, in awe of her. Perhaps because I didn't judge her. I didn't know enough to judge her. I was naïve. I wanted to believe only the best about the people I admired. At that time, I admired Gina more than anyone else I knew.

I was full of romantic notions that spring. I wanted to be in love, so I was, with Kurt Lesser, a junior. He had smiled at me once at a school assembly, looking a little guilty, as though caught in the act of noticing me. I seemed to see him a lot after that, in the halls, at the Friday night dances, where he held me awkwardly away from him; at Zimmer's, where he carefully avoided eye contact—even once, at Mass, an inappropriate grin on his face when I spotted him looking at me during the Offertory.

I was walking home from school one afternoon, by myself, when he drove up beside me on Green Street in his Studebaker, which had rusted out but was still triumphantly red. I felt my face warm, then flush, as he blurted out his invitation—a double date with Bob and Sally, both juniors (whom I knew only by sight), to a movie, that Saturday. I nodded hurriedly, as though I barely had time to respond. He said he'd call me and roared off, the worn tail pipe smacking against the road at intervals.

I turned in at Gina's front walk almost automatically, wanting to share this dream date with her, knowing she would applaud the discreet eye contact, the subtle encouragement, that had led up to it.

There was no answer to my knock, no shadow of movement as I peered through the beveled glass panel on the upper half of the door. I walked slowly down the porch steps, looking back, disappointed by her absence, not quite ready to accept it. I sat down on the last step, elbows on knees, chin on hands, unwilling to go further. I could go home and call Prue, but she was having trouble with dreadful Ed, her steady. She would be polite but lukewarm, resenting my euphoria, probably interpreting it as smug, self-satisfied. There was very little generosity in our teenage friendships, unless it proceeded from a position of superiority. My mother would be noncommittal, preoccupied, as she always was these days. There seemed to be no one to tell, even though telling seemed to be so important.

I was lost in thought when I heard the crunch of gravel and looked up to see Gina pulling up in the driveway in her small green Ford. She waved at me as she got out. Then she pulled two bags of groceries from the trunk.

"Where's Ellie?" I said, leaving my books on the step, running up to her to grab a bulging bag topped with a bunch of celery. I inhaled its sweet smell. Gina looked slightly heated, almost surprised to see me.

"Spending a few days with Grandma in Hillsville," she said, fitting the oversized key into the front door. "Phil's out of town, too. I'm restocking while they're gone. Come in. Thanks for your help."

She preceded me down the dim hall, through the living room, to the kitchen, where we put the bags on the table. I began to unload the bags, beginning with the sweet-smelling celery. Gina opened the refrigerator and the cupboards as she put things away. We had done this before. I had no hesitancy, or any feeling of intrusion.

I launched immediately into my account of Kurt Lesser. Gina murmured, laughing appreciatively once or twice. She looked at me as I was neatly folding the empty bags. She said, taking the bags, tucking them under the sink, "Nice going, Maggie." I felt the warm surge of gratification that I had been waiting for as I sat, impatient and forlorn, on the porch step.

"I have a few things to do, and a phone call to make," Gina said. "Come back later, if you can, right around dusk. We'll go for a ride."

An evening ride with Gina was an adventure, like our former early-morning walks, usually with Ellie chattering in the back seat, but sometimes with Ellie in Phil's care and Gina chain-smoking beside me, her voice, exhilarating, sometimes overpowering, swirling around me with the smoke.

I hurried through dinner, told Kate I was going "on an errand" with Gina, and was knocking on the beveled glass of her door at sunset, the days longer now, claiming the evening hours with soft, filtered light, warm breezes.

Gina called to me from the kitchen. I pushed the door open, walked down the hall to the kitchen. She was finishing an after-dinner cigarette. She nodded at me, grinding the stub into her plate, with the remains of a pork chop, some canned mixed vegetables, a few sticks of celery.

"Where shall we go?" she said, getting up, walking out of the kitchen without a backward glance. I admired this way of hers of turning her back on dirty dishes and unfinished tasks. I tried to imitate it at home, but Kate seldom let me get away with it.

"Let's just ride around," I said, grabbing a stick of celery from her plate, adding, "Maybe toward the lake."

"Right. Let us be off, my child. The roads and the lake await us."

She waved me ahead of her with a flourish. We hurried out to her car, laughing and jostling each other, as though we were late for an appointment. We were soon driving toward the edge of town, the streets quiet, tucked in for the night.

"I love this time of day," she said, shifting gears as we slowly eased our way out of town, "just before dark, when the light and the dark are so close to each other, or just before it gets light, in the morning. Remember our walks?"

I nodded, remembering, but I was silent. I sensed that Gina wanted to hear *her* voice, not mine. This perception, perhaps, was the clue to our friendship.

"When the weather gets warmer, we'll walk again, in the morning," she said. "It's a summer thing, those early walks. It's best when the days start before most people even think of getting up, and there's a promise of heat in the air."

We were on the outskirts of town now, heading toward Lake Erie. Gina turned north onto Overlook Road, a straight, sparsely populated road that led to the lake. She shifted into third gear, began picking up speed, leaning back, gripping the wheel with both hands, as if she were a pilot on the runway. When she was satisfied with the speed, she relaxed and lit a cigarette. She used both hands, just touching the wheel with an elbow.

"Let's live dangerously," she said, raising both hands and tilting her chin up as she exhaled. "What's the point of living if we don't take chances?"

I gasped as the car hit a bump, then veered sharply to the left. Gina touched the wheel lightly with her right hand, the hand holding the cigarette, and put the car on course without reducing speed. Lights from newly built ranch houses, or an occasional farmhouse, flashed by. There were no other cars on the road. I felt a surge of excitement as we raced over the pavement, invisible except for the dim centerline.

I had done this before, in a car full of teenagers, speeding down a country road on a Friday night, the driver cocky with beer and the need to impress us, terrify us, six of us shouting in fear mixed with delight until he lifted his foot from the gas pedal, and we could see the dark road stretched out in front of us. I had been sweaty with a relief I dared not express.

Now, with Gina, I pushed back the fear—the same fear I had felt on that wild, reckless ride—focusing on the thrill of being out of control.

"It's okay to be scared, you know."

Gina lifted her foot from the gas pedal, resting her hand on the wheel.

"It's even okay to say you're scared. Most of us are scared most of the time."

She puffed on her cigarette, took a sidelong look at me, smiled.

"Don't worry. I won't do that again."

"I'm not worried," I said.

Gina laughed.

"You're a good sport," she said.

I cringed, offended, but Gina didn't seem to notice that she was patronizing me. She was moving into her "talk" mode. For me, this meant that she was more than usually self-absorbed, confessional.

She was cruising down the dark road at a moderate speed now, relaxed, thoughtful. I glanced at her profile—the rather small upturned nose; the wide, generous mouth curling up in a smile as she looked straight ahead.

"Right now," she began, "I'm scared shitless and, believe me, it has nothing to do with driving with no hands on the wheel."

She sighed, rolled down the window a few inches, tossed out her cigarette butt.

I shivered as Gina rolled up the window again, but I wasn't cold. The air inside the car was close and smoky.

I felt as I did hovering on the edge of a rock ledge at the local quarry where we sometimes went swimming—blue sky above, green bottomless water thirty or forty feet below. Somehow, the sky always seemed closer, friendlier, than the still cold water of the quarry.

I wanted Gina to talk to me, to tell me what it was like to be an adult, a woman in full bloom. But I didn't want to leave the reassuring warmth of my childhood, that sun-soaked ledge, solid and familiar.

"You have a wonderful gift of silence," she went on. "A rare gift. Even teenagers these days seem to think they have something to say, and as for so-called 'adults'—Well, I guess we all pontificate. Wonderful word, isn't it? Pontificate. A child would never— Ellie would never—"

She stopped speaking as she released her foot from the accelerator and put it on the brake pedal. She pushed in the clutch with her left foot; we glided to a stop at the corner of Overlook and Lake Road, the beach ahead of us, just over the tracks. She shifted gears and we crossed Lake Road, crossed the tracks, parked in the small gravel lot adjacent to the beach.

"Grab that blanket," she said, nodding toward the back seat. "It may be cold out here."

I pulled the wool blanket off the seat, put it across my shoulders, grateful for its gritty warmth. Some loose sand from previous visits to the lake fell to the ground as I arranged it into a shawl.

"It's a glorious evening," said Gina, reaching for a jacket, also in the back seat. "Let's walk."

We did, in silence, to the rhythm of small, hushed waves lapping against the shore. The sand was cushiony under our shoes. It made soft, crunchy noises as we walked. I was still glowing from my recent compliment, unwilling to break my "gift of silence" even to comment on the beauty and stillness of the night. So I waited for Gina to pontificate.

"There's something—nourishing—about being close to the water. It's not enough to see it. You need to hear it, don't you agree?"

I agreed.

We walked on, listening to the waves, and the sound of our footsteps on the sand, until Gina, apparently nourished enough, began to hum.

"I miss Ellie," she said, abruptly breaking off her song. "Not that I want to have her here, now, but just knowing she'll be at home, in her bed, when I get back."

I said nothing, feeling a little jealous of Ellie—already missed, and so seldom away from Gina.

"Sometimes I just watch her sleep. A little frown on her face. Her eyelashes fanned out on her cheeks. She has the longest lashes—just like her dad."

I tried to remember Phil's eyelashes, but I could recall nothing remarkable about them.

"When she was born, I thought I was going to die. Good God, that was the longest thirty-six hours of my life. Pure agony, my dear. I'll never have another child."

"Really?" I said, genuinely surprised.

I still thought every woman wanted children. I didn't know any married women except Gina who had had only one child.

"Really," she said, emphatically. "Much as I love her. She tore me apart, physically, and every other way. And besides—"

She stopped speaking, stopped walking, seeming to forget to put one foot in front of the other. I looked at her, waiting. When she didn't move, didn't speak, I said, "Besides—what?"

"Oh. Well. It's just that I'm not—I probably can't—It's unlikely that—that I'll ever get pregnant again."

She whispered this, then set off again at a fast pace. I trotted until I caught up with her. We were both puffing, out of breath.

"There's a pile of rocks just ahead," she said, pointing. "We can rest there."

She ran toward them, flinging back at me, "Oh, how I wish I had been born a man, Maggie. How I envy their—carelessness."

I thought about Win as I climbed up on a huge, slanting rock, still somewhat warm from the sun. He was just that—careless. So confident of himself that he could be careless. I thought of my father's bursts of temper, how my mother stepped carefully around them.

"We're pitiful, aren't we, we women," Gina said cheerfully, hugging her knees, looking out at the lake from our platform of rocks. "In perpetual bondage to our bodies. From the moment we start bleeding to the moment we die."

The sun had set, leaving behind streaks of yellow and red on the horizon. The waves were hushed, as if listening. I tried to think beyond the flattering allusion to "we women," to make some appropriate response, but all I could say was, "I hadn't thought of that."

"Why do we do it, Maggie? Why? Why do we sacrifice ourselves at the altar of marriage and motherhood?"

"We don't have to," I said. "I'm not going to sacrifice myself for anyone or anything."

Gina's expression was surprised—and tolerant.

"Of course you're not, dear child. None of us sets out to be a sacrifice. You can be sure I'll do everything I can to see to it that Ellie . . ."

She stopped, as if to formulate her next words.

"It's just that life intervenes. Circumstances intervene. You set out in one direction and—before you know it—*whoosh!*—the wind has changed, and you're sailing a different course altogether."

"I know what I want," I said stubbornly. "Nothing's going to change that."

"Ah, yes, my dear, but between the wish and the deed ..."

I pulled the blanket more closely around my shoulders, crossed my arms, hugging close to me both the warmth of the blanket and the heat of my ambition. What I wanted to do with my life was so fragile a substance that I scarcely dared acknowledge it to myself, let alone expose it to someone else's judgment.

Gina looked across at me, while I stared out at the lake. She said, very quietly, "Tell me, sweetheart."

It was, I think, that endearment, which Gina used indiscriminately for the most part, that made me speak. And it was the fact that no one had ever asked me before. Certainly no one in my own family.

"I want—I want to go to college, first of all," I began. "I don't want to be ignorant *all* my life."

"Admirable, my dear," Gina said, pulling out a pack of cigarettes, extracting a book of matches from the cellophane wrap.

"Then—then I want to travel," I said, more emphatically. "See things. People and things I couldn't possibly know about if I were to stay around here."

Gina lit a cigarette, waving the tiny light of the match until it expired. She blew out smoke through her mouth and her nose. She nodded.

"And I want to be able to think about things, and figure them out. I mean ..."

I felt myself going lame, as usual, stumbling with the words.

"I want to be able to express what I'm thinking. What I'm feeling …"

I stopped, overwhelmed with the longing I felt to break free of my inhibitions, my shortcomings. Finally, I took a deep breath, struggling to express what, until then, had been incoherent thought.

"I want to go inside myself and be myself and express myself—somehow."

"Ah," said Gina.

She continued to smoke her cigarette. I saw, without turning toward her, the small white cylinder tipped with pinkish ash as it moved from her mouth to where her fingers rested on the rock.

I was trembling from the chill air, from the weakness that follows revelation. I was grateful for the silence, the space between us. I had never spoken of that sense of longing I felt sometimes—so beyond words. Superstitiously, I regretted the words almost before they were out of my mouth.

I said, hoping to wipe out those fragile words before they elicited a comment, "I also—I also want a husband and a child. Like you. But not—not until—"

"I know. Not until you've found your own—windless place."

She tossed away the scarcely visible cigarette butt with a practiced flick of her fingers. She had my full attention now and—unlike me—she always spoke with confidence in her words.

"What do you mean?"

"Just something I heard once. In a classroom maybe, or one of those deep dark discussions we indulge in at a certain time in our lives, when we're young, and eager."

"But what does it mean?" I said, again, my voice rising, knowing that I sounded very young, very eager.

"It has to do with a candle burning in a windless place," said Gina. "It was just an image that stayed with me. Something to do with repose, certainty—a sort of calm at the center …"

Her voice trailed off.

I let out a little gasp.

"Oh," I said, staring out at the lake, embarrassed by my tears, hurriedly wiping away the wetness around my eyes.

"Most of us never find it—never even look for it. Or we get waylaid. I was so sure, Maggie—so sure my life would be special, that *I* was special."

"You *are* special," I said, with all the force of my recent emotion.

"Thank you, my dear. You are my biggest fan. But the fact is—I got waylaid. I went looking for one thing and found—something else. Something along the way. Or maybe a lot of things. But not—that special thing. That special place."

"Why did you stop looking?"

I had to know more, so that Gina's failure could be my triumph. If she would only tell me where she went wrong, I could avoid that pitfall, that swamp that might suck me in and drag me down.

Gina didn't answer me for such a long time that I looked over at her, wondering if she had heard me. She had shifted her position and was sitting slightly higher on the rocks than I was. I had to lift up my head, stretch my neck in order to see her face. She was very still, staring out at the lake, except that she was shivering, despite the oversize leather jacket she was wearing, a jacket I had often seen on Phil.

"I guess I didn't stop looking," she said. "I'm just looking in the wrong place, with all the wrong—people."

"Oh."

I was puzzled, a little hurt, although I knew she wasn't referring to me, that I didn't matter enough to be one of the "wrong" people.

"Are you getting cold?" she said, a brisk, matter-of-fact heartiness in her voice. "I'm a little cold. Let's start walking back, shall we?"

I slid off the rock, rearranging the blanket across my shoulders. I was oblivious to the chill night air. I could have stayed on that rock until the sun came up over the lake, but Gina was ready to shift gears. I was just a passenger. It was Gina's ride.

It was fully dark now, with a moon on the wane shifting in and out of skimpy clouds. We walked quickly back to the car, Gina silent, preoccupied, hunched over, as though she were walking into a strong wind.

"I want to drive some more," she said, when we got back to the car. "Do you think your mom will mind if you stay out a little longer?"

"No, of course not," I said, knowing Kate was already upset at my abrupt departure. If I had stayed to listen to her objections, I was sure I wouldn't be here at all.

We got in the car. Gina turned on the heater. We were soon driving along Lake Road, the dry heat parching our skin, toasting our toes. I felt deliciously relaxed and sleepy. I was startled when Gina began to talk again.

"Not many men would do what Phil did," she said, as though we were in the middle of a conversation. I realized that Gina was continuing a discussion, to which I had just been admitted.

"Most men are too proud. Muscle-bound around their brains, around their hearts. Don't know what tenderness is. Would be embarrassed by it if they did. Phil is—kind—and he makes me laugh. Not enough, perhaps, to build a marriage on, but then there's Ellie. She makes it enough. She's the glue. Phil loves her just like—just like I do. She almost killed me. She messed me up inside. And yet, what I feel for her is this overwhelming—tenderness. I can't bear for her to be in pain. I won't admit she has any defects—even a speech defect. That's a laugh, isn't it? But there you are. And Phil, I can tell you, feels the same. He has never raised his voice to her. He has never been impatient with her, even though—God knows—"

She stopped talking, reached for her cigarettes, began the ritual lighting ceremony. I huddled down in the seat, still clutching the blanket around my shoulders, up around my ears, trying to be an invisible presence. I wanted her to talk to me as though she were talking to herself.

"It was while I was in what I call my 'wild' period, just before Phil and I got together, that I met—Ellie's father."

I gasped, then coughed, in a vain attempt to cover up the gasp. I peeked at her from my blanket shawl. She was smiling, looking straight ahead, her head tilted up as she exhaled a seemingly endless cloud of smoke. Gina loved dramatic moments.

"God, he was good looking. Tall. Muscular. Built like a god. Light brown hair always falling down over his forehead. He had this habit of combing it back with his fingers while he was thinking about something … Pale blue eyes. Long eyelashes—light, though, so you didn't really notice them unless he was close to you and looking down …"

She laughed, an abrupt sound, more like a grunt. She cranked the window down part way, tossed her cigarette out the window. Fresh air rushed into the car. I gulped at it as she closed the window. She sighed, shook her head.

"Within five minutes, I was hooked. All he had to do was reel me in. I knew almost nothing about him, except what he did for a living. I never knew anything about him, and I'll tell you something—I don't think there was much of anything to know."

I said, my voice hoarse, "What did he do for a living?"

"Plant manager. At a little tool and die company. Small potatoes—although you'd never know it to listen to him. He was full of himself. Loved to talk. Loved to hear himself talk. And, God help me, I loved to listen. I could have listened to him all day and all night. I didn't give a damn what he said. His voice—hypnotized me. Literally. There were times, when we were talking on the phone, when he said, "Hey, babe, you still there?" I would sort of shake myself awake, so I could answer him. I wasn't listening to what he said, you see. I was listening to—him."

Had I ever felt like that, I wondered? *Could* I ever feel like that?

"It's hard to explain that kind of love," Gina said, "or justify it. But it is love. Not a healthy love, or a lasting love. You don't look back on it and say to yourself, 'Oh, that wasn't the real thing. I know that now.' It *is* the real thing. It's overwhelmingly real. When a man makes your heart thump—and he's not even there in the room with you, he's not even around, he's just moving around in your head—that's real. That's as real as it gets."

We came to a stop in front of a red light. Gina turned left, away from the lake, in the direction of home.

"Where is he now?"

"Don't know. Don't want to know. Didn't know I was pregnant till after he went his way and I went mine. Then . . . I met Phil."

The car hummed, its motor warm, running smoothly. I pushed back the blanket, warm myself. Soon the lights of town were ahead of us. I began to stretch and yawn.

Just before we reached home, Gina said, her voice wistful, almost inaudible:

"Have you ever wished for something so much, Maggie, so much you could almost—almost—make it happen?"

When I didn't answer, she said, her voice so low I wasn't sure if I heard it:

"I wish I could love him."

CHAPTER 18

The Saturday of Win's graduation party was bright, clear—a perfect June day. The party was to begin late in the afternoon, with a dinner buffet, and continue long into the night. Wilifred Muncie and Frances Baird had helped my mother with last-minute preparations. Kate had planned so well that there was nothing to do but to make ourselves as festive looking as was the house and the back yard, where the tables underneath the open-sided tent were already laden with covered dishes. Festoons of crepe paper lifted in lazy spirals with every breeze.

I had invited Kurt Lesser to the party. We had survived several dates and dances, as well as some fumbling embraces in his rusty red Studebaker. I liked Kurt most of the time, tolerated him the rest of the time. I knew he would make a good appearance at my side, with his lanky dark hair combed severely back from his forehead, a sports jacket hanging from those broad shoulders. He wouldn't have much to say. He never did. But we were well matched in that respect.

Win had gone to pick up Peggy, his perennial girlfriend. My mother was upstairs, behind closed doors, where she was putting on the new dress that we had selected for the occasion. I was wearing the snug, sleeveless turquoise dress, also new, that had motivated me to turn away from snacks and desserts for the two weeks since my mother and I purchased it. It now fit to perfection. I looked at myself in the full-length mirror downstairs with wordless admiration. I had Kate's legs, smooth and tapering to slim ankles. The body beneath the turquoise dress was that of a woman, even though I still often felt I would never emerge from the clutch of childhood. I held my shoes in my hand, practical black leather (at my mother's insistence) with skinny two-inch heels (at my insistence)—knowing I would want to take them off almost as soon as I put them on. I walked through the living room toward the kitchen in search of the snack I no longer needed to deny myself.

The dining room looked unfamiliar, with extra folding chairs, and end tables neatly topped with ashtrays, matchbooks, stacks of cork table protectors, plates of nuts. I stopped to survey the room. Ahead of me was the kitchen, with its promise of food, but then I heard the stereo playing on the console in the room we called the "side room," just off the dining room. The song on the stereo made me pause, and listen. It was the Flamingos' "I Only Have Eyes for You," a tune Kurt and I had often danced to. It made me feel warm, even tender, though I suspected it was the song, not the thought of Kurt, that aroused me.

I padded into the dimly lit room to turn up the volume. Gina and my father were standing close to the wall opposite the stereo, their mouths locked together.

Without changing my pace or looking to either side, I reached for the knob on the stereo, turned up the volume, and walked out.

I saw—or thought I saw—my father's hand dislodge itself from Gina's breast as I made my exit.

I walked upstairs, sat down on my bed. When I looked up, my mother was standing in the doorway. She was wearing her new black and white floral print dress. Her blonde hair was swept up, away from her face. Her eyes and mouth were accentuated with makeup she rarely wore. A string of pearls hung around her neck, dipping toward the "V" of her dress. The swing skirt was short enough to show off her black hose and black heels.

"You look beautiful," I said, without emphasis. I could smell the sweet, slightly oppressive fragrance of her perfume. Chantilly. I added, "You smell good, too."

Kate smiled, said, "Come down soon," then was gone.

I remember everything about that afternoon and evening. The constant movement of people reflected on the polished hardwood floors. The smell of cigarette smoke, beer, liquor, and myriad foods for which I no longer had an appetite. The chorus of voices and laughter orchestrated by the stereo in the side room. The familiar faces crowded close to one another, nodding to me, calling out a greeting—or not seeing me in their quest to be heard, to be seen, to drink, to eat from their laden plates.

Outside, the fresh green grass was trodden on by many feet, ground down by many heels stomping out cigarettes.

The canvas tent cover billowed in the soft early evening breeze. Beneath it, our guests chatted as they decked their plates with ham, chicken, potato salad, bean salad, deviled eggs, cheese, slabs of white or rye bread, pickles, olives—all of the tempting dishes Kate had prepared and stowed away in our refrigerator, as well as in the refrigerators of accommodating neighbors.

Win, with Peggy close by his side, clutching his arm, moved in and out of groups, accepting congratulations along with hearty slaps on the back, melding with his own friends whenever he could. He dragged me into one group, urging me to, "Say hi to Benson."

Benson, who was still my ideal of young manhood, greeted me with a low whistle. But he was with his steady, and I was with Kurt. Luring him away from her seemed too complicated, too much of an effort. Kurt soon pulled me away, toward the tent. I went with him, although the heavy scent of many foods and many people beneath the canvas made me feel queasy.

With her infallible timing, Gina Gregorka walked into our yard toward sunset, with Phil at her side, and Ellie running ahead in her new dress—"pink, with lace edging"—that Gina had made for the occasion. Ellie ran up to me. She pirouetted in front of me, her dress billowing out, her spindly little legs spinning.

Feeling a sudden weakness in my legs, a trembling I could not control, I stooped down, so that Ellie and I were nose to nose. I gave her a hug.

"You look so pretty!" I said.

"Risha cake!" she said, peremptory, pushing me away. I pointed toward the tent, where Win's huge single-layer graduation cake was prominently displayed. She ran off, pausing to pirouette before an admiring clutch of adults.

"So do you, my dear," said Gina, as I stood up, smoothing down my dress.

"What?"

"You look very pretty yourself," said Gina. "Doesn't she, Phil?"

She linked her arm with Phil's, glancing from him to me.

"Indeed she does," said Phil, adding, with his usual chivalrous humor, "I'll bet there isn't a male here who isn't looking at you with a gleam in his eyes."

Still trembling—still timid about accepting compliments—I looked down. When I looked up, he and Gina had glided away, entering the thick of the party in Ellie's wake.

The sound of the party seemed, to my ears, to change subtly with Gina's entrance, her good-looking husband and lively daughter in tow. I could almost hear the women hiss, the men rumble, as she walked underneath the tent. Then I heard her loud, infectious laugh. The others joined in, the tension eased, the party resumed.

I watched her from a distance as the sun on the horizon reddened the sky and the moon ascended, plump, silvery. She approached my father with her hand held out. She said something that made him laugh, take her hand, greet her—and Phil—with his usual flourish.

Win came up to them soon afterward. Gina kissed him lightly, pressing her cheek against his, congratulating him. Win introduced Peggy, who nodded, smiled stiffly, and soon pulled him away again.

After that, I had only to listen for her laughter to know where she was. She must have greeted Kate, but I never saw them together.

The guests finished eating, then relaxed into the evening that, for everyone except me, it seemed, was perfect in its warm, soft, silent embrace. No one wanted to leave, so well had Kate prepared; so well had she and Frank presided; so well had the impeccable June day run its course. Frank lit a fire in the barbecue pit. Kate lit candles and lanterns. The guests grouped themselves around the spots of light like colorful moths, hands fluttering as they talked, laughed, gestured, holding glasses tinkling with ice, or mugs topped with froth from the beer kegs inside the tent.

The children, full of food and lemonade, had been sent home with older siblings or were nesting sleepily in their parents' arms. Ellie had resisted sleep as long as she could, then climbed onto Phil's lap, where she jabbered until her eyes clamped shut and her small mouth fell open in a wheezy pout.

There were always musicians at our neighborhood gatherings. That night they assembled outside, around the barbecue pit, with guitar, mandolin, banjo, harmonica, and many willing voices singing the old songs my parents and their friends loved.

Inside the house, where Kurt and I went to join the younger crowd, the stereo could be heard in all of the downstairs rooms. Win's friends, and my friends, were coupled off and dancing in the all-but-dark. One or two couples were necking in the relative privacy of the side room.

I was grateful that evening for Kurt's silence, my father's distance, my mother's preoccupation, Gina's obliviousness; for noise, music, the buffer of many bodies separating me from the necessity of looking at my father, or listening to Gina. Dancing close to Kurt, my head on his broad shoulder, I felt drowsy, content. I wondered if I had seen what I had seen. It was only a moment, after all. I had never directly faced my father and Gina. The side room was on the east side of the house—always dim in the late afternoon. Everyone was affectionate in greeting each other today. What better excuse for stealing a kiss?

I lifted my head from Kurt's shoulder, noting the couples who were kissing as they swayed to the music, or pressed against each other on the couch, or lumped together (Prue and her dreadful Ed) on the big easy chair in the side room. Then I looked up at Kurt, who kissed me soundly on the mouth before he allowed me to again rest my head against him. It was a day for kissing. There was no shame in it.

But I couldn't put away the hungry, furtive way my father and Gina had grasped at each other, the moan that rose to a gasp when I walked into the room. I kept thinking of the silence as I made my quick exit, Gina's arms hanging awkwardly at her side, my father's hand dropping away from Gina's breast.

I had often seen my father fondle my mother's breasts, or lightly caress her back, her buttocks. It was always Kate who pulled away when I walked into the room, or when I looked up from a book or magazine. Frank was unabashed in his displays of affection. He often said, jokingly, that he couldn't keep his hands off her.

Off Kate. Off my mother.

Using a headache as an excuse, I said goodnight to Kurt and left my friends before the party came to an official end. In my room, with the windows open, I could hear the stereo downstairs, the muted singing in the back yard, the bursts of laughter, the familiar but unintelligible voices. I pulled off my heels and unzipped my turquoise dress, stepping out of it with an indifference I could not have imagined a few hours ago. I got into bed, the dress a shapeless puddle on the floor. I closed my eyes.

CHAPTER 19

For me, there were no more days like those that led up to Win's graduation party. Something seemed to have vanished from our family—something that had resided in my father's stormy supremacy, my mother's tolerance and calm.

Win was more serious, more preoccupied. He was working full time at Superior Collision, and taking one or two summer courses so that he could meet entrance requirements at State. Peggy was the only girl he was seeing because (he said) he recognized at last all of her sterling qualities, or because (I thought) he was reserving his energy for work, summer school, and the upcoming demands of vanquishing the female population of a large Midwestern university.

I never confronted my father with what I had seen just before Win's party began, or alluded to it, or acknowledged it in any way. I concluded, at last, that perhaps I had not seen what I thought I had seen. My father edged back into his usual confident position—hot-tempered and opinionated, but often affectionate, cheerful. My mother continued to humor him, deflect his anger, ignore—as much as she could—his inconsistencies. Whether what I had witnessed between Gina and my father was appetizer, main course, or dessert, I didn't know with any certainty—just as I didn't know to what extent Win had been sucked into Gina's whirling vortex.

With Gina—"Mrs. Gregorka," as I now thought of her—I had more options than within my own family. I could simply avoid her.

I did, for most of that hot, restless summer.

There was a dry, parched quality to each day that succeeded that lush green June. The grass turned yellow. It grew slowly, with ugly bald patches here and there. The air was still, sluggish during the day, seldom cooling off enough at night to refresh and prepare us for another day of heat.

I mooned about, alone or with my friends, trying to make sense out of my tumultuous teenage emotions, now encumbered even more by an unexpected glimpse of clandestine adult behavior. It was one thing to pair an older brother and the woman accorded my uncritical adulation. It was quite another when one half of that pair was my father.

It never occurred to me to talk about what I had seen or not seen the day of Win's graduation party. If Gina and my father were guilty to the last degree, their secret was as safe with me as with Father Flint in the confessional. As an unauthorized witness, I bore my full share of guilt. I was guilty by association. I was guilty by relationship. I was guilty by being there, where I should not have been.

I thought about confessing my guilt to Father Flint, but instead confessed in vague terms to impure thoughts, lack of honor toward my parents, distortion of the truth. Father Flint was probably as confused by my confession as I was, but he absolved me of my sins, both real and imagined, and sent me on my way with a complicated penance of novenas, rosaries, and Stations of the Cross. I completed my penance with zeal and a previously unknown fervor. I felt, for the first time in my life, the joy of being a Catholic.

As a child, I had accumulated a tangled skein of impressions, which together meant that I was a Catholic. There were, first of all, the nuns: my grade-school guardians, swathed head to foot in black, with a starched white frame around their faces, and hands that appeared and disappeared from wing-like folds of material. I sometimes thought those hands might lift off, float away, like the angels on the holy cards the nuns dispensed for good conduct. The nuns taught us Latin by rote, as they did reading, writing, and the breathing heart of our sacred religion. God saw—judged—everything we did. There were no secrets from God—whether manifest as a bearded and magnificent Biblical father or his bloodied, exquisitely suffering son, crowned with thorns, hanging from a crude cross. The "Holy Ghost" or "Holy Spirit," for reasons I didn't understand, appeared in the shape of a dove.

To inspire us in our quest for a life worthy of these three mysterious entities, who hovered over us, reading our every thought, judging our every act, we had the lives of the saints, most of them brief, grisly, and abruptly terminated with acts of unspeakable torture, the details of which riveted our attention and halted the shuffling of our feet, the shifting of our eyes. As if to soften the blow from this vision of all-seeing eyes and all-suffering humanity, we were each accorded our own guardian angel, who watched over us to make sure we were not burned in hot oil, eaten by lions, or flayed alive—that is, unless we aspired to sainthood.

I was uncomfortable with the idea of a guardian angel. I didn't like the thought of an unseen being with gigantic wings hovering just behind or beside me, witness to my every move.

The nuns taught us to write a neat cursive hand, which most of us un-learned in the comparative freedom of high school; to stand up beside our desks and read with precision and accuracy; to repeat the multiplication tables with unerring speed; to recite Latin sufficient to participate in the Mass; to pledge allegiance to the flag, and to Father Flint.

Father Flint interrupted our studies at unscheduled intervals, lectured us into submission, quizzed us into humility. Even when we graduated from eighth grade and journeyed the six blocks or so to high school, we could not escape Father Flint. To him we confessed our sins, opened our mouths for Communion, gathered for the lessons in catechism that were to usher us into a pure and untainted adulthood.

It was to Father Flint I turned my attention when no other avenues of guidance seemed open to me. I fell into the embrace of my religion as, when a child, I fell into my mother's arms.

It was the responsibility of Mother Church and Father Flint to show me the way and the truth. They were to do this with no hints from me. Not even in the confessional would I reveal my father's betrayal, or Gina's recklessness. Nor could I describe my mother's careful avoidance of pain—for the baby who was born moments too late; for the son who was playing adult games before he was an adult; for the husband who adored her and deceived her with equal fervor. Especially, I could not confess my own portion of guilt and responsibility—for my insensitivity and self-absorption; for ignoring what I saw; for judging and condemning with no guidelines except my own ignorance.

Without any help from me except my obvious confusion, which was endemic in my age group, our parish priest could only do what he had always done: lecture us from the podium of his exalted station, hear our mumbled confessions, exhort us to cling to our fast-fading innocence, threaten us obliquely or, as he did one evening as I sat with my fellow teenage sinners, directly.

All summer I had been on my knees, literally and figuratively, in prayer and in penance. I wanted to understand why it was that adults, with their maturity and wisdom, continued to fall short of their—and my—expectations. Why, when Gina waved to me from the front porch or the back yard, did I wave back? Why, when Frank berated Kate for some trifling offense, did I defend her heatedly—but never accuse him outright? Why did I suspect myself more and more, Gina less and less? It must be, dear God in distant and objective Heaven, because I was wrong. There was some piece of the puzzle not available to me, still only an aspiring adult. Those who acted innocent *were* innocent. Look at Win. Look at Gina. Look at my father.

So, following the commencement of the school year, when Father Flint—attired in his usual mournful black, his pant cuffs peeking out from under his clerical gown, his stiff clerical collar edged in white and nicked in front, as if to hold his pale, balding head erect—addressed us at our first meeting of religious instruction, I listened as to an oracle, or a prophet of perdition.

Religious instruction—for those of us attending public high school—took place in the church, on Wednesday, in the early evening. It wasn't a gratifying turnout. Many of my fellow students scoffed at the idea of submitting to religious classes, after they had escaped the nuns. Even I had only appeared occasionally during the last year. But there were enough familiar faces in the front pews to make me feel comfortable.

I sat through the catechism in my usual listening state—half alert, half dreaming—watchful for the dark lashless eye, the square finger that might pick me out for an answer. I looked around the church, drawing comfort from the familiar altar with its near-life-size Christ on the cross, the side-altar statues of Mary and St. Jude—robed, eyes devoutly downcast, a bare foot peeping out from beneath their plaster gowns. The Stations of the Cross marched in bas relief along the walls, between high narrow windows, etched in colored glass, depicting scenes of suffering, grace, and miraculous works.

Something had roused the ire of the good priest, who lacked the humor and patience needed to control our high spirits, once unleashed. It was probably Prue's dreadful Ed, who would stop at nothing to elicit a laugh, or even a snort of approval, from his friends. Ed was sitting in the third row, trying to curb the grin that kept spreading across his face. A couple of his buddies were responding boisterously. Even Prue smiled a little, as she poked him soundly in the ribs.

"You can scorn the word of God, but you cannot escape it," said Father Flint.

My mind came back to the present moment at full alert. We were all familiar with, still frightened by, his sudden bursts of anger. Once, in grade school, he had grabbed an inattentive girl by her wrist, berating her for her lack of attention. He had thrust her out of the room, into the hall, then slammed the door in her face. We could hear her whimpering in the hall throughout the rest of his discourse. I had heard other stories of his temper, his impatience, but had never been under direct attack, which I attributed to my watchfulness, my reluctance to make myself conspicuous in a group.

"Do you think, because you are no longer children, that you are beyond the scope of the Church, of its edicts, of God Himself?"

Father Flint's voice rose to the pitch necessary to reach a Sunday congregation of two hundred souls. The two dozen of us, who half-filled the front pews, huddled on our hard seats, eyes cast down, awaiting the storm.

"Sinners, every one of you, and, in your pride, incapable of remorse. You have hardened your hearts against God. You have turned away from your Savior. I have seen it again and again. You go to high school. You find new companions. You engage in dangerous activities and late hours. You get your driver's license. You designate someone your 'girlfriend' or 'boyfriend.' You drink beer. You engage in sexual conduct. Your religious beliefs fall away from you as the leaves are falling off the trees at this moment. Which of you can raise your hand and tell me you are innocent of any of this? Raise your hand. I tell you, raise your hand!"

Of course, no one looked up, or raised a hand. We not only tacitly admitted our guilt but showed our pride in it with our silence. This subtlety, however, was apparently not perceptible to our spiritual leader, whose rage seemed to feed on his words.

"I know all of you. Each of you. I've watched you grow up. I've heard your confessions. I've given you my blessings again and again. Then I watch you drift away. To what? Who will guide you? Who will take you by the hand?"

There was a momentary guffaw, immediately suppressed, but it was enough to reignite Father Flint, whose rage had begun to subside under the impact of his own eloquence.

"Who dares to laugh when his own salvation is at stake? Who dares to make fun of the loving guidance of our Lord?"

In the silence that followed this challenge, we could hear the rustle of his priestly garments as he paced back and forth in front of us.

"I remember one who laughed and made light of his religion. He sat where you are sitting now. He scoffed at my questions. He ignored my warnings. He disregarded my injunctions. He walked out of this church, away from my instruction, in pride and in defiance. In pride and defiance he broke the commandments of God."

I could feel my heartbeat in the silence that followed. Everybody had heard this story, in one form or another. Everybody in my age group, at least. We had discussed it at great length when it happened, several years ago. I had listened with awe, and some pride, since it was Win who had stood up to Father Flint, who had walked away from him while the priest shouted denunciations at his back. Win didn't brag about this act of defiance, nor was he ashamed of it. He acknowledged it, then swept it aside. He never apologized, or went back, or confronted the priest again. When in church, at the insistence of our parents, he kept his distance, and declined to take Communion from Father Flint's hand.

"Do you see where it leads, this brazen defiance of God and his ordained representative? This young man has drifted further and further away from the teachings of the church, into a state of complete abandon."

I was staring at my hands clasped in my lap. They blurred and came into focus by turns. I was sure that everyone in the church on this Wednesday of a crisp fall-like evening was looking at me, or thinking of looking at me. I longed for the courage to walk away from this oddly callous man of God, but I could not move. I didn't have Win's courage, or his stubborn resistance to authority. It took all of my self-control to keep back the tears that obscured my vision.

Seemingly satisfied with the effect of his tirade, Father Flint bowed his head as he said, with solemnity, "Now let us pray for the forgiveness and compassion promised us by the Lord our God."

He led us in a closing prayer.

In a few minutes I was outside the church, breathing in the cool evening air. Prue put her hand on my arm, as if preparing to say something comforting, but I mumbled an excuse, crossing the street so that I could walk home alone.

Already the anger was setting in, replacing the feeling of hurt and betrayal I had felt in the church. This priest, who had known me and my family all of my life, had embarrassed and humiliated me in order to vent his anger, to make his point. Of course, he had been carefully unspecific. But he had scored a bullseye, and I had been the target.

I couldn't make the decisive gesture. I didn't have Gina's dramatic flair. But there was a measured finality in the anger I felt as I walked away from the church. The sense of confusion I had carried about with me for months dissipated. No one—not even the parish priest—could, by such obvious implication, expose my own brother. No one had that right—even the righteous Father Flint. He had gone too far. In doing so, he had earned my silent condemnation, of him and of his church.

Before I opened the front door of my house, I was Win's champion and, once again—as though in alliance against Father Flint and our narrow-minded townspeople—Gina's friend.

CHAPTER 20

I was nervous as I knocked on the door. When Gina opened it, the smile I had fixed on my face felt a bit wobbly.

"Hi," said Gina. "Come in."

"Majee! Majee!" shouted Ellie, running down the dark hall, throwing herself at me.

I stooped down, hugged her. She took my hand, pulled me toward the living room, chattering excitedly.

"Wishaskule," said Ellie, pointing.

I saw that school was in session, with several small neighborhood children seated in a circle on the floor, between assorted students of the stuffed and stiff-jointed variety. Rags lay uncomfortably among this group, his nose on the ground, the whites of his eyes rising like two new moons as he looked up at me.

"Hi, kids. Hi, Rags," I said.

There was a murmured response from the children, immediately hushed by Ellie, who had obviously designated herself the teacher.

"Mushatawkin*skule*," she said, putting a finger to her lips.

The children sat quietly while Ellie handed out coloring books and crayons—apple-cheeked Donald Morgan, scarcely out of diapers; Freddie Muncie, carrot-topped like his father; Lucy Granger, a little older than Ellie, mumbling protests against her friend's tyranny. But Ellie held them all in check, her will, as always, superior to that of any other child in the neighborhood.

"Cumminculer," she said to me, peremptory.

I sat obediently in the circle, took the book and crayons handed to me, searched for a page not yet scribbled with color. I looked helplessly up at Gina. She laughed and went into the kitchen, where I could smell hot chocolate heating up on the stove.

It occurred to me, as I filled in a circus scene with bold ropes of color, that Ellie never lacked for friends and visitors, no matter the ups and downs of Gina's reputation in our small town. The neighborhood children loved Ellie, who ordered them about like small robots. Gina always welcomed them, provided abundant refreshments, then left them to Ellie's devices.

Ellie walked around the outside of the circle, checking our pages, pointing a finger at unacceptable work. A small forefinger, the nail touched with chipped red polish, pointed at my page. I heard a "cluck" of disapproval from behind my left shoulder.

"Stayashideda*lines*," she said, tapping the finger here and there on the page where I had, indeed, ignored the lines and created my own color scheme. "Tigersher*not*green."

She sighed, dramatically, then moved on. I realized, with a pang, that I had missed her as much as I had missed Gina.

Last June didn't happen like I thought it did, I said to myself, as I swept a brown crayon over my green tiger. *It was just a friendly kiss, at any rate. It didn't mean anything. I blew it all out of proportion.*

Gina was leaning against the kitchen doorway, her arms across her chest, watching her domineering little daughter. She turned her head toward me for just a moment, nodding. Then Ellie ran up to her. They whispered together, and Ellie sang out, "Reeshesh!"

Four hungry students and a dog followed her into the kitchen.

During the next few months, I saw more of Ellie than I did of Gina. I became Ellie's "Nanny Maggie" (as Gina jokingly called me) when her mother went off for a few hours, an evening, sometimes overnight. Phil was often away from home, or came in late at night, when he would press some bills into my hand, then send me home with no questions asked.

I wondered at their relationship, so different from that of my parents, who accounted to each other for each moment of their lives. Phil and Gina seemed comfortable with one another, affectionate, appreciative of the other's humorous side, yet independent—while my parents seemed disabled, as if missing a vital part, when they were not together.

Gina had decided to keep Ellie out of preschool—perhaps because she didn't want her daughter criticized for her speech defect; perhaps because she wanted to keep her close to herself a little longer. Several of Ellie's friends had started kindergarten, so Ellie was more isolated that fall and winter. Little by little, she lost the hold she had on the older neighborhood children, whose confidence soared with their entry into school. She ranted at them, stamped her feet, but she couldn't cow them as she used to do. She had to settle for dominating the toddlers and the younger children, who were still awed by the noise she made.

"Iwanjacrosha*shtreet*!" she shouted at her mother.

For Ellie, independence and the path to adulthood were both encompassed in "crossing the street." She watched the neighborhood children, under the watchful eye of the safety guard, troop across the street, then watched until they were out of sight as they walked the few blocks toward the public elementary school, a cream-colored brick building sheltering the teachers and the pliable young minds they molded.

"Next year, my sweet," Gina would promise, "in all new clothes."

Gina would talk about the dresses she would make, the shoes they would buy—the smart little red wool coat they would shop for. Ellie would sigh, wipe away an angry tear, add an addendum here and there—"*Shiny*shuz," "Dreshjushlike*Looshy*"—then go off and play with her "little family" until the next morning, the next procession down the street.

Despite Gina's reluctance to let go of her child, she was often away from her in the afternoon and the evening, when her whereabouts were vague or unknown. Her instructions, at least to me, were, "I'll check in with you." I was awed by her freedom, which had no precedent in my experience. But I didn't ask questions, except once.

It was well into November, when the daylight hours are few and soon past, and afternoon melds seamlessly into evening. I had agreed to stay with Ellie after school, but I had lingered in a booth at Zimmer's with Kurt, Prue, and Ed, sipping a Coke, listening with some surprise as Kurt—usually silent, even glum—exchanged jokes and insults with Ed.

True, we had sat together the night before on the small tattered couch in the side room, kissing, watching the flickering TV screen. Kurt's hand, resting comfortably on my shoulder, had a tendency to slide toward my left breast. He had managed to pry my mouth open with his, slide his tongue in the direction of my throat. But could this progress in our relationship account for such confidence, such rollicking good humor?

At last, I glanced at the bug-spattered wall clock over the booths. I nudged Kurt to slide out of the booth so that I could leave.

"Gotta go. I'm babysitting," I said.

Kurt—still cheerful—drove me home, to save time, but I was still very late.

Gina greeted me with a frown and a puckered brow.

"Sorry," I said. "I was just—"

"It doesn't matter," she said, waving my words aside. Gina was never interested in excuses. "Ellie is cranky. She says she doesn't feel good, but I think she's just bored. Sometimes I wish I'd put her in preschool."

"Where will you be?" I said, taking off my coat, hanging it on the carved oak hat stand next to the door. I added, when there was no response, "In case she gets sick."

"She'll be all right," Gina said, grabbing her coat and scarf from the stand. "I'll be—" She paused. "I'll be—in touch."

She was out the door and in her car, the cold motor screeching indignantly, before I could form a reply.

"Doad*get*shick," said a voice on the stair.

I turned to see Ellie sitting on the top step, her elbows propped on her knees, her chin resting on her hands.

"I know you don't get sick," I said, climbing the stairs, sitting beside her. "But it's good to know where your mom is, just the same."

"Portentbishnush," said Ellie, not moving.

"I'm sure it's important," I said. "Otherwise, she wouldn't leave you."

"Majee?"

"Yes?"

"*Whaz*portentbishnush?"

"Well," I said, pondering, because there was a note of appeal in Ellie's voice, "it's something that you don't always want to do, but you have to do it."

"Why?"

"Because—because—it's important."

Ellie seemed satisfied with this explanation.

"Rajishshick," she said.

"Really? Rags is sick?"

"Inoshbital," she said, nodding, getting up. "Cuminshee."

I followed Ellie into the tiny sewing room at the end of the upstairs hall. Gina's sewing machine was set up against the wall. Her work-in-progress, mostly clothes for Ellie, was scattered around the room. On the opposite wall was a narrow, old-fashioned bed, scarcely wide enough for Ellie, upon which was a bright red quilt and Rags, lying in his usual position, muzzle between his paws, a clean white handkerchief tied around his head. Arranged around him were Ellie's limbless, eyeless, chewed and battered "little family." Her newer and more perfect dolls and stuffed animals had been excluded.

"So this is your hospital," I said, looking around with a critical eye, my hands on my hips. "Yes. This will do. We can make them better here."

Ellie, who had been looking up at me hesitantly, sighed with satisfaction. She planted her hands on her hips in perfect mimicry.

"Thishiz Majee," she said to Rags and the assembled patients. "Sheshα*dok*ter."

I nodded curtly as I pushed up my sleeves.

"Well, Nurse Ellie, let's get to work. We've got some nasty injuries here."

The phone rang, startling me out of a dream in which Kurt stood on the stage in the high school auditorium, drawing shouts of laughter from the assembled students, while I sat in the audience, whispering frantically to those students seated around me, "*What did he say? What did he say?*"

"—'Lo," I mumbled.

"You should have been home long ago," my mother said, in response to my sleepy greeting.

"Gina isn't back yet."

I pushed myself up to a sitting position on Gina's rust-red, gold-threaded sofa, with its numerous soft cushions, where I'd fallen asleep with school books and papers spread out around me, the lamp light shining in my face. Rags, curled up at my feet, sighed and smacked his gums.

"It's a school night," said my mother. "What about your homework?"

"I'm doing it," I said, rattling some sheets of paper.

"You'll have to tell Gina you can't babysit on weeknights if she's going to stay out so late."

"But I need the money," I said, mournfully. I didn't want restrictions placed on my friendship with Gina, so recently lost, then found again. "For clothes, and Christmas, and—things."

"When did she say she'd be back?"

My mother was circling around the issue, having told me I should try to earn money for "extras."

"Soon," I said, although I had no idea what time it was.

I had fixed supper for Ellie and myself, read her to sleep at 8:30, surrounded by non-hospitalized family members. Then I'd studied for a geometry test until the lines and planes blurred.

"Where's Phil?"

"I don't know. I'm sure he or Gina will be back soon. Don't worry." I paused. "Okay?"

My mother sighed.

"Is Ellie all right?"

"Of course. She's asleep."

"I left some pudding in the refrigerator for you."

"Thanks, Mom. See you soon."

I hung up, stretched, squinted at the grandfather clock, positioned between the two long paisley-draped windows. Just then it whirred, clanked, and bonged three times. It was 11:45.

I nosed around the kitchen, looking for something to appease my growling stomach. I was leaning against the counter, chewing on a banana, when I heard Gina come in.

She was humming. I went out to the living room to greet her. She danced across to me, grabbed my hand, whirled me around in an impromptu waltz. Rags, wide awake, was wagging his hindquarters, grinning.

"How are you, Nanny Maggie?"

"Just fine," I said, laughing. "How are you?"

"Better than fine. So fine. *So* fine."

She began singing the tune she had been humming—"Give me a kiss to build a dream on"—releasing me, dancing off on her own.

I watched her, my arms crossed, my head cocked to one side—an appreciative audience, but also a knowing one. I had watched my mother many times to see if she'd been drinking, and how much. I'd seen Gina drink, but I'd never seen her drunk. I was sure she wasn't drunk then, but she had been drinking. She was in one of her joyful, antic moods.

She was wearing an outfit I particularly liked on her—black, long-sleeved, high-necked sweater, with a pumpkin-colored skirt that flared out beneath her hips. Her short, glossy brown hair curled around her flushed face. Her cheeks were hot, red, as though bruised. She stopped by the sofa, sank down on it, crushing and scattering my homework papers.

"What's all this?" she said, pulling papers out from under her, flinging them up in the air.

"Geometry homework."

"Geometry homework," she echoed, "Geometry homework. My dear girl, life is tiptoeing past you, all beautiful and breathtaking, and you're doing geometry homework? What can you be thinking of?"

"I'm thinking of the test I'm having tomorrow."

"There is only one test in life," Gina said, leaning back on the soft, lumpy cushions. She stretched luxuriously.

"What's that?" I said, anxious to pass the test.

"Can you relish it?" she replied. "Can you possess it?"

"Oh," I said, disappointed.

She grinned at me, clasping her hands behind her head, looking at me from between the points of her elbows. "Maggie," she said. "What am I going to do with you?"

I shuffled awkwardly, shook my head, not knowing.

"Do you have any idea what's out there? What's ahead of you? I wish I could be you, starting out again."

"No, you don't," I said, with some confidence.

"You're right. I don't. Not tonight at least. Not tonight."

She closed her eyes. "I wouldn't be anyone else right now."

"Why, Gina?" I said irritably. "Tell me."

"Tell you what?"

Opening her eyes, sitting forward, she looked at me in mild surprise.

"Tell me where you've been tonight. Tell me why you feel like you do."

Her surprise became a little more pronounced.

"Why do you ask?"

"Well, why shouldn't I ask?" I said, feeling defensive, remembering my mother's voice on the phone. "I'm here with Ellie. You're not around. Phil's not around—"

"That's why you're here, my dear," Gina said, smoothly. "Because we're not around."

"I know, but—"

"I thought you wanted to earn some money."

"I do, but—"

"Was Ellie a nuisance tonight?"

"No, not at all."

"Well, then."

The silence buzzed around us. Then the grandfather clock whirred, clanked, bonged tediously—twelve times.

"I'd better send you home," Gina said, getting up from the sofa. "You have school tomorrow. Kate will be worried about you."

"I just talked to her."

"Oh?" She paused. "Is that why the questions?"

"She did ask me—"

"I'll get your money."

"Gina, you don't have to—"

"Pay you? Of course I do. Did Ellie show you her hospital? I don't know why the sudden concern for missing limbs and pushed-in faces. It never bothered her before. Maybe she's growing up."

She rooted around in her purse, pulled out a ten-dollar bill, which she held out to me.

"That's too much," I said, pushing it away. "Just give me a couple of dollars."

"Nonsense," she said, pressing the bill into my hand. "Buy something special with it. A pretty scarf, or some warm gloves. It's cold out there, and getting colder."

"Thanks," I said, shoving the bill into my pocket. Then, with a stubborn willfulness, a resistance to being bribed and gagged, I blurted out, "But where *do* you go, Gina?"

She laughed, surprising me, sweeping away the tension between us.

"And here I thought I was all grown up and didn't have to answer to anyone anymore."

"Mom says we're all accountable to each other, always."

"How very commendable of her."

I flushed, frowned. I was sensitive to sarcasm directed at my mother, except for my own insensitive attacks.

"Don't pout, Maggie. I'm going to answer your question."

"Maybe you shouldn't."

Gina took my hand and drew me down beside her on the sofa.

"Now. Where shall I begin?"

She pondered for a moment.

"Where were you?" I said, again, this time plaintively.

"Never mind that, for now. You asked me why I feel as I do. That's the question I'm going to answer."

"But—"

Gina waved aside my protest

"I was with a man tonight. Not Phil."

I was not surprised at this revelation and, after a moment, not even surprised at her telling me, her teenage babysitter, her unlikely confidante. But I still felt trembly.

"It wasn't—?"

She looked at me, questioning, but I couldn't go on. She blinked, as though my unfinished question had taken a moment to register.

"Frank? Your father? My dear child, no."

I turned away from her, sick with relief.

"I'm so sorry, Maggie. It didn't even occur to me that you would think— What you saw, Maggie, was all there was to see. Just a kiss. A harmless kiss. Prompted by curiosity, a private moment, as much as by anything else. I've always admired your father's—strength."

I took a deep breath, turned toward her again. She patted my arm reassuringly, leaned back again on the cushions.

"I knew you were upset, but there was no way I could make it better for you. Not then. You had to work it out for yourself. When you showed up on my doorstep a couple of months ago, I saw that you had."

I was finding it difficult to look at her. When I did, she was waiting for me, waiting to go on with her explanation.

"You see, Maggie, I had a lot of faith in you—in our friendship. And I was fairly sure you wouldn't want to hurt your mother."

I said, naively, "I couldn't."

"Of course. You *couldn't.*"

The relief I heard in her voice was unmistakable.

"Can we put it behind us now, for good?"

I nodded, more than willing to accept Gina at her word. I wanted to believe her, and so I did.

"I was with a man tonight, Maggie. Not Phil. Certainly not Frank."

She stopped, her eyes soft, faraway, her mouth curling up into a smile, as though there was something she couldn't share with me—some amusing private joke.

"He's the reason I feel as I do. He's the reason I run off in the afternoon and return late at night. He's the reason your babysitting business is booming."

She studied me for a moment.

"I shouldn't be telling you this. Sometimes I forget that you're—that you—"

Again, she hesitated.

"Sometimes I forget—how very young you are."

"It's okay," I managed to say. "I want to know."

I wanted to know everything about this man, how he made Gina feel as she did, why she had to turn away from Phil, her home, her child, again and again, to pursue this feeling. My need to know was greater than my sense that what she was telling me was inappropriate, greater than the slight but definite sensation of repugnance I felt. It was still hard for me not to admire Gina, not to want to *be* Gina.

She sighed, as though obliged to explain herself to me.

"I don't have any friends my own age. The women around here are all prehistoric, or shocked by everything I say and do."

She paused, considering, then added, "Your mother, of course, is beyond reproach."

Despite the tinge of sarcasm in her voice, I was grateful for the remark. I didn't want to be forced into a defensive position yet again. I had just reclaimed my friendship with this older, far more experienced woman. This friendship, I knew, was contingent upon my acceptance of her as she was.

"I need to feel this way," Gina went on. "As though—as though every cell in my body were buzzing." She laughed. "Not that we can go around feeling this way all the time, but …" She paused, then asked, "What about Kurt? Does he—?"

I was ahead of her question, putting myself beside him on the couch at home, in his car when we parked by the lake, on the dance floor when we—and all the other couples—seemed to cling to each other like adhesive. I shook my head, feeling no basis for comparison.

"Oh, well. There will be others. Many others. You're so pretty. Pretty Maggie," she said, dreamily. I could see her thoughts drifting away from me, back to the man who made her cells buzz.

"I like pretty things. Pretty people. I probably wouldn't love Ellie as much as I do if she weren't so— Does that shock you?"

I shook my head, emphatically, determined not to be shocked.

"This man," she said, "he's wonderful to look at. Kind of like Marlon Brando. Dark hair, brushed back. Riveting eyes. Strong, without being muscular. I don't like muscular. It's too obvious. When I first met him, I couldn't take my eyes off him. He had his sleeves rolled up to his elbows and—"

"Where did you meet him?" I said, primly, sounding like my mother.

Gina waved away my question as though it were an annoying insect.

"I think, when I first met Phil, I may have felt this way about him. I know I liked the way he looked ... I don't know," she said, dismissively, as though in answer to a question. "I don't remember."

"Are you going to divorce Phil?"

"Good God, Maggie, of course not. Haven't you heard anything I said?"

I thought very hard about everything she had said to me tonight, but I found no clue. Of course, that was irrelevant. Obviously, she had implied it, or thought it, and I had missed the signal.

Her irritation, at herself, or at me, was more pronounced as she said, "Shouldn't you be going home? You have school tomorrow."

"But you were telling me—"

"Far more than I should. This man and I, we're—just friends."

She got up from the sofa, pulled me to my feet. "Wrap yourself up and go home, my dear. Your mother will be worried about you."

The condescension in her voice was almost more than I could bear. I was bitterly disappointed in myself, for having failed to pass myself off as an adult. I gathered up my books and homework papers—still scattered on the floor where Gina had flung them—walked down the hall, put on my coat. Just behind me, Gina leaned against the stair banister, lost in thought, waiting for me to leave.

In another moment, I was outside on the porch. The door locked behind me with a firm brassy click. Huddled inside my coat, I walked slowly across the yard and up the front steps of my house. A few tears glided down my face toward my mouth. I tasted them. They were salty—and sweet.

CHAPTER 21

Win came home for Thanksgiving—bright, brash, as sure of himself as ever. I realized, when I saw how unchanged he was, that I had expected his first experience of college to have a humbling effect on him. But I saw that I was no more capable of predicting my brother's behavior than I was that of my parents, or my best friend Prue, or, especially, Gina Gregorka.

"Are they feeding you all right?" Kate said, touching his arm, as if to reassure herself that he was there.

We were seated at Thanksgiving dinner, in the dining room, just the four of us—my mother had insisted on this—prior to paying obeisance to both sets of grandparents and assorted relatives in Hillsville. Win's homecoming had eased the tension that had been accumulating in the past few months, some of which emanated from Kate, some from my own uneasiness.

"They feed us crap, Mom, but there's plenty of it, and there's always gravy or sauce to cover up whatever's hidden underneath."

Kate shuddered. Frank guffawed and slapped his son on the shoulder.

"That's the spirit, my boy. Nobody goes to college for the food."

"And how would you know?" said Kate, arching an eyebrow.

She looked very relaxed and attractive in loose crepe pants, an autumn-hued blouse, with a rope of beads around her neck. I watched her with curiosity, and a splash of envy.

"Yeah, Dad," said Win. "You're the original high school dropout."

"Not so," said Frank, unperturbed. "I graduated in the same class with your mother."

"Maybe at the same time, Dad, but not in the same class."

Frank laughed, appreciatively. He slapped his son again on the shoulder.

"You're right about that, Son. Your mom was at the head of her class, and she's been a class act ever since."

"Where were you in the class, Dad?" I asked.

"Somewhere near the bottom rung," Frank replied, striking the carving knife against the sharpening steel two or three times, then slicing into the turkey breast with sharpened blade and masterful dexterity. "Ready for more, Maggie?"

I nodded and handed him my plate. He placed three thin, perfectly carved slices of turkey breast on my plate, scooped out a mound of stuffing, positioned it carefully on the plate, and handed it back to me. I added giblet gravy and sliced into the fork-tender meat.

"This turkey is a work of art, Hon," Frank said.

He paused to look with pleasure at the dishes and bowls arrayed on the table. Mounds of mashed potatoes. A pitcher of gravy, brown remnants dripping down its neck. Sweetened cranberries boiled just to bursting. Bright orange winter squash. French-cut green beans with sliced almonds. Rolls nesting inside a napkin-lined basket.

"This whole dinner is a work of art."

He looked around the table, at each of us.

"This whole family is a goddamn work of art."

We laughed. Win said, slapping Frank on the shoulder in mock imitation, "You're goddamn right, Pop."

"What kind of grades did you get in high school, Dad?" I asked, as though Frank's joyful homage to our family had not intervened. I wanted a confession from my father, even if it was just an admission of poor grades.

Kate glanced at Frank with a demure smile. Win smirked, then pretended to choke on his turkey.

Frank said, serenely, "I was good at what I was good at, Maggie, and as for the rest ..."

"What *were* you good at, Pop?" Win asked.

"Well, when I wasn't dribbling balls on the basketball court, I was pretty good in art, and mechanical drawing."

The silverware stopped clinking momentarily, as we waited for Frank to continue.

"I had some talent, you know." He looked pointedly at Win, then at me. "Your mother will tell you that."

"You still do, Frank," Kate said. "You just don't use it very much anymore."

"There's not much call for art in the insurance business," Frank said. "Matter of fact, there's not much call for it in any business I know of."

"Art does a fairly good business at the colleges, Pop," Win said cheerfully, putting half a buttered roll in his mouth.

"College was never an option for me, Win," said Frank. "When I got out of high school, my first thought was to get a job, and my second thought was to talk your mother into marrying me."

"Yeah, how did he manage to do that, Mom? I thought you had better taste."

"Well, it did take a while," said Kate.

She glanced across the table at Frank, her long, light eyelashes catching the light.

"I had to stand in line, you mean," said Frank. "There were two or three admirers ahead of me, not to mention a couple of big, strapping brothers."

"My brothers liked you—after they got to know you."

"So they did. But we had to push each other around a little—do some man-type things together. Like jumping off the cliffs at the quarry."

"How high did you go?" I asked.

"Oh, thirty, forty feet. Even the top ledge once or twice."

"And then you won the fair lady," said Win, his mouth full. "Hey, Dad, I'll take some more of that turkey, but slice it thick. I don't want to see through it."

Franked carved precise quarter-inch-thick slices and arranged them on Win's plate, scraping the inside of the turkey for more dressing.

"I won the fair lady," he affirmed. "And I've loved the fair lady all my life."

His eyes glanced off me before he resumed eating. I thought of that moment before Win's party when I had seen my father and Gina locked together.

Did he love my mother *then*? Was he thinking of her *then*?

But I was determined not to disrupt this harmonious family gathering. I realized that I wanted to erase that look of unease I had seen when he looked at me. I wanted to love my father, to admire him, to forget what I had seen, or thought I had seen …

"I've seen some of your work, pushed away in a drawer," I said. "I thought it was good."

"Not good enough," said Frank, reflectively. "Just a few amateur attempts. I never had any training, except for a few high school classes, and after that …"

"You were too busy chasing after Mom, and jumping in the quarry," said Win.

"Something like that," said Frank. "Besides, what does it matter now?"

"You shouldn't waste your talent, if you have it," I said, hearing how pompous it sounded even as I said it.

"Yeah, Pop," said Win, who managed to catch the humor in my unlikeliest remarks, "You should throw us over, go live on a tropical island, paint your guts out—like Gauguin."

"I wouldn't mind living on a nice warm island, especially in the winter months, but I'd want Kate there with me, and even an occasional visit from you two."

The conversation continued—easy, agreeable, with most of the focus on Win, and Kate's cooking. We ate as much as we could, leaving an abundance of food still on the table.

"There's mince pie," said Kate, "and apple."

"I peeled, cored, and sliced every one of those apples," I said.

"In that case," said Frank, "I'll have a slice of the apple pie, Kate. Hot, with a scoop of vanilla ice cream on top."

"Mince for me, Mom," said Win. "Mags has been looking a little preoccupied. She may have planted a few apple cores in her pie."

I picked up plates and followed Kate into the kitchen. She sliced into the apple pie, warm from the oven, where she had placed it during dinner. She looked almost shy, almost embarrassed, by the happiness her expression revealed.

Watching her, I saw her as a young girl, not much older than me, her hair short and finger-waved, as I'd seen it in photos of her. She is walking down the street in Hillsville, wearing a light, flowery summer dress. Frank, stalk-slender and speechless with admiration, is at her side. He has trim black hair and a small mustache. The sun is shining down on Kate's pale yellow hair, catching at her long, light eyelashes.

CHAPTER 22

It was during the Christmas holidays, with Win again livening up our family circle, that I began to trace a change in my mother's drinking habits.

Kate had always been a companion in drinking, as in everything else, with my father. While Frank became more himself as he drank—livelier, more boisterous, more dominant—my mother became more *herself*—quieter, more reserved, more insular.

At any rate, preoccupied with myself, noting the rest of the world only as it impinged on me, I didn't see my mother change until the change was fixed in place. The impetus that moved her forward from day to day had shifted permanently.

Kate drank when Frank was drinking. That was her pattern, as it was with most of the things they did together. She matched him beer for beer, and was not far behind him when he was drinking hard liquor. Since my father drank for pleasure, as he did almost everything else in his life, except sell insurance, their drinking had few restrictions. It was bounded only by the enthusiasm that Frank brought to each social occasion, or the exceptional character of the beverage.

"If it's worth doing, it's worth doing well," he would say, holding a glass of Jack Daniels whiskey up to the light, eyeing it critically.

This pronouncement was rarely challenged, except by Win, who was heard to say, "If it's worth doing, it's worth doing fast," as he sped from one activity to another.

Left alone with the two of them, while Win installed himself on campus, I began to observe more—by chance rather than by choice. I did not want my parents to occupy my thoughts, which were preempted by issues vital to my own well-being and which revolved around my appearance, my popularity, my self-esteem. But Frank was difficult to ignore, especially when he was angry, and Kate obtruded herself on my notice despite her attempts to be inconspicuous.

During the holidays, there was a modest array of drinks for our guests. Liquor and soda. Beer. A bottle or two of wine. Eggnog chilling in the refrigerator. The house glittered with Christmas tree lights, tinsel, and the fragrant, leaping light of candles. Kate was always in the kitchen, cooking and baking, or cleaning up after cooking and baking. It was there that she drank alone—quietly, devotedly, like a nun at her solitary prayers.

Our kitchen was a spacious rectangle. The oak table at one end was hedged in on two sides by windows facing south and east, sunny during the day, at night veiled with cheerful red and yellow café curtains. Here Kate was relaxed—confident.

She seemed to prefer this turf to any other, even when she wasn't cooking. She sat at the table, reading the newspapers, *Ladies' Home Journal, Good Housekeeping*, or one of the other women's magazines she subscribed to, or a newly published novel she had checked out of the library.

Beside her was a beer, or sometimes a glass of wine. The expression on her face was one of peace, certitude. When she looked up at me, to make a comment or just to acknowledge my presence, her eyes seemed out of focus—as though she had been very far away and was only reluctantly returning to the present. This concession to what was real, to what was obviously predominant, never failed to annoy me.

"You're not even listening," I said, one afternoon during the holidays, stamping my foot like a small child, then turning away before she could respond.

"You said Sue was coming over later, to do schoolwork, and then you were going out."

"I said Prue was coming over, and we were going to make plans for the school dance, the Christmas dance, and then we're going out with Kurt and Ed."

Kate wobbled her head a little, in assent.

"I haven't seen Sue since I was in grade school. Sue lives in *Pittsburgh* now, for God's sake."

"Yes. All right. All right."

"Can't you even remember the names of my best friends?"

"Maggie. All right. Calm down. I just mixed up their names. There's no reason to get upset."

"There *is* a reason," I said. "You don't even know my friends. You hardly talk to them when they're here."

"That's not so."

"It *is* so."

I couldn't seem to put the brakes on this small explosion. I knew that she wanted only to end the argument, to be left alone, and this infuriated me more than anything.

"Prue even asked me once if you were mad at her."

"Oh, Maggie, don't be absurd. Prue knows better than that."

"How would she? You don't even remember her name. You think we're doing schoolwork during Christmas vacation, for Pete's sake."

"Maggie, that's enough."

I stopped, frustrated beyond words. I was angry, but there was no real basis for my anger. It was lodged inside me, inexpressible, somehow tied in with the half-empty glass of beer at her elbow, the look of impenetrable composure on her face.

"Sorry," I mumbled. "I'm going for a walk."

"Be sure you're dressed up warm," she said, as she turned back to her newspaper.

I heard her rustling the pages of the newspaper as I put on my boots, buttoned up my coat, hurried out the front door.

There were several inches of snow on the ground; new snow was falling in heavy, chunky flakes. I licked at them as I walked, my rage evaporating as quickly as the snowflakes I whisked off my face with a mittened hand. The anger was still there but tamped down, like the snow under my feet. Away from Kate, I was ashamed of my outburst. I wondered why I had wanted to hurt her.

It was late afternoon, windless, still daylight, the sun settling down behind me. I walked up the block, away from

Gina's house, where the houses rose each a little above the one before it, as the street gently inclined. Christmas tree lights twinkled in undraped front windows. I glimpsed neighbors as they moved about in their homes. The houses grew brighter as the afternoon grew more dim and lights were switched on.

Ahead of me, I heard a group of children shouting excitedly. As I grew nearer, I saw Ellie, Lucy Granger, little Donald Morgan, and a few of their friends constructing a snowman in the Morgans' front yard. As usual, Ellie's imperious voice dominated every other. I heard her piping commands before I singled out her red snowsuit.

"Makeum*bigger*," she said. "Makeistummy fadder. Lotsfadder. Dasnotfadnuff. Lemme do ut."

She was pushing a snowball almost as big as she was over the yard, which was already bald in spots where the children had built forts, tossed snowballs, and were now culminating their play with a giant snowman.

I waved and Ellie shouted, "Majee! Cuminhelp!"

She came running toward me, dragging me into the yard.

We managed to seat the "tummy" snowball on top of the base snowball. After applauding our success, we rolled a plump head, and created a crude face with sticks and stones. I lifted up Ellie so that she could plunk her cap on top of his head. The children jumped up and down, shouting their approval.

After dancing around the snowman in celebration, Ellie took my hand and I walked her home.

Phil opened the door, grinning at his daughter, pink-faced, chattering with cold and excitement. He hefted her up under her arms, where she dangled like a wet rag doll.

He carried her down the hall, shouting, "She's melting! She's melting! Gina, come quick! Our little girl's melting!"

I heard Ellie's paroxysm of giggles and Gina's, "Hurry up, Phil. We'll stand her up in the refrigerator," before I closed the door behind me and walked across the yard to my front door.

When I came in, my father had just gotten home, noisy and effusive as he shook off the frustrations of the day. I heard him stomping around the house, orchestrating the evening, as I took off my boots and wet coat. Then the back door slammed; there was a momentary lull.

In the living room, the Christmas tree lights were turned on; firewood was stacked near the fireplace. Win and Peggy were in the side room, seemingly watching television but actually engrossed in talk and each other—beneath the cover of the staticky sound and the rhythmically repetitious laugh track. My mother was in the kitchen, preparing dinner in her new West Bend electric skillet, with a mixed drink beside her, and the fresh, energized look she always wore when my father first came home in the evening.

"Maggie, will you help me?" she said, as I walked into the kitchen.

I looked more closely at her, made alert and suspicious by the unfamiliar animation in her voice. She was flushed, pretty, with little wisps of hair around her face and the merest suggestion of unsteadiness in her movements.

"Is Peggy staying for dinner?" I said, reaching into the cupboard for plates.

"Yes. I think so. Probably."

She stirred the skillet dinner she had prepared. I inhaled the pleasant aroma of sausage and potatoes, with an undercurrent of onion and black pepper.

"There's a bowl of applesauce in the refrigerator that needs to be heated up—and put those rolls in the oven, too. I'm sure it must be hot enough by now."

She was efficient and organized, as usual, but I was more than usually alert, looking for evidence of my suspicions. In terms of a musical octave, she may have moved up from C to E, but with Kate even such a minor elevation was telling.

My father came in the back door with a blast of cold air and a load of wood in his arms.

"Hi, Toots," he said, in passing. He stomped into the living room, puffing.

Soon we could hear the crackling of newspapers and kindling, the sputtering sound of damp wood as it caught fire. Win and Peggy drifted into the living room, drawn by the sound and smell emanating from the glowing fireplace. Their lowered voices, an occasional laugh or chuckle, rose above the rumble and popping of the fire, the clink of dishes and silverware, as I set the table for dinner.

"It's a beauteous evening," said Frank, gleefully, rubbing his hands as he came into the kitchen. "And you, my beauteous bride, are my evening star."

He stood behind my mother and wrapped himself around her, nuzzling her neck, kissing her.

"Frank, don't," she said, tolerantly. She stepped away from the counter, disentangling herself from his embrace.

"Yeah, Dad, stop it," I said, lightly, teasingly. I felt, as always, self-conscious as well as a little resentful when forced to witness my father's exuberant displays of affection toward my mother.

"Make me a drink, Frank," said Kate, unplugging the skillet and carrying it to the table. "Don't forget the milk, Maggie. Frank, bring in those candles from the mantelpiece. And tell Win and Peggy dinner's ready."

We ate Kate's tasty skillet dinner in the dining room, by candlelight. Everyone seemed to be in a festive mood fueled by the mellow holiday atmosphere, Frank's high spirits, the Christmas decorations, the dance and hiss of the fire in the next room, the snow falling softly against the windows. Before the end of the meal, Kate prodded Frank for another drink. He prepared it for her, grumbling but still jovial.

Win, as usual, seemed impervious to any underlying tension, enjoying the meal and Peggy's worshipful attention, matching Frank's boisterousness, praising Kate until she blushed like a schoolgirl.

"Mom, I may have to quit college and come back home. I really miss meals like this. I tell everybody who'll listen you're the best damn cook in town."

He touched his forehead in playful tribute, then handed his plate to her for a refill.

"More, please! And don't be skimpy."

I wanted only to be cheerful and unaware, but Kate's head was nodding; what little she said was increasingly slurred; she seemed unwilling to get up from her chair.

I covered for her, clearing off the dishes, making the coffee, feeling bitter, ashamed—even though no one else seemed at all aware of anything unusual in Kate's behavior.

Prue knocked on the door just as I was pouring coffee. I whisked her off to the side room, where we listened to the stereo until Kurt and Ed came by, honking the horn impatiently while we bundled up and said our goodbyes.

My mother was sitting in the living room by the fire when we left, sipping her drink. She was nodding and smiling with that increasingly familiar look of blurred complacency as she listened to Frank and Win's banter, and Peggy's appreciative laughter. I left quickly.

Kurt and I sat in the back seat of Ed's car while we rode aimlessly around town, discussing our options for the evening. We couldn't agree on anything, finally ending up at Zimmer's, where we sat in a booth, sipping cokes. Prue and her dreadful Ed said I was getting as glum and silent as Kurt.

Gina and Phil had planned a New Year's Eve party, to which my parents were invited. I was to take care of Ellie at our house, where she would spend the night. Kurt and I, and Prue and Ed, made up our own little party. Win and Peggy went off with their crowd.

It was the first time I had spent New Year's Eve with a boy. Even though we were under constant surveillance by a small child, I was nervous, uneasy about my role. Prue and Ed set the tone by turning off most of the lights in the side room, turning on the stereo, and necking ardently as they made minute concessions to the music they were supposedly dancing to. Kurt and I quickly followed suit. Ellie, in her footed pajamas and pink robe, danced with Mr. Bear, the stuffed animal she had selected to spend the evening with her.

Between Kurt's wet kisses, I glanced at Ellie, who was planting her mouth on the bear's stitched-on grin in exact imitation of the four of us, sighing and hugging his furry head between bouts of affection. I nudged Kurt, who nudged Prue and Ed. We watched Ellie until she looked up at us, as if for further instruction. Then we laughed helplessly, including Ellie, who fell back on the floor, still hugging Mr. Bear. She kicked her feet and rolled her head back and forth.

After that, as if by permission, we became kids together. We turned up the lights, turned on the radio for holiday music, got out Monopoly. I brought out bowls of pretzels and nuts, Pepsi and 7Up, enough candy and sweets to make us groan with surfeit. We were noisy, silly, reciting at the top of our voices, whenever someone gave us the least opening:

"Go to Jail! Go directly to jail! Do not pass GO! Do not collect $200!"

Ellie entertained us with her efforts to count her Monopoly bills and keep her little silver shoe out of jail, until she fell asleep next to me, curled comfortably around her bear.

At midnight, we shouted and kissed self-consciously. Then Prue and Ed left, I carried Ellie upstairs to bed, and Kurt and I watched television. I felt staid and adult as we sat up, waiting for my parents to come home.

They came home before the New Year was an hour old. I was fighting off sleep, relieved when Kurt politely wished them a Happy New Year and left. Frank was unusually glum; Kate seemed reluctant to speak but I could see that she had been drinking heavily. She was unsteady on her feet, impatiently dismissing Frank when he attempted to support her.

I heard her mumbling, "Leave me alone, leave me alone," as I went upstairs to bed.

Frank growled something and Kate replied, louder now, "I *won't.* I *won't* be told what to do. *You* go to bed. Just—leave me alone."

Closing the door of my bedroom, I discarded my clothes, leaving them in a heap on the floor, and put on my longest, warmest cotton nightgown. Then I opened the door and listened. My parents were downstairs, in the living room, still bickering, my father's words inaudible, my mother's tone unusually surly.

I went down the hall to check on Ellie, who was sleeping on a cot in the small back bedroom that was originally meant for my dead brother, Timothy, and was now called the "spare" room. She was hugging Mr. Bear, her mouth slightly open. I covered her with the blanket she had shrugged off, then watched her sleep for a few moments, calmed by her regular breathing, soothed by her look of dreamless innocence.

I went from there to the bathroom, where I brushed my teeth and peered at myself in the mirror over the sink. My parents' voices filtered up to me as I examined my teeth, my eyes, my hair, each small imperfection on my face.

I went back to my bedroom, closed the door softly until it clicked shut, and got into bed, burrowing deep under the blankets until just my nose was exposed to the chill night air. I fell asleep listening to the muted sound of their voices—the rising and falling rhythm of their dispute, the brief hush between bouts, as hypnotic as a lullaby.

CHAPTER 23

After the first of the year, with the social pressures of the holidays behind me, and Valentine's Day a good six weeks ahead, I decided to phase out my relationship with Kurt. If I continued to date him, I reasoned, in my sophomoric wisdom, his hold over me, both physically and socially, would continue to escalate. We were "going together," but not "going steady." That meant that, occasionally, I could accept dates, dance and flirt with other boys, with Kurt displaying only a minimum of jealousy. It also meant that our kissing and necking stopped short of any real intimacy—except for when he happened to touch my breasts, "by accident."

To go steady would alter all the ground rules. I did not want to enter that sphere—about which I fantasized but knew nothing—at least not with Kurt. As for Kurt, I was sure he would recover his balance in no time. Even with my own transcendent inexperience, I knew ours was no love match.

I had no voice, no way to express it at the time, but I was an idealist, not a realist. My friends took the practical approach—going steady ensured you always had a date. You didn't have to worry about staying home on a Friday or a Saturday night. You had someone to take you to football and basketball games, movies and dances, someone to meet after school, to walk you home, to drive you around in his car. You had something to report when your friends compared notes, good and bad, on their boyfriends.

In return, you proceeded, step by step, with your boyfriend, from kissing to necking to— Well, I didn't know much of anything beyond that—but I wasn't about to find out with Kurt.

I tried to discuss strategy with Prue, but soon discovered it was hopeless. Prue had been going steady with dreadful Ed since the beginning of time, and had long since passed the boundaries I was so carefully guarding. I didn't press her for details, since the thought of intimacy with Ed, with his bumpy teeth, his saw-toothed pinkish hair, made me cringe. Sharon and my other friends were either unsympathetic or overly eager, depending on whether they were going steady with no safeguards posted, or waiting for Kurt to put up the "I'm available" signal. I had never discussed dating strategies with my mother, and I couldn't imagine doing so. So I turned to Gina, as I had been doing since early in our friendship.

I knocked on her door on a Saturday morning. Hearing a muffled response, I opened the door and poked my head inside, calling out, "Gina?"

"In the kitchen," she said, sounding none too pleased. I walked down the hall and through the living room, formulating my request for advice.

Gina was sitting at the kitchen table, her turquoise silk kimono wrapped around her, a cigarette smoldering in the ashtray in front of her, bills and papers scattered over the table, as well as wadded and thrown on the floor. The kitchen was toasty warm; the radiators were clanking. The sweet homey smell of oatmeal raisin cookies emanated from the oven, mixed with the acrid smell of cigarettes. The combination of scents, which seemed somehow to define Gina, has stayed with me ever since.

"Smells good in here," I said, pulling off my coat. I arranged it on the back of the chair opposite her.

"Um," she said, not looking up as she examined a bill. She made a penciled note on a sheet of paper filled with columns of figures, doodles, rubbery bits of erasure.

"Can I peek?" I said.

"Um," she said.

I opened the oven door a few inches, inhaled the scent of the barely brown cookies.

"Just a few more minutes should do it," I said, closing the oven door.

"Um," said Gina.

"Where's Ellie?"

"Upstairs."

I sat down at the table and watched in silence as Gina continued her computations. She pushed back the long loose sleeves of her robe impatiently, dragging at her cigarette. Her hair was pulled back carelessly, tucked behind her ears. She raked stray tendrils back with her fingers, as if to draw blood from her scalp. The peacocks and savage, oversized flowers scattered against the background of her robe shifted and undulated with her movements, as though they were alive, blooming in some remote forest.

I gazed at the robe, hypnotized, thinking of the day when, uninvited, I had knocked on her door, wanting her advice on clothes and makeup for a school dance. She had come down the stairs in that robe. She had sent me away, abruptly—but not before I had seen a form, tall and shadowy, at the top of the stairs …

The oven timer buzzed.

"Will you do that?" said Gina, absently.

"What?"

"Will you take care of that?"

I got up, turned off the buzzing timer, opened the oven door. Satisfied that the cookies were just the right shade of golden brown, I grabbed hot pads, took the tray out, set it on top of the burners.

"Let them cool for a minute," said Gina.

"Okay."

"And put the other tray in the oven."

I transferred the tray from the counter to the oven, set the timer for twelve minutes, then carefully loosened the baked cookies with a spatula, arranging them on a plate.

"Help yourself," said Gina.

"Thanks."

I sat opposite Gina, savoring the taste of sweet, hot, crumbly oatmeal and soft moist raisins as I gazed out the window at the bleak January light, formulating my parting speech with Kurt.

"Shit," said Gina. "I hate my life."

I looked across at her in surprise.

"Is something—did something—go wrong?" I said.

"Everything is wrong. Everything has gone wrong."

Gina sat back in her chair, puffed on her cigarette, glared at me.

"I'm—sorry," I said.

She leaned forward, stamped out her cigarette as though it were a pesky insect, stood up, raising clenched fists above her head in a stretch that was also a threatening gesture.

"Why do I put *up* with it," she said to the ceiling. "I want so much *more*. I *deserve* so much more."

I nodded, in complete accord, but Gina seemed unaware of me. I was below the footlights, a breathing presence, but invisible.

"These bills," she said, acknowledging the scattered slips of paper with a scornful glance, "what do they have to do with me? With my life? Look at this. 'Mr. and Mrs. Philip Gregorka.' Do you see my name? Do you see 'Regina Gregorka' on any of these bills? No! I don't exist, except as an extension of him. Let *him* pay the bills, then. They're Phil's bills."

She stopped, the corners of her mouth lifting up in an unwilling smile. For a moment, she looked across the footlights at me. I nodded, almost applauded.

"They're Phil's bills," I echoed.

She laughed, a short, grim laugh, before she continued, wrapping her kimono more closely around her, tightening the knot in the sash.

"Do you know what I'd like to do?"

She paused, for effect.

"I'd like to chuck the whole thing. I'd like to walk away. I'd like to pack a bag, one bag, with this robe and a few other things I cherish, and just—go away. What would it matter? Who would miss me?"

"Ellie?" I suggested. "And me, of course."

"Ellie." She stopped pacing, considered. "Yes, Ellie would miss me. Who else does she have? Grandma in Hillsville could look after her but—who would guard her proud little spirit? Who would make sure she always thinks as well of herself as she does now?"

In the long silence that followed, the oven timer buzzed. I got up, pulled out the second tray of cookies, resenting the fact that Gina hadn't thought of me, but lacking the confidence to remind her.

"Thanks," she said, absently, as I scraped the cookies off the tray, adding them to the pyramid on the counter. I nodded, knowing that she was barely aware of me.

"Ellie," she said again. "What do I do about Ellie?"

"Stay with her?" I said. Then, low enough not to be heard, "Stay with me."

She sighed, sat down, as though suddenly deflated.

"Why do you have to be so logical?"

"Sorry," I mumbled, offended.

"And so sensitive." She cuffed me lightly on the chin with her finger. "You're a dear, you know that? Have another cookie."

She reached toward the counter, taking a cookie off the plate. I accepted her offering, and her apology, as I bit into it.

"Do you know what determines our lives? Yours and mine and Ellie's—and everyone else's? Do you know?"

I shook my head, wiping cookie crumbs from my mouth.

"Money. Dirty green money. Money to pay this."

She swept a forearm across the table and scattered a pile of bills.

"And this."

She pushed the rest of the bills off the table with her other arm, the wide sleeves of her robe dusting the table of morsels of paper and nibbles of eraser.

"If I had enough money. If I had my own money …"

She paused, then said, "I'd take Ellie. I'd take one bag. And I'd go away."

"What about Ellie's 'little family'?" I said, thinking of Ellie's sizable collection of stuffed animals and dolls.

"She'd have to pick and choose. Pick and choose. Just like me with my one bag. Too much baggage, my dear, and leaving becomes impossible."

"But you love all of your things," I said, unwilling to give her permission to leave, even in theory. "You've told me so, time and time again."

"So I do," she said. "My things—the things I own, the things I've acquired—are to me what Ellie's 'little family' is to her. My nest. My security."

She sighed.

"I suppose you're right. I can't go."

She leaned forward, a mischievous expression—exactly like Ellie's—on her face.

"At least not this week."

I sighed with relief. Did I do that, I wondered? Did I convince her to stay, or is she just playing games with me again? It didn't matter, though. She had committed herself to being here, in her house, in my life, at least for a while longer. I put the last bit of cookie in my mouth, brushed off my hands, satisfied.

Gina slumped in her chair, her anger draining away almost visibly. For the first time, I noticed a worry line etched between her eyebrows. I sat in silence while she stared at the ashtray overflowing with cigarette butts—the only thing she hadn't swept onto the floor—and tapped her fingers on the table.

"What about—him?" I said, at last, to break the silence.

"Him?"

She shifted, glanced across at me, as though she had forgotten I was there.

"Who?"

"You know. Him."

I struggled for a description of a nameless someone I had only heard her speak of on one occasion.

"The one who makes your cells buzz."

She looked at me—perplexed, annoyed. Then her face cleared. The worry line between her brows disappeared.

"Ah," she said. "*Him*."

She thought for a moment.

"Why, I'd forgotten I ever mentioned him to you."

"Well, you did."

"So I did. A lapse in judgment, surely."

"Why do you say that?" I said, hotly.

"Certainly not to offend you, Maggie, but you are, after all, so young. I must have been—carried away."

I crossed my arms and huffed, looking away from her.

She laughed, emitting a brief "Huh!" Then, seeing my quick look—angry, hurt—she said, "All right. I guess you're not so young. In fact, you seem to be maturing in great leaps, right before my eyes."

She added, before I could respond, "Did you tell anyone?"

"Of course not," I said, indignant. Then, curiosity overcoming my resentment, "Well—what about him?"

She shrugged.

"It was a mistake. *He* was a mistake. The peckerhead. He's off getting his kicks with someone else, someone not so *married*, he says. I just hope he dies of acute boredom, then roasts in hell."

"Oh!" I thought for a moment. "So I guess you aren't in love with him, after all."

"In love with him? I don't even like him. I *never* liked him."

"But you said—"

"Forget what I said. And, for God's sake, stop quoting me! Do you think I sit and reflect on everything that comes out of my mouth? Whatever I said I probably meant—then. But that was a hundred years ago. I don't remember. I don't *want* to remember."

I got up, feeling mortified. Mumbling something about having to get home, I slipped on my coat, which I had hung over the back of my chair. I walked quietly out of the kitchen, across the living room, down the hall, opening and closing the front door behind me with great care. I shuffled my feet as I crossed the lawn to my yard, thinking that I must have worn a path between my house and Gina's since she moved into the neighborhood.

As I closed the front door behind me, I leaned against it, thinking we had never talked about Kurt. Probably, we never would.

CHAPTER 24

We did, of course, talk about Kurt, and just about everything else, as we always had. Gina's moods shifted constantly. She had forgotten her angry outburst long before I did. Within a few days, she had hailed me from her front porch, whisked me inside, steered me into the kitchen—where she prepared "tea for two." Between sips of steaming tea sweetened with honey, she pried open my innermost secrets.

She was full of a strange electric energy. She scraped Kurt off my plate like yesterday's leftovers, and disposed of him with a few unkind words.

"Mr. Fresh-Catch-of-the Day? Throw him back in! You've got bigger fish to fry."

I laughed somewhat unwillingly at her comments, for I had considered Kurt a good catch, but I was also relieved that she approved of my "phase-out" plan, even applauded my logic.

"Of course you should move on," she said, propping her elbows on the kitchen table, her chin on her hands. "Look at you. You're not even sixteen years old, and so pretty. You shouldn't give any boy custodial rights. Not yet. How could a boy like Kurt—what is he, seventeen?—how could he possibly appreciate what you are, what you have to give? Most men are toads, anyway. Warty toads. They take and take—whatever you're willing to give—and consider they're doing you a favor. Now *you*—you take your time. Look around. Set your sights high. Kurt is just a rung on the ladder. You climb right on up, right on over him. He's not important. Believe me, you won't break his heart. He knows what he looks like. He'll smooth back his hair, smile that little crooked smile he has, and the girls will come running."

I frowned, wanting that little crooked smile directed at me and no one else.

"Relax," said Gina, reading my thoughts. "It will pass. In a few weeks, you'll wonder what you ever saw in him. In a few months, you'll have to think for a moment to remember his name. In a few years—well, you can't think that far ahead. A few years is a lifetime at your age. Dear child, how I envy you. You have so much to look forward to."

"But if men are warty toads—"

"Most men, I said. It's those few who are *not* that you're holding out for. They're the prize."

"What about Phil? Is he—?"

"A prize. Definitely. No one else would put up with me."

"What about—?"

"Hush now. I hear Ellie coming, and she's not quite ready for the warty toad discussion."

We waited for Ellie to make her entrance.

"Hello, my love," said Gina. "And how does your garden grow?"

"Shivabells 'n' cockershells 'n' petty maidsall 'n' a row," Ellie replied, like a windup doll in a frilly pink dress. Her speech was always clearest when she was reciting.

"Clever girl. Your reward is this magical apple."

Gina took an apple from the fruit bowl on the table between us.

"Eat it and you will grow up to be beautiful and wise."

Ellie took the apple from her mother and bit into it solemnly.

In the spring, I turned sixteen, without fanfare.

My mother baked me a cake and lit the candles after dinner. My father kissed me on the cheek, raised a glass of wine to my young womanhood. Prue presented me with a friendship bracelet. Gina gave me a locket, with a miniature image of her and Ellie inside, posing for a photographer in a studio setting—perhaps a Sears store.

"We had it taken especially for the occasion," said Gina.

Even though I knew she was flattering me, I was—as she meant me to be—flattered.

She gave me a framed duplicate of the photo, which I kept on my dressing table. She and Ellie were wearing their matching Christmas blouses, frilled at the neck, which Gina had made. It seemed to me they looked more alike than they ever had before. Ellie's smile, the expression in her eyes, the lift of her chin, were Gina's—as though Ellie had studied her mother's face and features until she could mimic every nuance.

When I mentioned this to Gina, she said, offhandedly, "Oh, yes, she's me all over again. I sometimes feel I should put out bulletins and warn the world. 'Look out. Ellie's coming.' She's going to do all the things I didn't do, and do them better than I ever could have. She's a winner, my Ellie. You'll see."

I often wondered, when I was with Gina and Ellie: where was Phil? Where was he when they had the photo taken that hung in a locket around my neck, that looked back at me from my dressing table, and from the living room wall of their home, where Gina hung it, enlarged, framed in gold, between the two long windows? I never understood clearly what Phil did during the long periods of time when he was away. Gina told me he sold hospital equipment and had to travel a lot.

"His territory is the entire Midwest," she said.

Phil was also in the Army Reserves. Periodically, he was away on weekends as well.

"I'm a grass widow," she would say, on those occasions.

Once, when I asked her what that meant, she said, with a hard edge to her voice, "It means I'm only as married as I damn well choose to be."

As much as I admired Gina, and liked Phil, I had only to compare them with Kate and Frank to realize that something was missing, or had gone away, or had never been there. Bumpy and hazardous as was day-to-day living with my parents, there was something between them that was as bottomless as the quarry water outside of town, where we tested our courage and endurance.

I was sixteen—no longer a child but not quite an adult—but no one close to me seemed to notice how I had changed, was changing. I looked different, grown-up, even to myself, but did anyone notice, except Gina?

I was still on a roller coaster ride with Gina as far as our friendship was concerned—sometimes thrilled with it; sometimes just wanting to get off, to be steady, grounded, still.

My mother was preoccupied. My father was away at work, or focused on the moment at hand, or talking about Win. Win was away but, even from a distance, I knew what was on my brother's mind. It was, as always, Win.

I looked, and felt that I acted, like an adult—most of the time, at least. The boys in my class, as well as some junior and senior boys, seemed to notice the change in me. They asked me out, asked me to dance at school functions, held me close, kissed me when they could, persisted even though I seldom encouraged them.

For this, I got little sympathy from my friends who, as far as I could tell, gave their boyfriends almost no discouragement. They seemed to consider my reluctance, my standoff attitude, odd.

"What are you waiting for? *Who* are you waiting for?" they would ask me.

The attention I was getting was what mattered. The boys who asked me out were what mattered. It was all about being popular, secure in the knowledge that no important event would find you without a date.

For this—the unwritten and largely unspoken rule book declared—you permitted your date, or your steady, to kiss you, to explore your mouth with his tongue, occasionally to touch your breasts—and then to proceed to more mutual intimacies—intimacies I had no desire to share with any of the boys I was dating.

I felt alone and lonely in my strange, not-yet-comfortable, sixteen-year-old body. I loved the attention it drew, but I wasn't ready for the responsibility of being what my appearance seemed to imply I already was.

One evening, that spring, while I was waiting for my date to pick me up, I went into the kitchen to tell my parents I was on my way out, and to say hello to the Muncies and the Bairds. They were sitting around the table, with beer and snacks close at hand. I reached for a potato chip.

"Who's the lucky guy?" said Fred Muncie.

I shrugged, giving Fred a sidelong glance and a smile.

"She's all grown up, your little girl," said Sam Baird.

"Not so's you'd notice," said my father, but I could see he was proud of me, proud of the impression I was making. "She has a ways to go yet."

"Your dad's blind or an idiot," said Fred.

"More likely the latter," said Sam.

Everyone at the table laughed, as they always did when the men exchanged insults, but I could feel the eyes of Wilifred Muncie and Frances Baird examining me, in my snug-fitting red dress, and even the quick look from my mother, who seemed to be having second thoughts about the style and color of the dress she had approved in the store.

My new dress was perfectly modest: sleeveless, with a boat neck; knee length, with a kick pleat in back. Even my mother could find nothing wrong with it—except for the color.

"Are you sure it's the right color for you?" she had asked me when I tried it on at Spangleman's.

"What's wrong with the color?" I had snapped back.

"Oh, nothing," she had replied, thoughtfully. "It's just so—red."

I had looked at my reflection in the huge department-store mirror, pleased with what I saw in the mirror.

My breasts were fully formed, unlike those of Prue and other girls I knew. The dress curved nicely around my waist and hips. My calves and ankles were slender and well shaped beneath the short hemline. I was wearing two-inch heels, my one pair of dress shoes, so I looked reassuringly tall. My hair (Gina told me it was one of my best features) was long and slightly wavy. I liked the feel of it on my shoulders.

"If that's your only objection ..."

I had continued to look in the mirror, my eyes shifting from my reflection to my mother's face.

"Well ..."

She had turned her head to one side, to avoid my look of defiance.

Holding out the price tag so that she could see it, I had added, "It's on sale."

"Well ..."

I had waited, in stubborn silence.

"All right, then."

"Don't stay out too late," my mother said, lifting her chin but not quite looking at me as I stood near the table, behind the Muncies and the Bairds.

"I won't," I said, frowning.

I wanted her to see me, to acknowledge that I was grown-up, admired by family friends, teased by them as though I were an equal, filling out in all the right places the dress she had bought for me, if reluctantly.

Wilifred and Frances asked me a few questions about school and my studies. I answered them politely; then, feeling all eyes on me, I said my goodbyes and walked out of the kitchen. The doorbell rang as I was making my exit.

That evening, with Roger, a good-looking senior who took me to a junior-senior dance in his own car, I felt different than I had ever felt before. I kept thinking of the glances of admiration I got from Fred Muncie and Sam Baird, the looks of assessment I got from their wives, the unspoken approval of my father—the certainty that I had, at that moment, passed through an invisible barrier. Somehow, my new dress, my date with Roger, the dance music—particularly the music from *Picnic*, my favorite movie—made me feel I had stepped out of my childhood as easily as I had stepped into that red dress.

On the way home, I wanted to shout out—something loud, something triumphant. But Roger was sitting next to me, no doubt anticipating the extended goodnight kisses that would complete the evening for him. I couldn't share my excitement with Roger. He was a part of the experience but as remote from me, from my feelings, as the full moon hovering in the clear night sky.

My mother was increasingly remote and withdrawn. She was drinking more than she admitted, or we elected to notice. Sometimes, in the afternoon, when I came home from school, she was already fortified for the long evening ahead—those evenings when I followed her movements, while Frank critically assessed her behavior.

"What is wrong with you?" he said on one such evening, refusing to acknowledge the evident. "I work ten, twelve hours a day. I come home and you're not even around."

"I'm sorry, Frank. I didn't hear you come in. I must have fallen asleep."

"But it's not even seven o'clock."

"I know. I was just—tired."

"I called upstairs. You didn't answer."

"I didn't hear you. The door was closed."

"Are you sick?"

"No. I'm fine."

"You look tired."

"Yes. I am. I'm tired."

"Have you had dinner? Has Maggie?"

"No, Frank. We were waiting for you. I'll start—"

"Never mind," said Frank, relenting. I could see that he wanted to enjoy what he called "the shank of the evening."

He headed for the back door.

"I picked up steaks on the way home. I'll go out back and heat up the grill. Maggie, would you make the salad? Your Mom's not feeling well. Will you join me in a beer, Katie, me lass?"

Of course, she didn't refuse. She never refused. I tried to remember when she had refused to join my father in a drink, or in anything else. I couldn't. She was yielding by nature. At that moment, sensing that she had already been drinking, I was unable to resist the impulse to denounce her for it.

"Why don't you go back to bed? I'll call you when dinner's ready," I said, as I tore up iceberg lettuce leaves, adding them to the chunks of tomato in the big wooden salad bowl.

"No, I—"

"I'll get Dad his beer. Go on."

"But I should—"

"It's okay. I'll take care of things."

"I'll just get the beer."

"Why? You've already had—what? Beer? Wine? Brandy? Vodka? That's why you fell asleep. Do you think I don't know? That's why you're so groggy."

"Maggie—"

"What? What? Do you even know what I'm saying? Do you even care?"

"Your dad—"

"Wants a beer, and some help with dinner. I know."

"You don't know. You don't know, Maggie. Don't try to fix it. You don't know."

I glared at her. She stepped back, as though I were going to strike her. Feeling rage, contempt, pity rising like bile in my throat, I swept my hand across the counter, tumbling the salad bowl and its contents onto the floor. The heavy wooden bowl clattered, spun. The damp vegetables crunched under my shoes as I ran out of the kitchen.

I heard Frank's, "What the hell?" and Kate's, "Just an accident, Frank. I'll take care of it," before I reached the top of the stairs. Once inside my bedroom, I slammed the door as hard as I could.

CHAPTER 25

For a while, after Win came home for the summer, my mother seemed her old self again. Win got his job back at Superior Collision, I took care of Ellie, worked part-time at Steed's Variety Store, and jockeyed for rights to Win's old Pontiac while I learned to drive.

"Take a lesson from Mom, young one," said Win. "Don't drive."

"She could drive if she wanted to," I said.

"But she doesn't want to. Take note. She leaves it to her better half."

"Well, I don't have a better half, and even if I did, *I* would be the better half."

For that show of self-approbation, I got a driving lesson. Others followed—with Win, my father, Gina—and once with Win and Gina together.

To me, Win, almost twenty, and in college, was the same big brother, to be bullied by and to bully, to tolerate and be tolerated by, in turn. I observed no dramatic changes in him. I still admired him—his height, his smile, his good nature. I was still jealous of the effortless ease with which he accrued my admiration and that of his friends, our parents—even Gina—who seemed to see him afresh as the days grew longer and warmer.

"He's certainly no warty toad," she said, one late Sunday morning, while we sat on her porch steps with Ellie.

Across the yard, in our driveway, Win, who had hailed us briefly, brooded beneath the hood of his car. He was wearing jeans and an old basketball T-shirt. While we were watching him, he lifted his head up and wiped at his face.

"Anything we can do?" Gina called out to him.

"Turn this heap into a new car," he called back, then continued to probe the engine of the dull black two-door Pontiac he affectionately called "Chief."

"He's the prize," she said.

Then, seeing my searching look, she added, "For some lucky girl. Is it still Peggy?"

"I don't know. I guess. He still sees her—sometimes."

Peggy, I was quite sure, was being relegated to an increasingly minor role in Win's life, but I was reluctant to say this to Gina. I was even more reluctant to ask myself why I didn't want to say this to Gina.

Gina continued to watch him, thoughtfully. Ellie chattered with her "little family," ranged on the steps. Porky, a stuffed animal that may have been pink, and may have been a pig, absorbed most of her attention. Rags sat next to us, sniffing the air, looking unusually alert.

"Where are your folks?" Gina said, still watching Win.

"Taking a ride. Dad said no lessons today. He wants to relax. My driving makes him nervous. So I stayed home."

"Hmm," said Gina.

"I don't suppose you'd like to go for a ride," I said.

"What?"

"Go for a ride." I steered an imaginary wheel. "You know. In your car. With me driving."

"Hmm. Maybe."

"Super! I'll go tell Win."

I started to get up but Gina grabbed my arm.

"Hold on," she said. "I'll tell him."

Gina got up and walked slowly across the lawn. She was dressed casually, in tan pedal pushers, loafers, and a yellow knit top with bold brown horizontal stripes. The stripes undulated gently as she walked.

"Shtay wish Majee," said Ellie to her assorted family. Then, turning to Rags, who was swishing his feathered tail and starting to follow Gina, she said, "You shtay too!"

Abashed, Rags sat down again, his tail stilled, his head drooping. I patted him but he ignored me, his eyes riveted on Gina. Ellie ran after her mother and tucked her hand inside Gina's, turning her head just long enough to smirk at Rags. Obviously, I thought, scratching the unhappy dog behind his long floppy ears, there's more than one form of sibling rivalry.

Win looked up when Gina approached. She said something that made him laugh. They stood opposite each other looking under the hood, while Win pointed here and there. Ellie bounced up and down, then sideways, still clutching her mother's hand.

At last, Gina pulled her hand free and pointed her toward me, but Ellie refused to leave. Win beckoned to Ellie, then lifted her up so that she could see the "Chieftain" hood ornament, and the engine beneath the hood. This seemed to make her happy for a few minutes, until she squirmed and whined. Win put her down.

Gina spoke to her sharply, but Ellie seized Gina's hand, whining even more plaintively. Gina shrugged her shoulders, said something to Win, then walked slowly back, Ellie pulling her, walking backwards in her efforts to hurry Gina back to her own front yard.

"What a ninny and a nuisance you're being," said Gina, pushing her daughter away as Ellie jumped, twitched, and whined.

"Did you tell him?" I said.

"Tell him what?"

"That we're going for a ride?"

"Did I say that?"

"Gina, that's what you … You said you were … Do you mean we're not *going*?"

I was whining, my voice rising. I sounded surprisingly like Ellie.

"I didn't say that."

"*Are* we going then?"

"Going where?"

"For a ride!"

I wanted to stamp my foot, have a temper tantrum. Didn't she know—couldn't she see—how important this was for me?

"Yes, of course," she said, as if prompted. "Ellie, come inside. I want you to stay with Daddy."

"I wanshagofe*ride*um."

"Not while Maggie is learning how to drive, my pet."

"I *wan*sha."

Ellie crossed her arms, tilting her head up toward Gina.

"I said no, Ellie."

"I shed *yesh*, Mommy."

Gina tried not to smile, but her almond eyes flashed me a look that was half helpless resignation, half humorous indulgence. She was enormously proud of Ellie's willfulness.

"Ask Daddy," she said, at last.

Ellie ran up the steps and into the house, her voice rising with excitement.

"Mommy sezakengoferideum Majee. Kinago? Kinago, Daddy?"

Phil appeared at the front door, still in his robe, Ellie bobbing up and down beside him.

"Is this student driver lesson number 27?" he asked.

Gina nodded, then shook her head in the direction of Ellie.

"Right," said Phil. "Ellie, you stay home with me."

Ellie opened her mouth to protest, but before she made a sound, Phil leaned over, whispering in her ear. Ellie listened intently, looked up at him, giggled, then pulled him down so that she could whisper in *his* ear. Phil nodded. Ellie looked at us, squirming with delight.

"You goferideum Majee," she said to Gina. "Willshtay wish Daddy. He needshatenshun."

"Just as you say, my sweet," said Gina, taking the car keys Phil pulled off the hook inside the door and held out to her. "Let's go, Maggie."

We raced for the car, Gina laughing at me. I took my place in the driver's seat with a sigh of satisfaction. Gina sat down beside me, waving to Phil and Ellie as I backed out of the driveway, hitting the bumper on the street as I turned the wheel. Gina clucked but said nothing until I shifted into first gear. Then she pressed my arm, said, "Wait," and called out the window, "Help! Student driver at the helm!"

In a moment, the passenger door was open, Win was sliding in beside Gina, and Gina was squeezed between us, laughing.

"Stay on the right side of the road, Maggie," said Gina. "No, the *other* right side. That's it. Use your turn signal if you're going to make a turn. No, *before* you make the turn. Try not to grind the gears. It wears them down."

"Mags could wear out a set of gears in an afternoon, given the chance," said Win, leaning forward to look at me, on his face a triumphant grin, his arm across the back of the seat.

"Well, here's my chance," I said.

Grasping the gearshift, which was mounted on the steering column, I shifted into second, grinding the gears. We surged forward, our chins lifting simultaneously. Win clicked on the radio, reaching across Gina, so that she was almost wrapped in his arms. Then he leaned back, tapping his fingers in time to the music of Little Richard's "Rip It Up." I pointed the car toward Overlook Road, where I would have the chance to pick up speed.

"Take it easy, Maggie! I'm getting seasick, and we're nowhere near the lake."

"Yeah, Sis. You're driving like a drunken sailor. Don't shift into third until you pick up a little speed."

"You're over the center line, Maggie. You'd better slow down. There's a car coming. Pity the poor unsuspecting driver."

"Mags, you can't go from three to one without pushing in the clutch and hitting the brakes. And, by the way, you don't need to press the clutch every time you press the brake pedal. You only clutch when you're switching gears."

He leaned forward and grabbed at the door handle.

"Say, could you let me out at the next stop? I just remembered an appointment."

We were laughing uncontrollably as I turned onto Overlook Road, just ahead of an oncoming driver, who honked his horn, then glared at me as he wheeled past us.

"If that had been a cop, you'd be in big trouble right now," said Win, waving at the irate driver.

"No, *you'd* be in trouble," I said. "You're supposed to be teaching me to drive, remember?"

"I'm thinking that's impossible," said Win.

"Maybe not," said Gina. "She's got good reflexes."

"I was the one looking in the jaws of death when we made that turn," said Win. "That car had to go through me to get to you."

"Did I mention Maggie and I are glad to have you with us?"

I propelled us down Overlook Road, Gina and Win by turns bantering with each other, clutching each other in mock horror as I swerved around corners or hit minor bumps in the road. Then, seeing a clear, straight stretch of road ahead of us, I remembered the night of the ride with Gina. Taking my hands off the wheel, I shouted, "Let's live dangerously!"

Gina grabbed the wheel.

Win said, "Jesus Christ!"

I put my foot on the brakes as the car swerved out of control. We swayed drunkenly for a few moments, then slowed down just as a car approached us over an incline.

"Sorry," I said, shifting down, brushing Gina's hands off the wheel.

"You jerk," said Win. "Where did you learn to drive with your hands up in the air?"

"From me, I'm afraid," said Gina, reaching for her cigarettes.

Her hands trembled slightly as she pulled matches from the cellophane, lit up. Then, as she exhaled, she relaxed and laughed.

"What the hell, it's my golden rule."

"What is?" said Win, leaning forward, scowling at me.

"What Maggie said: Let's live dangerously."

Win looked from me to Gina, his scowl rearranging itself into a grin as he unclenched his fists, relaxed his tense arm muscles.

"Give me one of those," he said.

Gina handed him a cigarette and lit it for him. Then, good humor restored, smoke tickling my nostrils as it escaped out the open windows, I shifted smoothly into third. I drove at a moderate speed to the end of the road, where it bisected Lake Road.

"Let's take a walk on the beach," said Gina, as we came to a stop. "A perfect restorative for jangled nerves."

"Can you make it across the road, Mags? Between cars, I mean."

I crossed the tracks, then parked the car in the gravel parking area where Gina and I had taken our evening walk on the beach.

"Bring the blanket, Maggie," said Gina.

She got out and walked on ahead with Win. I followed behind, suddenly relegated to a subordinate position. Gina took off her shoes and ran down the beach to the water, shouting, "Let's live dangerously!" Win ran after her, hopping on one foot, then the other, as he awkwardly pulled off his tennis shoes.

They played at the edge of the water, small waves nipping their bare feet and ankles as they chased each other, splashed water on each other. Clutching the old army blanket, I stood watching them, the early afternoon sun beating down on my head. Gina waved and beckoned to me, but I shook my head. I knew, with sudden insight, that she didn't want me there, at the water's edge.

I walked along the beach until I found a patch of shade beneath a rocky cliff. I spread the blanket on the sand and lay down on it, suddenly weary with rejection following close on the heels of excitement—as well as a familiar surge of envy, a longing for something I hadn't yet felt, that I suspected the two at the water's edge felt for each other.

For a while, I watched them play in the damp sand, racing the waves gliding in tireless succession against the shore. Then, hypnotized by the heat, the gentle whoosh of the waves, I rested a forearm over my eyes and fell asleep.

"Wake up, Noodle, and let's push off."

"We'd better get going, Maggie."

I opened my eyes and looked at the two faces peering down at me. The glaring light behind them cast their faces in shadow, but I had seen enough to know I hadn't been missed.

"I guess I fell asleep," I said.

"No kidding," said Win, grabbing the hand I held out to him, jerking me to my feet.

"We called you but you didn't answer," said Gina. "We had a long walk on the beach."

"Almost down to the lighthouse," said Win. "While you snoozed."

"I just—fell asleep," I repeated, stubbornly, hiding my disappointment at having missed the walk.

"Let's go," Gina said. "I promised Ellie—something—this afternoon. I think it was a Dairy Queen."

They started off. I shook out the blanket, folded it, tucked it under my arm, again trailing behind them. They leaned close to each other, saying things I couldn't hear. I sighed and looked down at my feet, kicking up small storms of sand with my canvas shoes.

Back at the car, Gina slid into the driver's seat. I got in the back, curling up on the seat and arranging the blanket under my head.

"Still sleepy?" said Gina, turning toward me as she backed out of the parking space.

"Um," I said.

As we drove back to town, I looked at the backs of their heads, listened to their murmured conversation. I felt as I used to when I was a small child and my parents, in the front seat, conferred with each other in low tones. In the space of a few hours, I had taken hold of my adulthood, brandished it, then let it slip away again.

CHAPTER 26

That summer, while I sat by with glum disapproval, and my mother turned away with something like despair, Gina and Win glided toward each other, then slid away, then glided toward each other again, like driftwood on the water.

I kept remembering the afternoon Win and Gina and I had spent at the beach, how engrossed they had been in each other's company, how I had resented their involvement with one another.

Then I would remember how Gina had admired Win when she first met him at our backyard barbecue two summers ago, how she had called him "young Adonis," the look of longing I had seen on her face when Win and his friends—rowdy, shouting with laughter, car radio blaring—had left the party in a red convertible.

And I would think about other things—like seeing someone at the top of Gina's stairway—had I just imagined it was Win?—when I stood at her front door last year, just before Halloween. Around that time, Win had been evasive, often absent from home, vague about his whereabouts, avoiding his usual friends, his usual hangouts …

Phil, whenever I saw him, was just the same as he always was. He seemed not to notice, or not to care. I wondered again at his and Gina's relationship, but could make no sense of it.

My father, for reasons of his own, refused to see what was happening.

"Nonsense," I heard him say to my mother. "Win and Gregorka's wife? Are you starting in with that again? That little adolescent crush? That was over and done with long ago. Never went anywhere. Never will."

His tone was so positive that it silenced Kate. But it also made me question my father's susceptibility to Gina. Was that far-from-innocent kiss I had interrupted just before Win's graduation party a payoff? Had Gina meant to silence Frank, to divert any lingering doubt?

I began to look at Gina from yet a different perspective, as though she were sitting at the three-way mirror on her dressing table, and I had shifted my admiring gaze from the full-front view to one side view—somewhat distorted—and then the other—even more askew.

It was not entirely by chance that I discovered Win and Gina's meeting place. I wasn't quite as simple as I had been a year or two ago. I sensed that there was an urgency to find a place, an opportunity, that would bring them together, and that they had pushed every other consideration, including me, into the background. So I watched, in a way that Kate could not, and Phil chose not to. I watched, because I knew Win was careless, and Gina was tugging at her restraints.

I sometimes reflected on my reluctance, or my inability, to judge Gina, even when she was blatantly wrong. I had condemned her once—when I saw her kissing my father—but, even then, I had managed to doubt that I saw what I saw. I had manipulated my own experience, the proof of my own eyes.

Much as I yearned to be an adult, I couldn't accept the disturbing clarity of it—the layered, multi-faceted awareness it brought; the need to judge or accept, to condemn or forgive.

At least, not then.

Gina was increasingly nervous and fretful—she said it was about money.

"As soon as Ellie starts kindergarten, I'm putting myself on the job market," she said to me one afternoon, as we sat with Ellie in Ellie's bedroom. "Auctioning myself off to the highest bidder. I've got skills. I was an office manager."

"Really?" I said. "You never told me. Where?"

"Construction company. Bunch of big oafs. But I kept them in line. Kept their books. Set up their jobs. Answered their phone. Typed up their invoices and work orders. Paid their bills. Practically ran the business."

"Will you go back there?"

"Hell, no. This round I'm going to do better. Just watch me. And I swear I'm going to spend every dime I make on clothes for Ellie and me. I'm going to lock the door to the sewing room and throw away the key."

"But you're so good at it, Gina."

"I have to be good at it. Otherwise—no clothes."

Gina laughed as she said this, but there was an edge of bitterness in her voice. No one that I knew was as clothes-conscious as Gina. Although she dressed casually, for the most part, she chose everything she wore with deliberation, wore everything she chose with a certain dramatic flourish, mixing styles and colors in a way I had never seen before—outside of a movie theater or a fashion magazine.

She dressed Ellie like one of her daughter's more decorative "little family" of dolls. Ellie's closet was jammed with outfits Gina had made for her, or brought home to her after one of her extensive shopping trips.

"Put Ellie in her Miss Muffet outfit," she said late one morning, as she ran off to shop, leaving me in charge. "She'll be an angel for you in that one."

I pushed through Ellie's closet, looking for a summery little dress that I vaguely remembered as polka dots on a blue background.

"Is somebody having a party?" I said to Ellie, as I pulled the dress off its hanger.

"Jushta*play*dresh," said Ellie, indignantly, as I slipped it over her head. "Partydreshiz here." She jabbed a finger in the direction of several lacy, foamy dresses, each hanging on a cloth-covered hanger. "Playdreshiz here," she continued, pointing to another section of the closet. "Coldayclozhiz *here*. Warmdayclozhiz *here*."

I nodded, impressed.

"Where are old clothes?" I said.

"No olclozh," she replied promptly. "Olclozh gotuh Savashun Ernie."

"Ernie? Who's Ernie?"

"No," said Ellie, stamping her foot, "Savashun Ernie."

"Oh. Salvation Army?"

"Yesh. Savashun Ernie warshmy olclozh. *All*my olclozh."

Gina came back from her shopping trip excited, happy, full of talk. She had been gone the entire afternoon.

"Maggie, I am a whole new person. I am full of the power of clothes. New clothes! Look at this slip. Wait. It's in this bag. Look at this! Feel the fabric. Silk. Can you see me in this? Never mind. I'll try it on for you. But first let me show you these shoes. Buttery leather. So soft it makes my fingers tingle. And there's a dress—where is it? Just cotton, but so— I found this necklace to go with it. It's in a little bag—can you find it? No, not there. That's lingerie. Black lace, and not much of that. Isn't it heavenly? And here—"

"Whadijubringfer*me*?" said Ellie.

"Don't worry, my pet. I didn't forget you. Oh, here's the necklace. Very plain—silver links—but attractive, don't you think? There's nothing like a simple piece of jewelry to make a statement. What else. Oh! Summer sandals. Just a few pieces of leather but so sexy. I'll wear my ankle bracelets with them. I stopped at a cosmetic counter and got a new polish. Just a touch on the toenails—"

"Whadijubringfer*me*?" said Ellie, again.

"Ah, yes," said Gina, musing. "What did I bring for Ellie? I thought there was something—"

"You fergot!" said Ellie, her mouth crumpling.

"I was sure I—"

"You sed you woodenfergot!"

"Well, I—"

Before the tears hovering on Ellie's lashes splashed onto her cheek, Gina scooped her up and hugged her.

"You silly child. Of course, I didn't forget you. Do I ever? Have I ever? That bag over there—no, not that one. The one next to it. That's it. Look inside. There's a new swimsuit for you. See it? Do you like it? Red, of course, but so smart and grownup. And shorts and a frilly top, for hot days. Oh, and look. Tennis shoes. Aren't they wonderful, Maggie? So small and neat and white. Well, they won't stay white for long, but who cares?"

The living room sofa was overflowing with shopping bags, tissue paper, clothes carelessly tossed aside. Gina and Ellie were chattering like two noisy children. Rags was sitting close to them, wagging his feathery tail, trying to get Gina's attention. Finally, he barked, once. We looked at him in amazement.

"Rags, you old dog, you," said Gina. "When did you find your vocal chords again?"

It was a standing joke among us that Rags had forgotten how to bark years ago, when he was a puppy. He rarely made a sound, except when he yawned. Gina crouched down in front of him and cupped his head with her hands.

"It's okay. We love you, too."

Rags, as if embarrassed, opened his mouth in a tremendous yawn.

"Rajizhbad," said Ellie, but she patted him on his head. Her perennial assessment of Rags was tempered by her fine new clothes.

"But wait!" said Gina, getting up, beginning to gather together her purchases. "What's this?" She pulled a small tissue-wrapped bundle from one of the bags. "I nearly forgot. This is for you, Maggie."

I hadn't even acknowledged the pangs of envy I felt as Gina pulled one purchase after another from her bag, or my covetous longing for the feel of silk, leather, lace, and fresh cotton against my skin. Shopping in my family was a rare, somewhat tense, event, punctuated by guilt for spending money we supposedly didn't have—always accompanied by Kate's reluctance to shop. For her, it was a necessary ordeal. For Gina, it was entertainment and diversion—spontaneous, stimulating, deeply satisfying.

I unfolded the tissue, feeling my skin turn warm with pleasure. Nested inside the tissue was a scarf, yellow threaded with brown, long and narrow and airy. The silk was so fine spun that it was almost weightless.

"I was trying to match your eyes. Did I? Let me see."

Gina wrapped the scarf around my neck, stood back to observe. "What do you think, Ellie?"

"Majee hazh yeyo izh. Jusht like Tigger."

I walked over to the gilt-framed mirror above the fireplace and looked at myself. Gina came up behind me, smiling at my image in the mirror.

"Yes. I thought so. Tawny. So unusual. You really should make the most of it, Maggie. A lot of young men would be quite willing to drown in those eyes."

As it happened, Ben Henderson took a dive that summer.

"You make me crazy," he said to me, as he came up gasping for air after one of our more affectionate encounters. "You're just a kid and you make me crazy."

But by then I knew him well enough not to be offended by his sometimes two-edged compliments.

"Benson," as he was called by almost everyone, was one of Win's best friends. After graduating the previous year, Benson went to work for his uncle at Henderson's Garage, just outside of town. Win called him "the grease monkey," but they still got together when Win was in town.

I had had a crush on Benson for as long as I could remember. He was a football hero in high school, big and broad, with a slow smile that made me wince with pleasure. He and his steady, Janet, were often at our house with Win and Peggy. But then, after graduation, Janet went to college, and Benson went his own way—slowly and deliberately, as he did almost everything.

Months later, but not until after my sixteenth birthday, Benson took another look at me.

"So, I see you're driving now."

He was sitting with Win on the porch steps as I opened the screen door and came out. He was leaning against one post, Win against the other, as though they were holding up the porch. I stepped between them and walked down the steps to the sidewalk, holding my breath, as I always did, when Benson looked at me.

"Yes. I guess. A little."

I exhaled and glanced up at him, looking for that slow smile. When I saw it, I caught my breath again.

"That's a fair description," said Win. "A little driving and a lot of guessing."

"The girl has to learn," said Benson.

I was wearing an almost-new outfit—canvas sandals, blue Bermuda shorts, blue-striped, sleeveless shirt. He glanced at my legs, then his eyes traveled—slowly—up to my face.

"Not in my car," said Win. "Not with my life hanging in the balance."

He stood up and stretched. "How about a beer, Benson?"

"Sure. I could go for a beer."

Benson stood up and turned to follow Win into the house. Then he turned back to me.

"See ya, Maggie."

"See ya," I said.

I stood on the sidewalk and watched him walk into the house. The screen door slammed behind him. I felt as though I had been standing on a darkened stage for years and Benson had finally turned a spotlight on me.

I took a deep breath and exhaled. Slowly.

After that, it was just a matter of time.

Benson called Win and talked to me instead. Benson picked me up as I left Steed's Variety Store. Benson stopped by the house while Win was out. Benson asked me out.

At first, he offered to give me a driving lesson. Then he offered to take me to a movie I just happened to mention. A drive-in movie. In Hillsville. After that, I saw him almost every day. We were going together, much to Win's chagrin.

"Jesus Christ, Benson, she's my kid sister. What do you want to go out with a kid for?"

Benson grinned and shook his head. He was waiting for me as I checked my reflection in the full-length mirror behind the door of the front closet. I was arranging my silk scarf—Gina's gift to me—around my neck.

"Where are you taking her, you bum?" said Win.

"Just for a ride," said Benson. "Maybe a movie."

"Yeah. Sure."

Win shook his head and scowled at us.

"Well, have fun, you two."

"We will," said Benson.

I would, perhaps, have seen more of what was going on around me if I hadn't been so preoccupied with Benson. But I saw enough. More than enough. So much that I wondered at the incomprehension of those around me.

My mother spent more and more time in her room. "I've been resting," she would say, if asked. Win accepted her explanation, but only because he didn't want to question her behavior.

Gina kept spending money, not only on clothes. Not since she had moved in and redecorated Mrs. Ennis' fusty old house had she indulged in such a frenzy of getting and buying.

She decided Ellie's room was too much a nursery, not the proper setting for a little girl soon to start kindergarten. So Ellie's old furniture went to "Savashun Ernie" and a new bedroom "shweet" took its place, finished in gleaming white. The small bed had scalloped headboard and footboard decorated with prancing lambs. The chest of drawers was scalloped top and bottom and repeated the lamb pattern. The miniature dressing table had a ruffled skirt, an oval mirror, a spindle-backed chair. A "trezhachess" at the foot of the bed, white wicker, held Ellie's "little family" of dolls and stuffed toys when they were in repose.

"Everything was on sale at Spangleman's," Gina said, after one excursion. "I couldn't resist."

She went off to shop for more. A dinnerware set edged in cranberry red. A bronze floor lamp with a leaded-glass shade. A set of mahogany stacking tables with bow legs. A ceiling fan for the kitchen. A fireplace set on a stand with poker, shovel, and log lifter in heavy brass-plated steel with ball handles.

When I asked her why she had purchased a fireplace set in the summer, she shrugged.

"I hated looking at that old wrought iron set. It was the only thing left from Mrs. Ennis. I threw it out as soon as I got this."

When Gina wasn't shopping, she was complaining about the bills that inevitably followed.

"I'm only trying to take care of things," she said one afternoon, as we sat in her little sewing room on the second floor. She was sitting at her sewing machine, making a sunsuit for Ellie.

"I can't make every stitch of clothes Ellie and I wear, can I, Maggie?"

I shook my head, wanting to talk to her about Benson, but not knowing how to start. When Gina was in one of her "talking" moods, there was no stopping her, no interrupting her. Gina did most of her thinking out loud, and she liked having someone like me to listen, quietly and without comment.

"Phil likes nice things, a comfortable home. That costs money. Yet he's amazed and appalled when the bills come in. He says we don't need anything. He says Ellie has more than she knows what to do with. He wants to know what I'm getting all dressed up for. Good question! Who cares what I look like, what I wear? Phil certainly doesn't. He says I look good in anything, or nothing. He has no clothes sense. He has no decorating sense. He just looks at the bills, sighs, looks at me as if he doesn't know what to make of me. Well, he doesn't. Never did. Do you know Phil says he never dreams? I'm married to a man who never dreams! When I say I'll get a job, he says, you *have* a job. Right here. So I'm doing my job. When Ellie goes to school, it will be different. Things will be different. I'm just marking time."

She stood up, stretched. She had completed the task at hand; she was ready to move on.

"Maggie, can you stay with Ellie while I take a run to Hillsville? I put a few things in layaway the other day at Justine's. Summer things. Shorts and a wraparound skirt with a sleeveless top. A few other things. It will only take me a couple of hours. Can you stay?"

Then the shopping stopped, abruptly. Gina came home empty-handed, with little to say, looking as if every cell in her body were buzzing. She had started leaving Ellie with another sitter, Izzy Shoemaker—she said because of my job at Steed's Variety Store—so I wasn't needed as often.

At home, Win had even less to say. He snapped irritably at me when I teased him for his silence. He no longer came directly home from his job at Superior Collision—he said because he was hanging out with friends. But I was often with Benson, and Peggy was rarely at our house. Most of his other friends weren't in town for the summer.

One afternoon, when I was out on my bicycle, and Izzy Shoemaker was taking care of Ellie, Win whizzed past me in his old Pontiac.

When Win passed by, I was more than a mile outside of town, moving leisurely in the direction Gina and I used to take on our morning walks. When Win was out of sight, I picked up speed, gulping down air to swallow my apprehension. I was almost sure I knew where he was going.

Less than a mile further on, on an unpaved road, there was a wooded rise that dipped down to the bridge where Gina and I had taken our first early morning walk. The bridge, made of unpainted planks that shuddered when you drove over them, was built over the creek I was following. On the other side of the bridge was a tractor path that led into the woods. At the end of the path was a little shack owned by Fred Muncie.

I had played in those woods. I had been in that shack many times. For years, Fred and Wilifred hosted clambakes and corn roasts in the cleared area surrounding the shack. I sat around the open fire with family and friends, scooping slippery clams out of their shells, biting into fresh corn on the cob, once or twice witness to the slow roasting on a spit of a tender little pig. Years ago, on frosty days, my father and Fred, sometimes with Pete Granger and Sam Baird, sat around the wood-burning stove inside the shack, passing around a fifth of whiskey still in its brown paper bag, filling the shack with cigar smoke, while Win led me, sometimes with Fred's two daughters, Jean and Patricia, on missions of exploration in the woods.

Jean and Patricia were a little older than Win, giggly, not averse to tussles and mock wrestling matches with Win when they were well out of sight of the shack. They had both gotten married and were living in Hillsville.

After Fred had a mild heart attack, four or five years ago, he rarely visited his property. The old shack was usually deserted.

I followed the creek until it nose-dived down a little waterfall. It took a sharp turn before it righted itself and continued on. At the next intersection, I turned off onto the dirt road that led down to the water. On the near side of the bridge was a path that followed the creek. It was invisible from the road, but I knew it well from my youthful excursions in the woods. I hid my bike in the trees, then followed the path until I was directly opposite the shack.

Outside the shack, side by side, were Win's old black Pontiac and Gina's little green Ford coupe.

I sat down on the trunk of a tree that had been pushed sideways by strong winds in its youth. It had stuck fast to the earth, sending out shoots that spread out over the ground like a leafy centipede. We had often, as children, walked the length of its slender torso, and hidden under its spray of branches.

I wondered what to do with what I knew. It was too big for me, yet I had chosen to know. I had wanted the certainty.

Win, not yet twenty, and Gina, not yet thirty, had wanted certainty also. The certainty of each other. I wondered what it was like to risk everything for that, or if they had even considered the risk. I realized for the first time how alike they were. Win probably never thought about the cost. For Gina, risk was just another purchase, subject to impulse—sometimes resulting in worthless goods, sometimes well worth the price.

"I'm looking for treasure," she had said to me, after one of her shopping trips. "I don't always find it, but I'm always looking."

Yet, she was aware of her shortcomings, her impulsiveness. There was the day she had looked at her new bronze floor lamp with the leaded-glass shade and called it "hideous." She had laughed—at the lamp, at herself for buying it—but she had acknowledged her mistake.

And then there was the night of the ride—my first ride with her—when she took her hands off the wheel and shouted, "Let's live dangerously!"

That evening, when we had walked on the beach, when she had talked to me about finding my own "windless place," she had seemed to see right into my soul, to give substance to the longing I felt but could not express.

Was this Gina's windless place—this one-room shack with its raw pine floor, rough-hewn table and straight-backed chairs, wooden boxes that served as extra seats, crude shelves and hooks for tools and supplies, narrow cot on rusty springs, small pot-bellied stove with a pipe that took a right turn before it jutted out through the tin roof?

Gina loved luxury. She enjoyed her lavish wardrobe, her expensive furniture. But she had chosen to be here, to be with Win, because he could give her something she couldn't buy or acquire—that fleeting experience of youth she had so treasured before she herself was twenty.

I clutched at my stomach, feeling suddenly ill, wanting to vomit onto the rotting debris beneath the fallen trunk on which I sat. I wanted to be rid of the "adult" concerns I had been preparing for so anxiously, to expel them from my mind, my body. I wanted to be a child again, to not know what had made me no longer a child. I wanted my mother to guide me as only she could, my father to take the wool off his eyes, Win to go back to dating Peggy, Phil to stay home long enough to look after his wife and child, Gina to …

A squirrel scampered up to me, sniffing the air and twitching its tail. After appraising me and finding me harmless, it wheeled around, thrusting out its tail like royalty adjusting a magnificent train, looking back to catch its effect. I waved a hand and sent it scurrying up the nearest tree.

I stood up, wanting to feel the sun on my skin. I walked quickly back down the path to the road, picked up my bicycle, pushed it up the hill. I glanced back over my shoulder for any sign of a car, as though *I* were the one in hiding and not the two in the shack behind me.

At the intersection, I got on my bike and pedaled furiously until I approached the sidewalks and tree-lined streets of town.

CHAPTER 27

I have since learned that not everything we do has consequences—at least not immediate consequences. But, at the time, I waited for all of our lives to ignite simultaneously, as though that meeting in the woods between Win and Gina needed only a witness—my witness—to make all of us combustible.

Nothing, however, happened. June passed into July; summer settled in, undisturbed by all that was disturbing me. The days were hazy, oppressive. I was by turns wary, confused, irritable, indifferent, sorry for myself, enraged with everyone else.

"Jesus Christ, Kate, what's possessed this girl of yours?" said my father. "She snaps at everybody like a mad dog."

"She's your girl, too," said my mother, mildly.

"Not likely," said my father, who was home for lunch and in buoyant humor. "We're remarkably good natured on my side of the family. I think you put something over on me with this one, Kate."

"Why don't you both just leave me alone!" I said.

I slammed the door as I walked out of the house.

Having made a dramatic exit, I stood on the front porch, uncertain what to do next. I couldn't very well go back in the house. I quelled my first impulse, which was to run next door to see Gina. I thought of getting on my bicycle, pedaling over to Prue's, but it was too hot, and Prue was as puzzled by my moodiness as was everyone else.

Win had walked to work that morning. His Pontiac was parked across the street, in the shade of a maple tree, windows open to keep it cool inside. Still unlicensed (temporary permit only), I hesitated, but only for a moment. I crossed the street, got inside the car, adjusted the seat forward and the rearview mirror down, felt around for the keys. They were just under the front seat, beneath a torn piece of carpeting. I started the car, shifted into drive, glided quietly down to the end of the street. Once out of sight of our house, I relaxed. In a few minutes, driving slowly, I was outside of town.

It was the first time I had driven by myself. Feeling a surge of freedom from all the ties of family and friends, I turned onto Overlook Road, then pushed down on the accelerator. The Pontiac balked, like a horse being kicked by its impatient rider, then bolted, sputtering and coughing. Gathering strength, it charged down the empty road.

I laughed out loud and banged on the wheel, shouting encouragement. The sensation of being on my own was intoxicating. It was like being kissed by Benson—sweet, disturbing, a little dizzying.

Seeing no one ahead of me or behind me, I stretched my arms out, shouting, "Let's live dangerously!"

Win's Pontiac charged ahead, smooth and on course. Long seconds later, I saw the bend in the road that signaled the end of Overlook Road's unswerving course. I put my hands on the wheel, lifted my foot from the accelerator, and coasted around the bend, savoring the screech of the wheels as they hugged the road on the curve. Moments later, seeing the end of the road ahead and a car approaching, I reluctantly pumped the brakes.

I stopped at the intersection of Overlook and Lake roads, blinking at the cars passing by in both directions, surprised by the tears running down my face. As fast as I whisked them away, more tears spilled out, until it seemed as though I were watching the road through a summer rain. At last, seeing a break in the traffic, I crossed Lake Road, bumped over the tracks, and parked on the gravel lot next to the beach. Two other cars were parked nearby. I could hear the shouts of children playing in the water. I looked at my hands, knuckles white with the strain of grasping the wheel, then slowly loosened my grip, turned off the ignition, and pulled out the keys, tucking them under the seat. I brushed at my wet face as I got out of the car and walked down to the beach.

"Stupid, stupid, stupid," I murmured, as I walked down to the water's edge and watched the children diving like plump young dolphins. "It's not my problem. It has nothing to do with me. It's *their* problem."

The two mothers on the beach glanced at me without interest, then turned back to each other, deep in conversation. I passed them and walked toward the rocky area of the beach, where visitors seldom ventured. I had been there with Gina, and with Benson. I wanted to sit there and look out at the water. I wanted to listen to the waves as they grazed the shore.

I walked until I came to the rocky ledge that slanted down toward the lake, where Gina and I had sat, the night of that wild ride; where Benson's kisses had warmed me like the afternoon sun. I climbed up on the ledge, sat down, pulling my knees up to my chest.

Four or five summers ago, swimming in this area of the beach, I had almost drowned. I was with Win and Patricia Muncie, Fred Muncie's daughter, who had a car and a crush on Win. Wanting to stretch my limits, I had ventured farther out on the water than I ever had before. I swam until I felt pleasantly tired; then, spotting Win and Patricia at the edge of the water, I started back. I was within hailing distance when I felt the pull of an undertow.

In an instant, my body was dragged under, as though an anchor were attached to my feet. I clawed up to the surface, gasping for air, struggling to keep my head above water. I could see Win and Patricia; they were splashing. chasing each other in the soft, wet sand at the water's edge. I was sure if I just raised my arms, they would see me, but when I did I sank below the surface again, drinking in the churning, fishy-tasting water as I was pulled under.

When I surfaced again, choking on the water I had swallowed, I was exhausted, desperate to make a sound, any sound that would carry the short distance between myself and the two whose shouts and laughter reached my ears like the murmur of a radio tuned a few decibels too low. I felt myself getting weaker. I knew I couldn't shout, I couldn't gesture, I could only tread water and hold my head up—and even that seemed too much of an effort. I wanted to let go. I felt the relief of yielding to a force stronger than me, more tenacious than my will to live.

It was at that moment that Win grasped my arm and pulled me out of the sucking patch of water. I floated on my back, too tired to swim, letting him guide me to shore. He dragged me onto the sand, then stood over me, breathing hard.

"You brainless ninny," he said. "How often have I told you about that undertow? This is Lake Erie, remember? Not some neighborhood swimming hole!"

"I'm all right," I said, in answer to his unspoken question. "I guess I forgot."

After that, he never said a word to me about it, nor, as far as I knew, did he ever mention the incident to anyone else. There were no anecdotal rescue stories, no taunting, no payback. There was, in fact, a quiet generosity in his reticence, as though, having done what the situation demanded, he had dismissed it from his mind. I hadn't thought of it in years and—I was sure—neither had he.

The lake blurred before my eyes. I rested my head on my arms and wept—for Win, for Gina, for myself, for what I knew—and what I didn't want to know. Then I remained motionless, listening to the ongoing lament of the seagulls, the soft answering sigh of the waves. When at last I raised my head and looked around me, there was no one on the beach. The sun was still hot overhead.

I looked out at the water, toward the area of the undertow. There was nothing on the calm turquoise surface of the lake to indicate its whereabouts, but I knew it was there. I also knew that most of the people around here swam all of their lives and never hit an undertow. It was probably not that they knew so much more about the lake than I did. It was probably just luck.

I stayed looking out at the lake until the sun cast long shadows against the rocky ledge. I realized it was getting late. Win would soon be missing his car. I scuttled across the sand, feeling surprisingly light, almost buoyant, as though something caught in my throat had dislodged itself and I could breathe deeply again. I drove back to town without incident; parked the car in the exact same place across the street from the house—seat back, rearview mirror up, keys lodged beneath the torn carpeting.

When I walked into the house, my mother called out, "Maggie? Is that you? Your dad's still out on a call, and Win's not home yet, but they should be here any minute. Will you help me with dinner?"

CHAPTER 28

And so I became a conspirator. Protecting Gina and Win with my silence. Without their knowledge or consent. For reasons as murky and undefined as the lake after a summer storm.

I was less jumpy and caustic. My father, who was not attuned to subtleties, said. "We seem to have our girl back." My mother just looked at me questioningly. But I had nothing to say to her. I shrouded my feelings, as she did hers. We were alike in that.

In the little time I spent with Win, he seemed just the same, but Gina was different. She was softer—there were fewer sharp edges poking out—or so at least it seemed to me. I saw her often, if only briefly, whenever she asked me to stay with Ellie—even though Izzy Shoemaker was always standing by to take my place. But Gina paid me well—too well to refuse. With that and my part-time job at Steed's Variety Store, I was saving enough money to go back to school well dressed for once.

I saw less of Prue and Sharon. They seemed young to me, preoccupied with trifling concerns. I couldn't confide in them, so I hadn't much to say when I was with them. It was only when I was with Benson that I felt at peace. Nothing seemed to disturb Benson. Nothing agitated him. When we were together, we talked about inconsequential things. We laughed a lot. We kissed—a lot.

I liked kissing Benson. I had kissed Charlie and Earl and Kurt and Roger because it was expected of me, but I kissed Benson because I wanted to. There were no road signs blinking when we kissed: this leads to this, which inevitably leads to this. We kissed playfully, affectionately, because Benson was playful and affectionate. Whatever else there was he held in reserve, perhaps to be experienced later. It was exciting to contemplate, but far enough away that I could enjoy what I was feeling in that moment.

We saw each other two or three times a week. Sometimes he kept me company when I was with Ellie. Ellie ran to greet him, shouting, "Benshun! Benshun!" and then did everything she could to monopolize his attention. She insisted he play games with her, or read to her. If the reading selection proved too short, she said, "Wanta book wish chapterzh init!" Benson laughed at her imperious commands, and I tolerated them, so Ellie usually got what she wanted. But sooner or later she grew bored, or sleepy, and went off to play with her "little family," or nodded off. Then I had Benson to myself.

Once, Ellie said to him, "Yur fingerzhur dirty," and Benson had actually blushed. He scrubbed and scrubbed, after work, but the grease was embedded in his hands and nails. I was careful not to draw attention to his hands because I knew they were clean, if stained, and I knew he was self-conscious about them. I liked the fact that he worked with his hands and got dirty and greasy, then cleaned himself up—for me.

Gina raised her eyebrows but smiled tolerantly when she came in one afternoon and found us nuzzling each other on the sofa.

"So you're Benson," she said, although she had met him the summer before.

To me, later, she said, "He's like a big teddy bear, isn't he?"

I felt a flash of anger and wanted to snap back, "So what kind of a toy is Win?"

But I was careful what I said to Gina. I no longer confided in her—perhaps because I was afraid she would confide in me. It was enough that I guarded their secret, hers and Win's, that I shared their guilt. It was more than enough.

I had kept Gina's secrets before, without reflecting overmuch about her integrity—except for the incident with my father. I had resolved that issue, at least to my own satisfaction. Gina was attracted to men. Men were attracted to Gina. Her marriage hadn't wiped out the impulse. Phil didn't seem to care, or was determined not to show that he cared, perhaps because he didn't want to confront her. Nor did I. I didn't want to look too closely at what was wrong with Gina, nor at what was wrong with me.

I felt justified when I opened Gina's front door and she called out to me, "Come in, Maggie. We've been waiting for you," and Ellie rushed to me, breathless with excitement, chirruping, "Majee! Mommy shez we kin play till dark!"

"Pigeon-gray dark?" I asked.

"No! More dark!"

"Black-crow dark?"

"Yesh!"

But I felt guilty when I walked into my own home and my mother, looking pinched, distracted, said, "Oh, Maggie. I thought you were Win. He's still out. Are you hungry?"

And so the summer days marched by, one after the other. Benson taught me how to parallel park, among other things not directly connected with parking. By August, I was licensed to drive.

One early evening in August, I knocked on Gina's screen door in answer to her request for a sitter. Phil had been gone all week. He was not expected back for at least a day or two. As usual, Gina did not tell me where she was going—just that she was "going out."

Ellie's voice floated down from the top of the stairs, "Cumunup, Majee. Weramost ready."

I ran up the stairs, giving Ellie a quick squeeze before I walked into Gina and Phil's bedroom. Gina was sitting at her dressing table, looking at herself in the ornate three-way mirror. She was frowning. The dressing table stood between two long screened-in windows that faced the front of the house. Creamy white curtains billowed out on either side of her, catching the fresh evening breeze.

Ellie came up beside her, propped her elbows on the table, her chin in her cupped hands. She frowned at Gina's image in the mirror in perfect imitation of her mother.

"I look ten years older than I did yesterday," said Gina.

"You look nyshe, Mommy," said Ellie, using her little fingers to pull her bottom lip down, then smiling at the effect.

"I don't want to look nice," said Gina. "I want to look gorgeous."

"Whaz gorjush?" said Ellie.

"It's the way you look when you're young," said Gina, picking up a bottle of Tabu cologne and spraying her wrists, then touching the scent behind her ears. Absently, she repeated the process with Ellie. I felt slightly repulsed by the faint undertone of patchouli.

"Shmelz shweet," said Ellie, sniffing at her wrists, then sniffing Gina's wrist.

Rags, who had been lying close to Gina's feet, raised his head long enough to sneeze; then, with a sigh, he settled his muzzle on his front paws again.

"Yes, my love. Sweet and spicy. Like you." She leaned close to the mirror and squinted disapprovingly.

"Kin I gowishyou, Mommy?" said Ellie.

"Not tonight, Ellie. I have—important business to take care of. You're staying with Maggie."

"Wannagowishyou," said Ellie.

She stood back from the mirror, crossed her arms in front of her, cocked her head at Gina's image.

"Maybe next time," said Gina, smiling at Ellie in the mirror. It was one of their favorite games, in which the only rule was to look at the image in the mirror, not at each other.

"*Thish* time," said Ellie.

"Insubordinate child."

"Whaz insubbrodnek?"

"It means you're going to do exactly as I say or else."

"*Won't*," said Ellie.

"*Will*," said Gina.

At that moment, the screen door squeaked open and slammed shut. We heard Phil call out, "Hey, where're my girls?"

Gina's expression in the mirror changed from smiling indulgence to surprise, quickly followed by annoyance. Her brows came together and her mouth, freshly touched up with bright red lipstick, turned down.

"Phil?" she said. Then she glanced at me, adjusted her expression from disbelief to pleasurable surprise, and added, emphatically, "Phil! We're up here! Ellie, it's your daddy!"

But Ellie had already raced down the stairs and hurled herself into Phil's outstretched arms. Rags lumbered down the stairs behind her; he got a scratch behind the ears for his efforts. I followed at a sedate pace, exchanging a brief greeting with Phil before Ellie thrust a small hand puppet in my face, saying, "Look, Majee. Isha fox!" I nodded at the newest member of Ellie's "little family," admiring its lush, reddish tail.

Phil ran up the stairs three at a time to greet his wife.

I took Ellie out on the front porch. We sat on the swing, taking turns wriggling our hand inside the little puppet, making it nod, clap its paws together, talk to us.

"My name ish *Foxy*," piped Ellie. "Whaz *yer* name?"

The swing chains squealed rhythmically. I could hear the murmur of voices overhead. I felt a grim twist of pleasure as I tried to catch the tone of the indistinct words.

"Gunna goshow Daddy," said Ellie.

She ran inside the house and up the stairs. The murmur changed to laughter, first Phil's, then, more subdued, Gina's, as Ellie recreated the little puppet scene we had rehearsed on the swing. Then Ellie clambered down the stairs again, with Phil close behind.

"How's Maggie?" he said, coming out on the porch and scooping up Ellie, who tapped him on the nose with the fox paws.

"Maggie's good," I said.

"How good?" he said, teasing me.

"As good as I need to be," I replied.

Phil and I always engaged in friendly combat—and never went beyond.

"Will it mess up your plans if I send you home? Here. For your trouble."

He tried to thrust some money in my hand but I refused it.

"My mom says never accept money I haven't earned," I said, archly.

Phil smiled. "You *are* growing up."

"See ya," I said. "Bye, Ellie."

Ellie held up the little fox puppet and made it wave. "Bye, Majee."

I walked across the lawn, glancing back at Phil and Ellie huddled together on the porch swing.

At the bedroom windows, above the swing, a light breeze was still tugging at the curtains on either side of Gina's dressing table. They billowed and flapped, fluttering against the screens.

CHAPTER 29

My mother was sitting at the upright piano when I walked in, practicing some sheet music that may have been Chopin.

"Oh?" she said, raising her eyebrows but not looking at me. She didn't stop playing.

"Phil came home," I said. "Gina thought he was in Milwaukee."

"Did she cancel her plans?"

She was struggling with the chords.

"Yes," I said.

"This piano needs tuning," said Kate. "The keys are sticking. It's so humid."

She hit a smooth spot and the music flowed beneath her fingers.

"Where's Dad?"

"Out in back. Gardening."

"Where's Win?"

I tried to sound casually interested.

"He's gone out for the evening. He didn't say where."

She hit a rough spot again and banged ineffectually, the melody and chords going off in two separate directions.

"Maybe it's not the piano," she said, pausing for the first time to look up at me. "Maybe it's me."

"No, Mom, don't stop. You were doing well. I like to hear you play."

"You should have continued your lessons," she said, closing the sheet music. "I let you off too easily."

"I hated the practice. All those boring exercises."

I bumped against her as I sat down on the piano bench, pounding out a monotonous chord exercise I happened to remember. Kate laughed softly, then added a light, playful melody.

For a few moments, shoulder to shoulder, we harmonized, plucking at the keys haphazardly, somehow creating a smooth, rhythmical effect. Then my fingers slipped and slid, there was a jarring discord, we both stopped at once.

"Sorry," I said.

"Nonsense," she said, squeezing my arm. "It was fun."

She got up and lowered the cover over the keys.

"I'll get it tuned and we'll try again."

I nodded and watched her as she walked out, heading for the back door to join my father. She raised her hands, smoothing her damp, upswept hair. There was such grace in the movement that I blinked admiringly, as though she were walking offstage.

Perhaps it was that graceful exit, perhaps it was those few moments of closeness while we sat side by side on the piano bench, while Kate's melody synchronized with my simple chords, but not long after that I tried to talk to her.

I began by looking for an opportunity.

This was not easy because I had to find her alone, sober, and undistracted. Kate was often alone, she was sober much of the time, but she was almost always distracted. We quarreled about this endlessly—or rather I complained and Kate responded. She preferred to call it "busy." I said she never listened to me. She said she heard everything I said to her. I said she never looked at me, never gave me her full attention. She said that was nonsense, she was always looking out for me. I said looking *out for me* and looking *at me* were two different things. She said I was being irritable and silly. Was I feeling all right? I said I was trying to tell her how I felt but she wasn't listening.

So it went on, with minor variations, like the practice exercises I used to pound out on the piano.

Kate was sitting at the kitchen table when I opened the discussion, a few days after our session at the piano. It was just before sunset; the table was cleared; the dishes were washed. Frank and Win had just left to take an evening sail with Peggy and Peggy's father, who owned a boat—the Peggity—big enough for all of us. He had taught Win to sail years ago, and often invited the family along.

The light flushed golden red through the windows over the sink and spotlighted the linoleum—as clean as the dishes piled neatly on the rack to dry. I had watched Kate carefully; I knew she wasn't drinking. Frank, who would doubtless celebrate the glory of the evening with a drink or two shared with Peggy's father, had also gone off sober, cheerful at the prospect of a sunset sail. Kate could have gone but had refused, not liking to sail. I had refused because I was expecting Benson, but not until later, after Henderson's Garage closed.

I sat down across from my mother and clasped my fingers together, looking at her. Kate looked up in mild surprise from the newspaper she was reading.

"There's something I'd—like to ask you about," I said, feeling awkward, self-conscious.

"What is it?" said Kate, still with that look of mild surprise.

"It's about— It's about —" I paused and then blurted out, "I just want to know—when to stop—protecting—someone."

"Protecting? How?"

Kate fingered the edge of the newspaper, as if she wanted to turn the page, and waited for my response.

"Just—you know—not talking about what I—know."

"Is this person in trouble?" said Kate. "Is it one of your friends?"

"No," I said; then, "Yes."

"I see."

She glanced at me quickly, then glanced away, as though it hurt her eyes.

"Well."

She examined her hands, slightly smudged with newspaper ink. Kate had square-shaped hands, with short, blunt, unpolished nails. I thought of Gina's hands, each nail a perfect red oval.

"You have to do what's right."

"But that's what I don't *know*," I said, irritation stirring inside me. "I don't *know* what's right."

"Of course you do, Maggie. We all know what's right and what's wrong."

"How can you say that?" My voice rose. I stopped, swallowed, said, "I don't always know."

"Of course you—"

"I don't know, I tell you. I don't know."

Kate looked down at her newspaper. I saw her eyes move beneath her lids as she read a few lines. She looked up and said, almost apologetically. "I'm not helping you, am I? Maybe you should ask Dad—or Win."

"I'm asking you," I said, acknowledging the futility of our conversation but not willing to end it. Perhaps I wanted to watch her squirm a little.

"Is your friend— Is she—?"

"Nobody's pregnant, if that's what you mean."

Our roles had shifted. Now it was Kate asking questions and me holding back.

"What is it, then? Who is it you're—protecting?"

"I can't tell you until I know if it's right or wrong to protect them, can I?"

I was viciously sarcastic. Kate winced and looked away from me.

"I can't help you unless you tell me a little more, Maggie."

"Well, then, you can't help me."

The silence settled over us like a haze, fissured by the sudden busy hum of the refrigerator. A drowsy bird twittered in the bushes just beneath the windows. I wanted to cry out my frustration, but the sound that I made was a harsh grunt. Kate looked at me. Her eyes gleamed, like a rabbit caught in a headlight—or perhaps it was the reflected brilliance of the setting sun.

"Do you want to think about it a little more?" she said.

"Think about what? You haven't said anything."

"I'm trying—"

"Then just tell me. When do I stop protecting this—someone?"

"Is it Gina?"

I was startled into honesty.

"Yes," I mumbled, not looking at her.

"What has she done?"

Her voice was calm, but there was a fearful edge to it.

"Nothing—that I know of."

I thought of my father and Gina frantically grasping each other in the side room, of the two cars, Win's and Gina's, parked outside Fred Muncie's shack. Then I pushed the images away. What did I know, after all?

"But you suspect—"

"I'm guessing. I'm not sure. I'm probably wrong."

Kate examined her hands, wiping ineffectually at the ink stains. I watched the evening settling in. I watched my mother, wondering if I had said too much.

I needn't have worried. Kate could no more confront the reality of my need than she could the thought of Win and Frank in their separate but analogous snares. We were irritants, to be smoothed away by the application of alcohol, and a continual dose of life's little distractions.

"Perhaps you shouldn't be spending so much time there. Maybe you shouldn't take care of Ellie—"

"I need the money."

I snapped out the words, challenging her.

"Of course, Ellie is a sweet child but—"

"Ellie's not the problem."

"Of course not, but maybe you should distance yourself—"

"Like you do?"

I waited.

"What has Gina done, exactly?"

Her voice was timid, almost a whisper.

"I don't know, *exactly*." I couldn't resist the impulse to mock her. "Probably nothing."

Even as I forced the words out, I could feel the tension between us ebb. I could see the furrow between Kate's brows smooth itself out to the merest indentation. I could sense, almost palpably, her relief.

"If you saw something, or heard something—"

"No."

"Or if Gina told you something—"

"No."

"Then you're not—?"

"I'm probably just—"

"I know."

Kate smiled at me, the relief apparent in her voice.

"I've done the same thing. You think you know something, then you begin to doubt what you know, and then—"

She folded back a section of the newspaper, smoothed down the crease.

"Gina is— She's— Well, I guess you know she's not one of my favorite people."

"But then, who is?" I replied, but so low that Kate could ignore it.

"I like Phil, and Ellie—well, Ellie's not to blame for anything, is she?"

I looked away from her. I shook my head.

"She's barely five," she said, thoughtfully. "Timothy would have been—"

I nodded. It was useless to say that Timothy, my younger brother, was dead, while I was sitting across from her, needing her. She was giving me what she could. I rejected the habitual urge to stomp on it.

"I'm going out with Benson later. I guess I'll get ready."

"All right, Dear."

As I walked upstairs to my room, I realized I was clutching at that whispered endearment, so rare, and repeating it back to myself, again and again.

That night—as Benson and I sat in his roomy, comfortable Buick, watching the moon glide across the lake, and Win, Frank, Peggy, and Peggy's father sailed across its waters somewhere close by, and Kate soothed life's irritations with her hidden store, and Gina sat with Phil, trapped in the house she had filled with her treasures—I said to Benson, "Let's do whatever comes next."

And we did.

CHAPTER 30

It seemed as though Ellie could think of nothing but going to school. Her "little family" of dolls and stuffed toys sat in rows, attentively awaiting their next lesson. The day was divided into class time, "Reeshesh," and after school. There was a new collection of pencils, crayons, work paper of various hue and heft. The current date on the calendar was X'd out before bedtime, as just another day, scarcely worthy of note, while the first Tuesday in September had a circle carefully crayoned around it, which Ellie pointed out to me regularly.

"Firsht day of kinnergarten," she said. "Only thish many more dazh."

She counted them carefully, while I acknowledged her accuracy.

Her wardrobe was, as usual, supremely important. Gina continued to nurture her own vanity by encouraging Ellie's clothes pride. Almost everything in Ellie's closet was deemed unworthy and relegated to "Savashun Ernie." When I wasn't taking care of Ellie, I often saw the two of them emerging from Gina's little green Ford, juggling bags and boxes of new clothes and shoes. Shopping seemed to give Ellie an energy charge, just as it did Gina. I always smiled when I saw them hauling in their goods.

One afternoon in late August, I followed them into the house so that Ellie could show off her new purchases.

"Risha coat," demanded Ellie, clawing through various bags, looking at her mother accusingly. Rags sat on his haunches, watching her, unusually alert.

"I'm sure it's there somewhere, Ellie. We couldn't possibly have forgotten it. Try the box on the stool."

Ellie tore away the box, impatiently pulling at the tissue paper.

"See, Majee? See it? Ish red. Fer kinnergarten when it shnoze."

She held up a small wool coat. I admired it extravagantly, even though I'd never seen her in a coat or jacket that *wasn't* bright red.

Other items followed, one by one. I nodded and approved, until Gina called a halt, suggesting she arrange her new clothes in her closet.

"Cumunupun sheeum, okay, Majee?"

"Okay," I said. "In a minute."

She ran up the stairs, stumbling over dangling sleeves and slippery bags. Gina followed her to the foot of the stairs, watching her progress.

"Have you noticed how her speech is improving?" Gina said, coming back to the living room. I was frowning, my thoughts on Gina and Win rather than on Ellie. Before I could adjust my expression, she raised her eyebrows questioningly.

"Yes. I have," I said, trying to sound neutral and pleasant.

Ellie did seem to be speaking more clearly, but I wondered if it was genuine improvement, or just that I had adapted to her speech patterns. I didn't say this, though, not wanting to challenge Gina's assessment.

"How pretty you look today," she said, as though by rote. "That tan is very becoming."

"Thanks," I said, just as mechanically. "I've been in the sun a lot."

"And how is Benson?" she said, a hint of the old cheeky mockery in her voice.

I tried to suppress the warm flush that crept up over my tan, but I had yet to reach that level of sophistication.

"Benson is—just fine," I mumbled.

"Not a warty toad, I take it?"

"No," I said. "He's the prize."

She nodded, opened her mouth to say something, then thought better of it. She gathered up the remaining bags and packages, swept them to one side, then stretched herself out on the sofa, reaching out a hand to nuzzle Rags, who was, as usual, as close as he could get to her. She looked graceful, comfortable, at ease. I wondered at her composure and even envied it.

"We haven't talked for quite a while, have we?"

"No," I said. "We haven't."

"Why is that?"

I shrugged. I couldn't seem to look at her.

"Tell me about Benson."

I flushed again. She had said the one thing that made me set aside the urge to flee upstairs to Ellie and her new clothes.

"Well," I said, stumbling, self-conscious, but eager. It still seemed so natural to confide in Gina. "He's—special. He makes me laugh, and I like to—to—be close to him."

"Does he make your cells buzz?"

Her voice was so amused and affectionate that I laughed.

"Yes! Yes, he does."

She laughed with me. Some of the chill fell away. I felt, as I used to feel, nourished by her scrutiny. She reached for her purse, pulled out her cigarettes. I watched her as she pulled the book of matches from the cellophane wrapper and lit up.

"He doesn't—he isn't—like the other boys I've gone out with. He's—"

"Not the little-boy type," she said.

"Why, no, he's not!"

I looked at her gratefully.

"He's beyond the little-boy stuff."

"Yes! Yes, he is."

"And big and soft and cuddly, like a—"

She stopped. But then I saw Benson as she did, solid, somehow furry, with his thick brown hair, brown eyes, big hands and feet, winsome grin, small white teeth.

I giggled.

"Oh, all right. Like a teddy bear."

"Ellie's Pooh Bear," said Gina. "Or maybe—"

"Charger," I said.

She nodded and we both laughed.

Charger was an enormous brown teddy bear that Phil had brought home to Ellie after a lengthy absence, when she was recovering from chicken pox. The teddy bear was bigger than Ellie when she got him, and was still so unwieldy that we laughed whenever we watched her moving him around. Because of his size, Ellie left him in charge when she wasn't able to supervise her "little family." Thus, he became known as "Charger."

"I like Benson," said Gina, musing, blowing out smoke. "I think he's good for you."

I realized that, despite all, I had been waiting for her approval.

"It's funny, the people we need," she said. "It's not always what we expect."

I was curled up on one of Gina's matching green silk armchairs, my shoes on the floor. I began to tug at a loose thread on the edge of the arm, where many hands had rubbed, wearing away a small corner of the material.

"I think we're all born with something missing," said Gina. "Not something obvious, but something that we know belongs to us. Something that we know should be there, that will make us feel whole. So we grow up, wanting this—something—looking for it. When we find it, *if* we find it—"

"Yes?"

I was afraid she would stop, and I needed to hear all of what she was saying.

"Of course, it's not the same—what's missing—for everyone."

Gina puffed on her cigarette, exhaled thoughtfully

"Take me, for instance."

She slid an ashtray closer, flicked her cigarette over it.

I pulled at the thread on the armchair.

"I should have ordered matching arm covers for those chairs."

"Sorry," I said, releasing the thread.

She shook her head, dismissing her comment and my apology.

"With me—for me—it seems to be something I look for in men. Whenever I meet a man, I wonder—does he have it, what belongs to me, what I'm missing? Sometimes it seems that he does. I thought that Phil— He seemed so— But then—"

"Maybe it wasn't meant to be Phil, or any man," I said. "Maybe it's Ellie."

The corners of her mouth turned up, her face softened, as it always did when she was contemplating Ellie.

"I have thought that. Many times. Ellie's like an extension of me. Or maybe a very small, compact model made in my image. But still, she doesn't belong to me; she's just mine for a little while—while she's small, and helpless."

"She'll always need you," I said, thinking of Kate.

"Perhaps. But I can't be that missing piece for her, any more than she can be, for me. What I'm talking about doesn't come parent to child. What comes parent to child is—expectation, I think. Yes. I think it's expectation. Every child comes into the world burdened with it. Like Original Sin."

She sighed, impatiently.

"It's a wonder any of us survive. We're all handicapped before the race begins. That missing—something. Weighed down with our parents' expectations, and our universal guilt. You'd never know it to look at Ellie, though, would you?"

I shook my head.

We listened for a few moments, hearing the creak of the floorboards overhead, the barely audible rising and falling drone of Ellie's voice, as she moved around her room, chattering to her "little family."

Gina said, "I suppose I'm still looking for it, that missing something, in all the wrong places, but—I won't know what it is, or where it is, until I've found it."

"Then— Then— you haven't found it?"

Gina sat up straight, stomped out her cigarette in the ashtray, looked directly at me. She said, reluctantly, "I don't know."

I must have turned pale under my tan because she said, gently, "Are you all right?"

I nodded, my eyes averted.

"Majee, cumunup right *now*," Ellie called from the top of the stairs.

"She'll be up in a minute," Gina called back.

"Is it Win?" I said, seeing my mother's face as she said to me, *Is it Gina?*

Gina's almond eyes squinted slightly. She took a deep breath. Then, looking away from me, she shook her head, as if to shake off the question.

"That's not *fair*, Gina," I said, hearing how young I sounded as I said it. Like Ellie, with one of the older neighborhood children. One she couldn't quite bend to her will.

"Of course it's not fair," she said, soothing me, as she would Ellie.

"I'm not a child!"

"Of course you're not." She let a moment pass. "That's why I said—what I said."

"You can't have Win," I said. "He's ours. He belongs to us."

"Of course he does."

"And you have Phil."

"Yes. I have Phil."

She got up from the sofa, walked across to me, sat on the arm of my chair. She put her hand on my shoulder. I shrugged her hand off, covered my face with my hands, and cried. I felt ashamed, but I couldn't stop.

When I looked up, Ellie was peering at me quizzically.

"Whazamatta?" she said.

"Maggie's having a good cry," said Gina, still perched on the arm of my chair.

"Why?" said Ellie.

"She just felt like it," said Gina. "Sometimes, it feels good to cry."

"Oh," said Ellie.

After a respectful moment of silence, she added, "Cumunup now, okay, Majee?"

"Okay," I said, with a small sob.

"She'll be up soon, Ellie. Will you play quietly until she gets there?"

"Oh, okay," she said, resignedly.

She ran off, clattering up the stairs. Rags, who disliked the disturbance I was making, followed close behind her.

"I'm sorry, Maggie," said Gina, patting my shoulder, comforting me. " I thought you were ready to hear this. I was wrong."

She got up and paced. I leaned my head against the back of the chair and closed my eyes. When I opened them, Gina was sitting on the sofa again, curled up, as I was, her shoes tossed aside, her feet underneath her. She was puffing on another cigarette.

"Are you going to tell Kate?" she said.

"I don't know."

"Kate is—Maggie, maybe you don't want to hear this either, but your mother is—so fragile. Last New Year's Eve—"

"She got drunk. Here. In your house."

"Yes."

"Why? Why did she get drunk?"

Gina shrugged. "I guess she thought Frank was—a little too friendly."

"What do you mean? What happened?"

"It was New Year's Eve, Maggie. Everybody is a little too friendly on New Year's Eve."

She added, almost under her breath, "Everybody except Kate, of course."

Then she went on, "At any rate, the friendlier we got, the more Kate drank. She sort of—hung back, got quieter and quieter, although she was pleasant enough, whenever we talked."

I rearranged myself on the chair, wiped at my damp eyes, quivering with a sort of defensive rage, as though I were Kate.

"I don't know your mother very well, Maggie. I don't know anyone who does, except for your father. But it was almost as though she wasn't really there, with us. The more she drank, the further away she seemed to go. After midnight, after things wound down, I told Frank to take her home. Her speech was slurred, she was very unsteady, but it was more than that. We were all drunk by that time. She reminded me of a china figurine, teetering on the edge of a table, ready to fall off and break into a dozen pieces."

She took a drag on her cigarette, then blew out a long column of smoke. I was silent, picking at that loose thread again, wanting to unravel the upholstery as Gina was unraveling me, making me feel like a child again—angry, helpless, frustrated.

"I'm sure I'm not telling you anything you don't already know."

When I didn't respond, she went on, "Of course, we're all pretty fragile, if you look close enough. By the time we grow up, we've all got hairline cracks here and there. But Kate …"

She took a breath.

"When we first moved here, I tried to get to know her. We are, after all, next-door neighbors. But I don't know her any more than I did two years ago, after that first get-together in your back yard. Win says—"

I looked up, waiting for her next words. Gina's face changed, perceptibly. She seemed to be thinking of something—remembering something—that made her happy.

"Win says she was born out of her time. She should be wearing long skirts and petticoats, lace down to her wrists and up around her neck."

She stopped talking. I waited, knowing there was more.

"Frank told me once—"

She hesitated.

"He said …"

"What did he tell you?" I said, my voice shrill, demanding, knowing I wasn't meant to hear this, that whatever Gina said would be a betrayal, would dishonor both my parents.

"He said—he said she wasn't comfortable—he couldn't remember when he last saw her—completely naked."

I stood up, planting my bare feet on the floor.

"Why would he tell you that?"

Gina started; she bit her bottom lip, as if to bite back her words.

"I don't—remember," she said, quickly. "Maybe he didn't. That is, I'm sure he didn't tell just me. Or maybe he said it in company, just to tease her. You know how Frank likes to make your mother blush. It was probably during one of those so-called 'adult' party discussions, when we're all more than a little drunk and saying embarrassing things about our spouses ..."

I scooped up my shoes, started walking toward the front door.

"I've got to go," I said.

I didn't trust myself to stay in the same room with her. I wanted to scratch at her face, see the blood flow down her cheeks.

"Maggie?"

I stopped, rooted to the carpet, as though my bare feet were embedded in its exotic flower pattern. Gina was standing just behind me. I could hear her breathing. I could smell the cigarette she had been smoking. Her voice was cracked, high-pitched—not the confident tone I was used to hearing.

"Will you stay a little longer? Can we talk a little more?"

"I can't."

"Are you sure?"

"Yes."

I padded barefoot down the hall, pushed open the screen door, walked out onto the porch, still warm underfoot from the afternoon sun.

As the screen door banged behind me, I heard Ellie running downstairs, calling out to me, "Majee, wherrur you going?"

I didn't answer her. I didn't turn around.

I never saw Ellie again.

CHAPTER 31

If we could just finish things. If I could only go back in time, curl up on Gina's green silk armchair, and talk to her, and listen to her. If I could just run upstairs with Ellie, sit cross-legged on her pink quilted bedspread, admire her new clothes, and "ooh" and "aah" while she chattered. If only Phil would call me "Blondie," and tease me about being so grownup …

Gina called me, once, early in September, to see if I would stay with Ellie, but I said I was too busy, with school, and working at Steed's Variety Store, and homework, and Benson. She didn't ask me again. Ellie's alternate babysitter was Izzy Shoemaker, a sophomore. I saw her now and then in the halls, between classes. She was the younger sister of one of Win's friends, which is, I suppose, why Gina asked her to take care of Ellie.

Prue said it was about time I got out from under Mrs. Gregorka's thumb. She said everybody was talking about

Gina, and the only reason I didn't know about it was because I spent so much time at her house, babysitting Ellie, who should have been with her mother, anyway. Sharon fluttered around me like I'd just come back from a long trip, more interested in Benson than in Gina. She asked me a few questions about Gina, and a lot of questions about Benson and me. She'd never dated anyone who was out of school.

I was an upperclassman that fall. It felt good to walk down the halls in my new clothes, nod to my friends, feel the eyes of the junior and senior boys following me as I walked past them standing in hunch-shouldered clumps, knowing that it wouldn't take much to lure a chosen one or two of them off their perch. After all, Gina had taught me well.

After school, we gathered at Zimmer's, or I went to Steed's, where I could count on seeing someone or other I knew, someone my own age, among the staid middle-aged browsers and shoppers. Benson would pick me up after work or stop by late in the evening, after Henderson's Garage closed. My mother was always gracious when Benson came by, even if she'd been drinking, and my father was embarrassingly hearty.

Win had gone back to State after the funeral, where, for all I knew, he might have continued to see Gina, or he might not have. He never talked about her, or asked about her. Of course, we were all preoccupied, "with everything at sixes and sevens," as my grandmother, Kate's mother, often said.

After things calmed down, nobody talked much about Gina, or Ellie. For a while, though, it seemed as though nobody talked about anything else.

Lucy Monroe had been leaving Johnson's Dry Cleaning, right next door to Reinhart's Bakery, when the accident happened. She told Prue's mother it sounded just like somebody hit a baseball on the street. There was a screech of brakes, then a hard "pop." Mrs. Monroe had been at least eight months pregnant then. She said it gave her such a start she thought she might have the baby right there on the street. Fortunately, Mr. Johnson took hold of her just as she got dizzy and started to lose her balance. He helped her to her car. She had a little baby girl, right on schedule, and Prue's mother said she called her "Rebecca Eleanor," in remembrance of Ellie.

Poor Mrs. Prelski hadn't been seen since the accident. I had heard that her family took her away for a while. Someone said she had a daughter in Duluth. The newspaper story said she had been "questioned and released." It also said she was 77 years old, and hadn't even had a parking ticket in more than thirty years.

The "incident'" happened just after noon. Ellie was "pronounced dead" at 4:00 p.m.

Of course, no one blamed Mrs. Prelski. They all felt sorry for her, and hoped they would never have to live out the last years of their lives with that kind of guilt and pain. Ellie Gregorka had run right in front of the car. Mrs. Prelski wasn't doing more than 25 or 30 miles an hour. It was the way she was hit, they said, and the way she hit the pavement, head first. If she had lived, they said, she would have had "closed-head injury," and would have been "a helpless, drooling little puppet of a child," barely able to hold her head up.

Later on, Fred Muncie gave my parents and me a first-hand account of the accident.

"I was down the street, just coming out of church, when I heard the commotion," Fred began. "Sounded like all hell broke loose. During the week, I like to sit in church for five minutes or so on my lunch hour. It's dark, and quiet. Peaceful. Almost never see anybody there, not even the padre. The whole place kind of belongs to me, you know? Well, anyways, I was coming out of church, almost blinded by the light, when I heard these sirens. Not like your ordinary sirens, speed calls and that. These horns meant business.

"Everybody was headed toward Reinhart's Bakery, so I just followed along, thinking the place might of caught on fire. Couldn't see no smoke, though. Then I saw that crowd in the middle of the street, and Jim Haas, the sheriff, re-directing traffic. I knew, right then, it was an accident. A bad one.

"I pushed my way through the crowd. Jim saw me, and nodded. Then he looked down at the street where the medics were surrounding this little bundle, covered with a blanket. It was so small I thought it was an animal, maybe a dog. I wondered for a second why all the fuss. Then I saw them put the bundle on a stretcher. I saw it was a child, and I saw Lil Prelski looking out through the windshield of her car, her eyes all glazed over, blood running down the side of her face. Everybody was craning their necks to see better, like spectators at a circus. I stood there like a jackass and made the sign of the cross. I was that spooked."

He stopped for a moment and rubbed his forehead.

"I didn't even know it was the Gregorka kid at that point. I hadn't asked around. It was just this sick feeling I had, standing there in that crowd, the sun beating down on my head, that God had snapped His fingers and snuffed the life out of that little bundle. Just like that. A hell of a thing, that kind of accident. Lil Prelski will probably never get over it. Good woman, Lil. Sits in the same pew every Sunday. Well, used to. She hasn't been around lately. I hear she left town for a while. She was married to Stan Prelski, remember him, Frank? Counselor Stan? Had an office up above the bank? Drew up everybody's will for fifty years, at least. A deacon in the church till the day he died."

Fred looked around at us.

"What do you hear about the Gregorka woman? Phil's wife? I hear it hit her pretty hard. Son of a gun, she had a voice. I used to listen to her singing up there behind us in the choir and think, Christ, she sings like a goddamned bird. Good looking, too. Pleasing to the eyes. Pleasing to the ears. Just as well we couldn't see her up there in the choir. Distracting, that kind of woman."

There was a pause, then my father said, "I guess she and Phil split up. Last I heard she was staying with her mother, back in Hillsville. Ready for another beer, Fred?"

Later, Fred said to my father, "Did I tell you somebody broke into the shack over the summer? Didn't do any harm. Everything's just about like it was, maybe even a little cleaner. Definite signs of life, though—tires tracks and all. It sure as hell wasn't raccoons. Not unless they're given' out drivers' licenses to critters with furry tails and a mask."

Of course, there's always somebody who has to make a joke out of somebody else's loss. I suppose it makes that person feel less afraid. Death is so absolute. There's no reprieve, no second chance. Maybe that's why the Church invented Purgatory, that waiting room for the soul, where those of us who aren't very good and aren't very bad languish until we're more deserving of our reward. The thing is, Purgatory must be very crowded because most of us aren't very good and aren't very bad. Even Gina. Besides, she was already in Purgatory, in her mother's house, in Hillsville, waiting for whatever came after Ellie.

Anyway, it was Prue's dreadful Ed who actually made us laugh over Ellie's death. Even me. We were at Zimmer's, having a Coke and talking about school, the movie we'd just seen, other things. It was the first time Benson and I had double-dated with Prue and Ed. I wasn't keen on our going out together, but Prue wanted to get to know Benson, and Benson didn't care. He was easygoing to a fault, my Benson. I thought a movie would be best, because we wouldn't have to talk much, or spend too much time looking at Ed.

I don't know how we got on the subject. I guess it had been during that time when, sooner or later, we all talked about Ellie, and Gina, and the accident. Most everybody was careful what they said around me, but Ed doesn't know about tact, even though it's a one-syllable word. He just opens his mouth and out the words come, like one of those candy machines with a glass head. Put a coin in, the jaw drops down, and the candy slides out of the slot.

Prue said her mother said everybody tried to be nice to Gina after the accident, after Gina came home. But there was a lot of speculation about where she was when it happened, and why nobody could find her. The accident happened on a Friday. Gina didn't get home until Saturday morning. That was when I saw her run into the house, screaming Ellie's name.

I heard that scream. I was on my front porch, sitting back in the shadows on an old rocker Kate had put out there during the summer. I was waiting for Gina to come home, as was Phil, and Gina's mother, and Mrs. Boetcher, and everybody else in the neighborhood. They had located Phil right away, through his head office, but neither he nor anyone else knew where Gina was. Even Izzy Shoemaker didn't know for sure. She didn't know Gina very well, or Ellie. I had always been Ellie's sitter. I had always been available.

Mrs. Boetcher was right. When Gina drove up in her little green Ford coupe, barely stopping the car before she got out and ran into the house, calling her daughter—Ellie's name an endless drawn-out howl of pain—Mrs. Boetcher said she sounded just like the police and ambulance sirens we hear occasionally in our small town. In fact, I've never heard a siren since that I haven't heard and felt Gina's scream somewhere inside that sound. I don't think that will ever go away.

I stood up, the rocker throbbing gently behind me, but I stayed in the shadows, that scream hanging in the air like smoke. I heard Phil's voice through the open windows, then Gina's, then Phil's, then silence.

After that, old Mrs. Ennis's house, that Gina had refurbished and filled with her treasures, with Ellie, and with her own vivid presence, seemed to shut down, to sag, like an elderly face. I have never since been inside that house, not even for the open house that Phil and Gina's mother arranged after Ellie's funeral.

Benson said, while we sipped our Cokes at Zimmer's, "Did anybody ever say where Mrs. Gregorka was that day, the day of the accident?"

Prue shook her head and looked at me. I looked down at my Coke.

"I heard she was in Cognito," said Ed.

He sucked up the last of his drink with a resounding "*Thwip*."

"What?" I said.

"Somebody told me that," he said.

"Told you what?" I said.

"That she was in Cognito."

"Where's that?" said Benson.

"That's what I said," said Ed.

"You idiot," said Prue.

"I looked it up on the map. I thought it might be on the other side of Hillsville, toward Ryeburg and Belton. No sign of it, though. Maybe it's further south."

"You're brain dead," said Prue.

Then she tittered, and Ed grinned. Benson looked sheepish, having fallen into Ed's trap, then smiled with his usual good humor. Prue leaned back in the booth, shaking with laughter. Ed glanced around at us expectantly.

After a few moments, we all roared, like a dam let loose, the booth vibrating. At the tables and booths around us, there was a brief hush while the other patrons paused to analyze the disturbance; then the babble of talk resumed.

I wiped at the teary edges of my eyes and looked at Ed. I didn't want to laugh; I wanted to cry; I wanted to rant at his over-the-top twisted sense of humor. But the joke, tasteless though it was, had been irresistible. It had released us, for a moment, from the grip of Ellie's death. In that moment, I almost—but not quite—liked him.

The speculation about where Gina was during those hours after the accident probably outlasted any other morsel of the gossip. Mrs. Granger said there was no excuse for it, no excuse at all.

"And to leave that poor little child in the care of a young girl like Izzy Shoemaker, and not say where she was? Inexcusable."

Mrs. Granger had stopped by to return a casserole bowl belonging to my mother, a bowl Kate had brought to a picnic the previous summer, and that Mrs. Granger "just happened" to come across that very morning.

"I hope you haven't missed it too much," said Mrs. Granger.

"I haven't missed it at all," said Kate, very polite, as always, but sending me a sidelong glance.

"Of course," Mrs. Granger continued, "we feel sorry for them, for Gina and Phil Gregorka, but how do you account for it? For that kind of heedless behavior? And think what it's done to Izzy Shoemaker. The guilt. The load of responsibility on those young shoulders."

I had seen Izzy often enough at school to conclude she wasn't overwhelmed by her carelessness. She giggled and chattered with her girlfriends like any teenager. She didn't appear in the least dejected. She was even somewhat smug, I thought, about her temporary notoriety.

"She told her mother, Fran Shoemaker—you know her, don't you, Kate?—that Mrs. Gregorka said she would be back on Saturday, and that Izzy was to stay until Phil got home, which would probably be Friday night but might be Saturday if he got held up, so Izzy was to bring clothes enough for overnight, as well as her schoolbooks. She gave Izzy the name of Ellie's doctor, and Phil's central office number, and a lot of instructions—so much Izzy said she couldn't remember any of it—and said she would call Izzy. She couldn't leave a number, she said, but she didn't say why. Can you imagine? When Izzy told her mother, Fran said she never would have let her sit if she had known, but it was too late, and Izzy should make the best of it."

Mrs. Granger stopped to catch her breath.

Kate nodded, but said nothing.

"Well. That was Friday morning, before school. Izzy said she parked her things in the spare bedroom Gina—Mrs. Gregorka—had shown her, then she and Ellie left for school. Izzy held her hand all the way there. She said Ellie chattered like a magpie the whole time, but Izzy couldn't understand what she was saying—that speech problem, you know—although Ellie got along just fine with her little friends, despite that handicap. So Izzy just nodded and smiled. Then she left Ellie at her classroom door and said she'd come back for her at noon. Ellie said something, but Izzy couldn't understand her, then Ellie went into her classroom, Izzy went to her classes at the high school, and that was that."

As Mrs. Granger seemed to be waiting, Kate said, "Why, then, wasn't she there to meet Ellie at noon?"

Mrs. Granger nodded with satisfaction.

"Yes, indeed, that's the question on everybody's lips. Izzy, to give credit where credit's due, says she was there at noon—only a few minutes late. She told her mother she couldn't get her locker open, or she forgot a book, or something of the sort. Anyways, when she got there, Ellie had run off by herself, probably forgetting Izzy's instructions, or not having heard them, or not having understood them. That speech problem, you know."

She paused.

I wondered what link there was between Ellie's speech defect and her ability to understand Izzy's instructions, but I kept quiet.

Then, she went on.

"Miss Steuben was just gathering up her things when Izzy came by looking for Ellie. She said, no, she hadn't seen Ellie leave, and didn't she leave with Mrs. Gregorka, as usual? And wasn't she a bright, enthusiastic little girl? Izzy left and ran after Ellie, going just as fast as she could, but by then it was too late. She heard Mrs. Prelski hit her brakes just as she came around the corner. By the time she got there, she had to push through a crowd of onlookers to see what had happened. Fran said Izzy said she sat down on the curb and cried, until the police started asking questions. Fran says she keeps telling Izzy it's not her fault, but she's afraid the poor thing will be scarred for life."

I cried for Ellie too, when I heard, cried and cried, until Kate, standing outside my bedroom door, her words a little slurred, said, "It's okay now. He's okay now. I know he is."

I lifted up my head and listened, wondering who she was talking about, but then she went away. Later, I thought it must have been that she was thinking about Timothy, my little brother who died just before he was born. Or could she have been thinking about Win?

Kate called Win Friday evening, to let him know about the accident, and to see if he could come home for the funeral, which was scheduled for Monday. But nobody at the dorm knew where he was. They hadn't seen him since Friday morning. They thought he might have stayed over with a friend. They would give him the message as soon as he got back.

My mother was never far from the phone that evening, and the next morning. When Win called, on Saturday morning, I was close by, listening to her.

"Yes. Yes, I know, dear. Yes. A tragic accident. Everyone's so upset. I thought you should know. That dear child. She just ran across the street and— What? Yes. She was coming home from kindergarten. No. It was noon. The students are still on half days. Hmmm? No. Maggie wasn't taking care of her. She hasn't had time lately. She feels so guilty. She's devastated.

"It was Izzy Shoemaker. That's right, Paul's younger sister. No, we don't know where she was. Probably right there with Ellie. A child can slip away so easily. It just takes a moment—

"Yes, they got hold of Phil right away, but your father said Gina didn't call home until a little while ago, to check on Ellie. No, Ellie was taken to the hospital, but she never woke up— I think it was late in the afternoon. They said—"

She listened for a moment.

"Well, I saw Gina's mother, with Phil, so I suppose— No, I don't think anyone else is there, unless Gina is already back— Yes, Win, I'm sure. There's no mistake. I know people say things that are— But— Ask who? Win, try to— No, I haven't been over there but your father— Yes. Frank was over there last night, after Phil got home from the hospital, and again this morning. Gina's mother was making all the arrangements—"

She stopped again, listening.

"What? Did he say what? Well, of course, Phil was frantic. He didn't know how to get hold of Gina. She didn't say— Nobody knew— Phil tried every place he could think of. He even called the police. They looked for her car, checked hospitals—"

It was then that I had gone out on the porch and sat down on the rocker. I could still hear my mother's voice on the phone. It was unusual to hear her talk so much. I listened, my mind hovering between avid curiosity and a stony indifference.

"You'll be here when? Tomorrow? Yes, tomorrow night is fine. The funeral is Monday morning. Well, yes, they have to go ahead with these things, even if Gina is—

"Yes, I'm sure it will be in all the papers. There was a story about the accident in the *Gazette*. This morning. On the front page. The photo just showed a lot of people and the ambulance—

"Green Street. Yes. Near Reinhart's Bakery. Right at the intersection. You know Ryeburg Road has a fair amount of traffic— Mrs. Prelski, maybe you remember her, she goes to our church; her children— No, she wasn't speeding, Ellie just—

"No, Win, it wasn't her fault. Even Phil doesn't blame her, the poor soul. Phil is—

"All right, dear. I'm sorry to have to tell you all this—

"Yes. I know. We'll see you— All right, dear. Yes. Bye."

Gina must have called about 8:00. State was three hours away, according to Win, if you drove at a good clip. She was probably half-way home by now …

The sky was a deep September blue, with a few clouds scudding by. The air was warm, soft, slightly crisp, expectant.

Gina told me once that she hated this time of year, that she could smell death in the air, but for me it was a time of heightened sensation, of ravishing clarity. Perhaps it was just because it was the time of year when school began.

For Ellie, that had been the magic of September, the September she looked forward to all summer long as she marked the days off on her calendar. For those few days, I thought, as I sat on the rocker, she had awakened each morning to blue sky and the wonder of "kinnergarten." She had run to the window to salute the sun, then to her closet to choose her costume for the day, then to wake up Gina, perhaps to climb in bed with her and nuzzle up to her, while Gina yawned and smiled and said, "Yes, yes," to Ellie's excited babbling, perhaps to invite Rags to share their first moments of the day, and, of course, Phil, waking up on the other side of the bed, if he was there.

And then to wash and dress and dash through breakfast and hurry Gina to the door and hug Phil and pat Rags and clatter down the porch steps and wait impatiently for Gina to take her hand and lead her to this new playground, this "kinnergarten" of noisy children and new books, a real desk with a chair attached to it and a top that opened up so that you could store pencils and gum, and the small red canvas bag Gina had bought for her, and chalk scraping across a blackboard as wide as a wall, and a kind lady who smiled and clapped her hands when she looked at Ellie's work pages.

Better than playing school. Better than being teacher to the neighborhood children and a select few of her "little family."

At the funeral, there was a photo of Ellie. It was propped among the banks of flowers, close to the small glossy white coffin. The photo had been taken by Mr. Mac of Mac's Studio, a local photographer who had been running a special on children's portraits over the summer. Ellie was wearing one of her frilly 'partydreshiz,' her plump elbows resting on a table, her chin on her hands, and she was looking out at us with such an eager smile; there was such crackling energy in her face that I couldn't look at it. I turned away, and looked at the cross over the altar, with the near-life-sized Christ hanging in pale, semi-naked agony, his face turned up in exhausted supplication, painted drops of blood frozen in place where the crown of thorns pierced his forehead, and the nails were driven through his hands and—placed carefully one over the other—his feet.

He had hung there for three hours, they say. For me, that Saturday morning, while I sat on the porch, in the shadows, rocking back and forth, watching the clouds hurry across the sky as if they were going someplace, those hours seemed to stretch out endlessly. The neighborhood was quiet, the occasional bawl of a child hushed imperatively by a parent. We all seemed to be waiting.

Children are impatient, though. Apple-cheeked Donald Morgan, four doors up the street, may have listened when Mr. and Mrs. Morgan said to him, "Poor Ellie

Gregorka was hit by a car. She was running across the street. Remember what we told you about crossing the street? No, she won't be getting better. She was too badly hurt. Her parents are very sad."

But it's Saturday morning. The sun is out and Donald can almost feel its warmth on his skin. He eats his cereal and drinks his juice, looking glum, not meeting the sidelong glances of his mother and father. Then Mr. Morgan looks at Mrs. Morgan and shrugs. Mrs. Morgan nods, then says to Donald, "All right. Play outside if you like. But no shouting. And no noisy games. And don't cross the street, even if Joey begs you to. And no—"

Donald is already out the door, his sturdy legs carrying him far away from the sound of his mother's voice, the sun in his eyes, heading straight for his tricycle, new on his birthday last February, now lying on the front walk, on its side, scarred and dented.

Soon he is pedaling down the street full tilt, wheels squealing, "Push on, push on, push on." He's heading for Joey Granger's back yard, next door to us—not even glancing at Ellie's house, two doors down from the Grangers.

And then the sounds of the neighborhood pick up, as other children run outside, and Mr. Granger revs up his lawnmower to shave his yellowing grass, and Mrs. Boetcher sweeps her porch, and Helen Mowby's voice is raised in angry rebuke as yet another child tramps through her late-blooming flowers. A few cars sail up and down the street, propelled by the warm September breeze.

And I realized that no one was waiting, except me, and maybe Kate, and Phil, and Gina's mother. The momentary sensation of Ellie's death had already peaked, shock had been followed by sympathy, sympathy by curiosity, and even curiosity was fading into the pressing concerns of the day.

"Most of us can count on our fingers the number of people who care about us, really care about us," Gina had said to me once, on one of our early morning walks. "And most of us don't need both hands to add them up."

We had walked to the cemetery that morning. Gina had been sitting on one of the carved marble stones, resting, smoking a cigarette.

"But there are all of our friends, and our family," I had said.

"After my father's funeral—I wasn't much older than Ellie—I said to my mother, 'There were nine people at the cemetery, Mommy. I counted them. Is that a lot?' My mother said to me, 'It's enough.'"

"Was your father very old?"

"Not even forty. Bad heart. They were both past their prime when I was born. I was a late child. Rather a nuisance, I think. Certainly a handful. 'What shall we do with the child?' they used to say, as though I were an unexpected guest they didn't have room for."

I don't remember any other time when Gina talked about herself as a child. Her life seemed to begin in her teens. Maybe that's why she watched my progress with such interest.

There were more people at Ellie's funeral than I could count on my fingers. The whole neighborhood turned out, along with relatives and friends of the Gregorkas I'd never seen before, and some people I was sure Phil and Gina had never seen before. The stories in the papers had caused a mild sensation. A lot of people, it seemed, came out of curiosity.

"You'd think people had some goddamned other things to do on a Monday morning," Frank said, after the funeral service, as we drove in slow ceremonious parade out to the cemetery where Gina and I used to watch the sun come up. "Did you see the number of gawkers in that church? I'd lay odds they never set eyes on Ellie before, or the Gregorkas."

Father Flint, dignified in his flowing black vestments, conducted the funeral service with self-conscious flair, as though in tribute to the public attention given Ellie's death.

Win, sitting between me and Kate, gripped his arms across his chest and lowered his head, like a bull about to charge.

But Father Flint couldn't begin to upstage Gina, who sat in the front row between Phil and her mother. Gina was wearing a red suit and a frilly white blouse that cascaded around her neck and emerged from beneath the cuffs like drooping petals.

Ellie had danced with excitement when Gina brought home that outfit.

"Ishjushlike mine!" she had said, and then she insisted that I stay so they could show me. A few minutes later, Gina and Ellie had walked slowly down the stairs, smiling at me, smiling at each other—so pleased with themselves. I stood at the foot of the stairs and applauded.

Even though the glossy white casket was closed, I knew Ellie lay with her hands crossed over her favorite "partydresh"—red, with white frills at the neck and cuffs.

I had never seen Win as angry and glowering as he had been the night before, when he came home for the funeral.

"Is everybody asleep in this godforsaken town?" he said, as we sat in the living room. "Can't they see a kid crossing the street?"

"That's not fair, Win," said Kate. "It wasn't her fault. Ellie ran right out in front of Mrs. Prelski's car."

"And where were you?" Win said, ignoring her, turning to me. "I thought you took care of Ellie."

"Not lately," said Kate. "Maggie has been too busy."

"Too busy. Shit. Too busy."

"There's only one person responsible for that child's death and that's her mother," said Frank.

"Don't say that," said Kate, visibly wincing.

"Why not? It's the goddamned truth. Where was she? What was she doing that was so important she couldn't take care of her own kid?"

"She'll mourn that child till the day she dies, Frank. That's punishment enough."

"Why should she be punished at all?" said Win. "What did she do that was so wrong?"

"I didn't mean—" said Kate.

"She's not a fucking kangaroo," said Win. "She couldn't carry Ellie around in a pouch everywhere she went."

"Nobody said—"

"It's a goddamned crying shame, that's all," said Frank. "She was a cute little kid. Never understood a word she said but she was cute as a button. She shouldn't be planted in a goddamned marble orchard with all those old farts."

Win glared at him but said nothing.

"We can't change that," said Kate.

"Nobody can change anything," said Win. "What's the use of talking about it?"

"I need a drink," said Frank.

"I'll have one with you," said Kate.

They both got up and went into the kitchen. Win and I sat on, in silence. Finally, Win said, "I didn't mean it. What I said. I'm just so damned—"

He stopped. I bit my lip, unwilling to show Win my anger, my sadness, my guilt.

"Are you all right?" he said.

I nodded.

We sat on, silent mourners, somehow closer during those wordless few minutes than we'd ever been before.

After the funeral, before we went to the cemetery, Win murmured something to Kate and left. We didn't see him again until Thanksgiving. His game fell off after he went back to State; he almost lost his basketball scholarship. He did better during the Christmas holidays, though. Once or twice, I heard the old heedless assurance in his voice.

I'm glad Win wasn't there when Gina finally got back, her "Ellie-e-e-e-e!" bringing everybody in the neighborhood outside, as though the accident were happening at that moment and not the day before. My father wasn't at home either. My mother came out on the porch and looked at me, questioning me, but I couldn't answer her, not even with my eyes.

My father carefully distanced himself from Gina after the accident, while giving his support and sympathy to Phil. He spent some time with Phil on Friday night, and again on Saturday morning, and he and my mother went to Tibbit's Funeral Home on Sunday. They told me Gina wasn't there, that Phil and Gina's mother were greeting the guests. Gina's mother told Kate they wanted an open casket but Gina "raved" at the suggestion, so they had decided to put Ellie's photograph next to the closed coffin. It was a shame, though, Gina's mother told Kate. Ellie looked so pretty, and Mr. Tibbit had done such a good job.

"Gina should have been there when people came to pay their respects," said Frank on Sunday afternoon, after they had been to the funeral home. "Phil shouldn't have been obliged to make excuses for her."

"I suppose she was still too upset," said Kate. "Gina's mother said she was there in the morning, but then left as soon as people started coming."

"Phil's upset, too," said Frank. "Damned upset. Cried like a baby Friday night. Said Ellie and Gina were his whole goddamned world and now Ellie was gone and Gina was missing— Where the hell was that woman all that time?"

Kate glanced quickly at me, then said, "Nobody seems to know, Frank. She was always a loving and conscientious mother, though, wasn't she, Maggie? No one ever faulted her for that."

"It's a hell of a thing, that's all I can say. Disappearing like she did, and then holing up in that house all day yesterday, and then ducking out of the funeral home. A hell of a thing."

CHAPTER 32

When I opened the front door and walked out, early Sunday morning—the day before Ellie's funeral—the air was soft, moist, bracing. I carefully closed the door, pulling my sweater around me to ward off the pre-dawn chill. It was so still my footsteps echoed on the sidewalk as I walked quickly out of town. Even the birds were reluctant to wake up. They chirped, then were silent, chirped again, then were silent again.

I began to feel warmer. My cheeks glowed as I stepped up my pace. By the time I left behind the shaded streets, I was wide awake. I crossed another street and followed Old Creek Road as it opened out into fields, a few ranch houses set far back from the road, the occasional barn, with unpaved roads like spider veins branching off on either side. Farther on, another mile or so down the road, was the wooded hill with the gently descending dirt road that led to a plank bridge, a tractor path skirting the water, and the one-room shack owned by Fred Muncie. But I wasn't going there. I was headed for the cemetery that sprawled over the crest of the next rise, surrounded by a wreath of trees, with a bank thick with scrub alongside the creek.

The light was edging the horizon as I reached the path that led into the cemetery. It touched the marble stones and gave them a pale iridescent sheen. I walked between them, through the wet green grass, toward the knoll, where I could just make out a dark figure sitting on a wrought iron bench.

"I thought here would be good," said Gina, as I approached her. "It's quiet, away from the road. There are trees, and the creek just below. And this bench. I can sit here and talk to her. There are things I need to say to her."

I stood at the edge of the bank, looking down at the creek. I could hear it gurgling as it made its way over and around the small rocks, mounds of dirt, branches and leaves—obstructions put there by nature, man, and numberless generations of beavers.

"I like it here," I said.

"It has been sanctioned by our many walks hereabouts, hasn't it, Maggie? And the talks we had here."

"Yes," I said.

"Those talks were—a kind of rehearsal. I wanted to say those things—a lot of those things—to Ellie, when she was ready to hear them."

"I know," I said.

Not knowing, but wanting to say that I understood.

"Did you? How dear you are, Maggie."

I gulped, wiping at my face with the back of my hand, but Gina wasn't looking at me. She hadn't noticed.

"I wish—I wish I had been there."

"Been there?" I said, choking on the words.

"With Ellie—there—when it—before it—I wouldn't have let it —happen."

I heard her sigh, or perhaps it was the sound of the creek below us.

I looked around at the reddish flush on the horizon. The early morning bird chorus picked up, swelling with the light. The sky was pale blue, almost transparent.

"It's—so beautiful," I said.

Gina did not reply. I sat tentatively on the opposite end of the bench, the cold iron chilling my backside, my legs. Gina did not move. I think she had forgotten I was there.

"I don't know what I was looking for," she said. Not to me.

She was staring at the marble stones, some flat against the ground, others rising up in shapes as alike and various as the human face—oval, round, blunt, sharp—stones inscribed with the marks and scars of a long life, blue-gray in the rising light, identifying what no longer claimed identity, was no longer there, beneath the surface—had, in fact, changed substance, become indistinguishable from its neighbors.

I sat beside her, speechless. Once again, we watched the sun rise up, bringing with it a pure, bright, unsullied day.

Gina said, "I knew it would be sunny."

As if she wouldn't have it any other way.

Then, she said, "Do you remember the hospital?"

I started, thinking of Ellie in the hospital after the accident, in the deep sleep she never woke up from, doctors hovering over her bruised, unresponsive body. I had pictured her there, again and again, since Friday. But Gina hadn't been there, nor had I.

"Do you remember how she loved those pitiful remnants? That bear with no eyes and one ear, its stuffing coming out? And that putty-colored lamb—it must have been one of her first stuffed toys—barely identifiable after Rags got hold of it? And all those dolls, from the time she was not much bigger than them? And that p-p-p-pig?"

Her voice rose to a high-pitched stutter, then she stopped, drew in long breaths, as if she had been running.

I nodded. I said, reaching for a response, "She had that hospital for a long time. Sometimes I was the doctor and she was the nurse."

"I know," said Gina. "She told me."

She took another deep breath.

"She never gave up on them. No matter how bruised and broken and old and dirty they got to be."

"They were her 'little family,'" I said. "She had to take care of them."

"Just like I took care of her."

I could think of nothing to say, so there was a long silence.

Then Gina went on, as if she were simply continuing a thought, "Every time Phil or I brought home a new doll or a new stuffed toy, we would say to Ellie, 'Now you can throw out Lucy Bear'—or Tom the Giraffe, or Miss Blue—that was the doll with the missing arm and leg, and not much of a face, either. Ellie would cross her arms, set her mouth, and say, 'No. I won't.' We got so we would tease her, knowing what she would say."

We listened to the gurgling of the creek, the swelling chatter of the birds; then Gina said, "Most of us get rid of the things we disfigure and break, even as children. I wonder what it was in Ellie—"

Her voice hovered in the air, like an unfinished chord.

"I didn't stop loving her, you know. Not ever. I just forgot about her, for a moment."

"Forgot—?"

"Just then. Just for that moment, when she let go. I wasn't there for her."

"I don't—"

"It doesn't matter. We were—I was—someplace else, not holding her in my thoughts. That's when it happened."

"How do you—?"

"I just do. I know. It wasn't when the car hit her. I was still holding on then. It was later, when she was in the hospital. I was someplace so— I didn't want anyone else there with us, even Ellie—"

My mind buzzed and whirred and circled around her words, trying to understand, wanting to keep up with her. My confusion must have been evident in my blinking eyes, my mouth open to form a question, because Gina said, "Never mind. It doesn't matter now."

"Were you—?"

I began, then stopped, while I formed the question I had thought about for so long.

"Were you in that—place?"

Gina's eyes narrowed, her expression suddenly cool, hostile. I shook my head, anxious to explain myself.

"That—special place you told me about once."

"I never told you about— What place?"

"You called it—a windless place."

I all but whispered the words.

Gina looked at me solemnly until I blushed. Then her face cleared. Her almond eyes flickered.

"Yes. I suppose I was in that—place—or at least I thought I was. What made you remember that?"

I shrugged.

Gina said, as if to herself, "Was I? Was that it? … The calm at the center …"

I waited for her to go on, but she didn't. She squinted at the sun and said nothing. At last I shivered, despite the sun.

"Maybe you'd better go home," she said. "It's chilly here."

"I'll wait for you. We can walk back together."

"No. Don't wait for me." Gina's voice was flat, emphatic. "Phil will be out here later, with one of Tibbit's gnomes, to look at the—to see where—where we'll put Ellie."

"I could—"

"No. I want—I need—this time, before they get here. It's good you came, though."

She paused.

"Why *did* you come?"

"I don't know," I said. "I just woke up and got dressed and—here I am."

"Yes. Here you are," she said.

But it was as though she no longer heard what I was saying, no longer cared.

I got up, pulling my sweater around me.

"Well, I guess I'll go home then."

When she didn't respond, I said, "I'll see you—"

I stopped, thinking about the funeral, where I would see her next.

"Yes. See you," Gina said, absently.

I waited a few moments, awkward as an uninvited guest, then raised my hand in a farewell salute. But Gina didn't notice. I stumbled across the smooth plots of grass until I reached the footpath that led to the road. On Old Creek Road, I was again surefooted. I covered the mile or so back to town in less than twenty minutes.

I didn't see Gina after the funeral, and we didn't see much of Phil either, before they both moved away. Phil said that Gina was staying with her mother, and Phil was on the road a lot, as usual. Old Mrs. Ennis's house was put up for sale again. I never got to know the new family that moved in next door. I wanted to remember it as belonging to Gina, and Phil, and Ellie, and Rags.

Benson told me it was time to leave all that "baggage" behind me. It wasn't my fault, he said. I wasn't even there. It's the parents who have to take responsibility for what happens to their kids. I was just a babysitter, and I wasn't even babysitting any more when it happened. Ellie was a good kid but spoiled, used to getting her own way. Izzy Shoemaker was just a kid herself, and careless to boot. And where was Mrs. Gregorka? Why wasn't she there? Why hadn't she at least left somebody responsible in charge of Ellie? It was a crying shame when women had kids and then chucked them while they went off who knows where to have a good time.

For a while, Prue and Sharon treated me like I was a convalescent, still wobbly on my feet. They hung around me, especially at school, where I was an object of curiosity—though not as much as Izzy, who told her story to the local paper. They took my arm and led me away from huddled groups of students in the hall or on the school grounds, talking to me ardently as they glanced over their shoulders, as though we and we alone knew the real story. After a while, though, everything went back to normal. Prue shifted her attention back to dreadful Ed, and Sharon resumed her ransacking of the Varsity players. That year, she was focusing on the basketball team.

My parents and I continued to collide on a daily basis, at meals and other required family rituals. I never realized until Win went away to college how much he had buffered our encounters, the pricks and nettles falling away harmlessly when he laughed at us, calling us a nuclear family always poised to explode.

I knew Kate missed him far more than I did, but she didn't say much. She quietly prepared our meals and fended off Frank's temper tantrums, much like she fended off household dust and dirt. She sewed for me now and then, catered to Frank, read her magazines. She seemed most serene when she emerged from one of her afternoon "rests," or when she shared a clinking ice-filled drink with Frank, and maybe a few close friends. When she started to slur her words, or became unsteady on her feet, Frank took her home, or excused her and took her upstairs—cursing, grumbling, impatient with her if she stumbled or resisted.

No one could rouse Frank's temper more easily than Kate but, once the storm was past, he was as affectionate with her as a love-struck bridegroom.

It wasn't until April, months after Ellie's death, that I began to think Benson might be a little warty, after all.

I was seventeen.

"A dangerous age," Gina had said to me. "Too many possibilities."

But that was a long time ago, when I first knew her, and Gina had been talking about Win.

True, I would muse, Benson had helped me through that bad time last fall, and always took my side—even against *me*, when I blamed myself. He was a rock. In fact, I called him "Rock Benson" sometimes, to tease him. But he still worked at that garage his uncle owned, and he didn't seem to have any plans for the future.

"I like what I'm doing," he said, when we talked about it. "I like working with my hands all day, then getting cleaned up so I can be with you. I like being with you."

When I asked him if he wanted to go to college, if he wanted something else, something more, he shrugged, and smiled that slow smile of his.

"Like what?" he said.

He and my father and Win and Ben Henderson, Benson's father, used to hunt together. That past winter, Benson and my father had gone off hunting once, just the two of them. They took Lulu, Mr. Henderson's basset hound. They came back red-faced, cheerful, with a ferocious appetite and a smug, self-satisfied air about them.

"Nothing like it," Frank had said, when they sat down to eat, tearing at the cold beef and horseradish sandwiches Kate put in front of them. "Cold morning. Air crisp. Open fields, deep woods, frost crunching under my boots. What more could a man ask for?"

He turned his head and nodded at Lulu sprawling at his feet, ears fanned out, showing the whites of her sad brown eyes as she looked up at Frank.

"Except a good dog."

He lowered a choice piece of beef into Lulu's upturned mouth.

Benson nodded and ate, nodded and ate.

"And the sound of her," Frank had said, "when she catches the scent of a rabbit, that excited, high-pitched bay tearing into the silence. I tell you, Kate, there's nothing like it. Nothing like it in this world."

Benson grinned, his teeth pasted with bread and bits of meat. I frowned, looking at his hands, dark against the bleached white of the bread, striated with the dye of his trade, the fingernails scraped clean but still gray.

I had been tempted to say—as once Ellie had said to him—"Yur fingerzhur dirty."

People change when you get up close to them. Your family you're used to seeing up close, "warts and all," as my father used to say, but people you admire you want to go on admiring, even if you have to step back to do it. I remember when it took my breath away if Benson looked at me, if he so much as dropped me a "Hi."

Kate used to say that experience is never wasted, but I wonder. Sometimes, when you trim all the excess fat off an experience, there's not much left. Of course, my mother never wasted anything. Sunday's roast beef became Monday's casserole became Tuesday's soup. But I wasn't like Kate. I'd often duck out with Benson, or eat with Prue and her mother, when I saw those bones simmering on the stove.

Looking back, I still see Gina as she wanted to be seen, as I wanted to see her. That bout of hero worship has stayed with me—perhaps because my friendship with Gina ended, abruptly, at the cemetery, the day before Ellie's funeral. I never spoke with Gina again. I didn't see her change or decline. I didn't see her without Ellie. She was always, for me, the Gina that I knew during those two years when I was on the cusp of being a woman, and she was a woman in her prime. It's how I choose to remember her—just as I choose to remember Ellie as a little girl I came to love as though she were my own—a precocious little girl with a great big capacity for life.

I remember, years ago, when my father shot our old dog, Brandy, an Irish setter he adored. He came back with his rifle slung over his shoulder, his eyes angry and bloodshot, cursing the day she was born. As usual, when strong emotions were involved, he hid his feelings beneath a display of temper.

"She was a pain in the ass from day one," he had said to Win, Kate, and me, hanging up his rifle inside the back door, then sitting down at the kitchen table with us to unloop the strings of his high-top boots. He fumbled impatiently with the boot strings, yanked off the boots. "Jittery out in the field. She'd either lose the scent or we'd lose her. Brought me a goddamned possum once instead of a pheasant. Took years to train her. Goddamn good riddance, I say. Should have taken one of her pups and got rid of her when I had the chance. There's nothing worse than a decrepit old bird dog."

It was the only time I ever saw Win cry. He had been about fourteen or fifteen then, big for his age. The tears slid down his cheeks as he listened to Frank. He didn't even bother to wipe them away. I reached out a hand to him but he pushed it away without even glancing in my direction.

"She was mine too!" Win had sobbed, his voice high, unnatural. "You didn't even tell me!"

"No, and why the hell should I," Frank had said, his voice like sandpaper. "You think you could change anything? Take the rheumatism out of her bones? Prop up her hind end? Give her a new lease on life? No, goddamn it. I had to do it, just like I do everything else around here. All the real work."

He had stomped out of the kitchen in his thick socks. We heard his feet on the stairs, muffled, but making maximum impact with each step.

After a while, when people would ask me about Gina, I'd shrug and say, "I don't know. I don't see her anymore. She moved away."

I'd say this irritably—as irritably as my father in a temper—because I didn't want them to come back and ask me again, later on.

As for Ellie, I still miss her—sometimes more than I can say—and I tell myself, well, why shouldn't I?

She was mine too.

About the Author

Toni Fuhrman is the author of three novels, including *A Windless Place, The Second Mrs. Price,* and *One Who Loves.* Her novels are intensely personal explorations of intimacy and obsession within the context of strong family ties. Toni grew up in a small Ohio town near Lake Erie. She now makes her home in Los Angeles, where she is working on her next novel. Her personal essays on writing and reading are at **tonifuhrman.com.**

Acknowledgments

Thank you, Stevan Nikolic, Editor-in-Chief, Adelaide Books, for publishing my novel. I am grateful for your careful supervision, and for your dedication to literary fiction.

I suppose writers can work alone, but ideally we need group support consisting of a mentor, fellow writers, friends and family—in other words, a coach, a team, and a cheerleading squad.

Thank you, Holly Prado, so lately departed and so dearly missed, whose friendship and guidance—especially during the years in which I was a member of her ongoing writers workshop—were vital to me as I wrote and rewrote this novel, as well as my previous two published novels. Her life as a poet and a creative spirit inspired me, and her common sense kept me grounded.

To my fellow writers, many of whom were in Holly's writing workshop—thank you for your friendship, support, and encouragement. You keep my creative life humming.

And special thanks to my friends and family, who believe in me and cheer me on, including Marcia Barbour my go-to design authority, and my pre-pub readers: Barbara Lanctot, Barbara Potyk, and Virginia Woodrow.

Made in the USA
Middletown, DE
13 May 2021

39417989R00177